A TASTE OF PASSION

She touched the cloth to his lips and not even the icy chill of mountain springwater could cool the fire that leaped within him at her touch.

Her eyelids fluttered. Her lips parted. The fingers pressing the cloth to his mouth trembled. Tremors shook him, as well, from the effort of denying himself. He wanted nothing more than to tear the cloth from her, to draw her head toward his and claim those strawberry-stained lips with his own.

And so it seemed at first that it was a dream, when the cloth landed on his knee and her fingertips, smooth and chilled from the water, traced his lips with a gentle curiosity that threatened to drive him insane.

"Your lips are soft," she marveled. "They can look so harsh." She leaned closer; he felt her breath against his skin, and then with a movement that might have been an attempt to turn her head away, or might have been an attempt to steal a kiss without his knowing, she brushed her lips over his in a featherlight caress . . .

Books by Donna Jordan

JUST THE WAY YOU ARE

SCHOOLED FOR SEDUCTION

Published by Zebra Books

SCHOOLED
FOR
SEDUCTION

Donna Jordan

ZEBRA BOOKS
Kensington Publishing Corp.
http://www.kensingtonbooks.com

ZEBRA BOOKS are published by

Kensington Publishing Corp.
850 Third Avenue
New York, NY 10022

All Kensington titles, imprints and distributed lines are available at special quantity discounts for bulk purchases for sales promotion, premiums, fund-raising, educational or institutional use.

Special book excerpts or customized printings can also be created to fit specific needs. For details, write or phone the office of the Kensington Special Sales Manager: Kensington Publishing Corp., 850 Third Avenue, New York, NY 10022. Attn. Special Sales Department. Phone: 1-800-221-2647.

Zebra and the Z logo Reg. U.S. Pat. & TM Off.

First Printing: November 2002
10 9 8 7 6 5 4 3 2 1

Printed in the United States of America

One

While others in the room wrung their hands and beseeched their sovereign for calm, Vincent Kenby stood in the shadows, studying his lord's face. The mottled skin, the bulging eyes, the flaring nostrils, all declared the Earl of Ardleswyck's fury so emphatically that a deaf man could interpret the lord's shouts.

Vincent carefully memorized all the facial distortions betraying his lord's temper, to ensure he would never let them mar his own features.

Vincent knew nobody could call him a vain man, but he also knew it would take more than anger to twist his features into ugliness. He held no real concern for his appearance, and yet took great pains to guard his expression. He had learned it was prudent to shutter his feelings.

His lord never paid any mind to Vincent's expressions. Each woman who warmed his bed believed she would be the first to breach his defenses. When she left, as each one invariably did, his ears would ring for days with accusations of heartlessness, coldness, indifference. Never selfishness, for he spent freely on his women. Never meanness, since he practiced courtesy and respect to a knightlike degree. "You never

smile at me," they would whimper. "I can never tell
how you feel inside."

Everybody knew emotions ruled a woman's heart
and mind. Everybody expected men to be above such
silliness. Vincent knew little difference separated the
sexes in that regard.

Some of the bitter glances directed his way told him
that his competitors for the earl's ear mistook his im-
passiveness for calm. It suited him to let them think so,
for it would keep them worried and fretting over his
perceived confidence. It would gain him no advantage
to betray the dread coursing through him, dread that
deepened with the earl's every shout and pounding of
fist into palm.

The earl's level of agitation always matched the degree of trouble Vincent would be expected to sort
out—and Vincent had never seen the earl in a rage so
intense. A horrid mess awaited him, of that he had no
doubt.

The earl pounded his fist into a wall. Blood trickled
from his knuckles along his fingers to mingle with the
fine grit of cracked plaster. "Vincent!" he roared.

With his name echoing through the suddenly quiet
chamber, Vincent moved out of the shadows. The earl's
counselors and advisors stepped aside in the grudg-
ing manner of those who had made way for him many
times before. They left a clear path between the earl
and his most trusted counselor. Vincent knew that if resentment and jealousy could strike a man down, he
would never survive his passage among his colleagues.

"Aye, my lord?"

"The goddamned son of a whore and a pig cursed
me with his dying breath."

Vincent inclined his head slightly in acknowledgment. There had been dozens of witnesses to the curse wheezed out so laboriously by the dying Earl of Hedgeford. No sense in denying it ever occurred.

Around him, those who did not agree with Vincent's methods of dealing with the earl, cried out words they thought might placate the furious man. "Deserved to die!" shouted one unwise soul. "Nothing wrong with what you did!" exclaimed another. "Let him rot in hell!" added yet another fool.

Vincent watched his lord flinch with each supposed encouragement sent his way.

He tried, for just a moment, to put himself in the place of a man such as Ardleswyck. He'd achieved his current position by doing just that—imagining himself as someone he had not been born to be. Most times he succeeded. But in this case, he found it impossible to judge how one might feel after coming to blows with his lifelong friend over a minor matter involving insignificant tenants.

He supposed one's soul would writhe with regret when that friend took an apoplectic fit and died squirming in agony on the ground, while lips that once always welcomed you with a smile and a friendly greeting formed hateful words, while the last precious breaths were expended to heap curses upon your head.

No, he could not imagine what the lord must be feeling, partly because Vincent had never known a friend so dear. Nor would he ever, ever allow himself to fall victim to a passion so intense that it would blind a man to the ramifications of his actions. Passion clouded a man's mind, robbed him of intelligence and strength.

If Vincent had been there when the earl lost his head, he would have hung onto his lord's fists or let

him pummel himself rather than allow him to strike
the other man. The satisfaction of downing an oppo-
nent soon faded, while the acrimony always lingered.
The victor might find his grain stores fired, his live-
stock run off, his dogs poisoned. There had even been
cases where the defeated one petitioned the king for financial retribution.

Vincent understood his lord well enough to know
that much of the earl's violent rage, much of his incoherence, stemmed from devastation as well as anger.
From guilt as well as righteousness.

The other advisors and counselors pressed close,
eager to placate the earl with assurances that he had
been right to escalate the minor dispute into a full-
fledged fight.

"Vincent," the earl practically whispered, and in that
moment Vincent felt full force the anguish of a man
who had failed to extend the comfort of his hand while
his best—and perhaps only—friend, died.

Only God could ease the earl's conscience. Only
time would dim the memory of a friendship so dear.
Only the earl's most trusted lawyer could cope with the
political aftermath of that brief, violent incident.

"There will be repercussions," Vincent said.

The earl nodded. Just once. An abrupt, reluctant acknowledgment of the mess he had created.

Once again, the others in the room fell into silence.
In the welcome quiet, Vincent's mind settled on a hope
so bright he dared let it lighten his heart a little.

"Hedgeford's heir has ever been like a son to you,"
he reminded his lord—unnecessarily, he hoped. "Now
that he assumes the title, he will take your daughter to
wife. The joining will let you both set aside the pain."

He thought for a moment that he had succeeded.

The earl's jaw worked, his eyes moistened a bit, and then Vincent's most ardent competitor ruined it all.

"Hedgeford will use your daughter and your own money to wreak his vengeance. He is a hot-tempered lout." The man narrowed his eyes at Vincent, all but daring him to interrupt. When Vincent did not, he smirked, and turned his full attention upon the earl. "I would caution you against turning over a rich dowry to the devil spawn son of a man who cursed you with his dying breath. Set aside the betrothal, my lord."

All semblance of order vanished as men burst into argument. Vincent, unable to believe such a stupid suggestion had been articulated, made certain his amusement did not show.

The earl's eldest daughter, Catherine, had been betrothed to Michael, now Earl of Hedgeford, well before Vincent had come into his lord's service. The marriage had been arranged so long ago that nobody ever spoke of Catherine, save to link her name with Michael of Hedgeford. Truth to tell, nobody spoke of Catherine at all, not even her mother. The girl had been sent to a convent in Italy years ago to prepare her for the role of wife, and when she returned it would be straight into Hedgeford's bed. She'd been rooted from the family as thoroughly as a rose torn from a hedge.

Vincent, who had lived among monks, had never understood how immersion in a house of religion could prepare a woman for marriage, a man's bed, for bearing his children. But the nobility seemed fond of the concept, and he had never found the matter of sufficient interest to press for an answer.

The suggestion to set aside the betrothal was a ludicrous idea tossed out by a man so eager to curry the earl's favor that he had forgotten what he knew of the law. It was bad enough that Vincent had to be ever on his guard against ingratiating fools, who all too often found the earl willing to hear what they had to say, willing to grant them as much credence as he accorded the opinions of those more learned. It was worse to think a man of his own standing might allow his jealousy of Vincent's position as the favorite to lead him into making suggestions that could directly hurt the earl's interests.

But even as he assured himself that the earl could not treat the idea seriously, he saw his lord's attention swing to the man who'd made the ridiculous suggestion. The others saw, too, and opportunistic as always, lent their words of encouragement to the babble.

"My lord, the betrothal must be honored," Vincent said, attempting to quell the stirrings of foreboding.

"Nonsense," spouted the fool who had started it all. "King Richard himself never honored his betrothal to the princess of France."

This roused a chorus of agreement. Nobody bothered to remark that kings had more leeway in such matters than their minions, and nobody mentioned that Richard's refusal to wed the French girl had caused a serious breech in relations with France.

"Catherine has been specially prepared for this match. It seemed such a good idea at the time." The earl appeared to be speaking to himself, so soft and odd were his words.

In the vehement arguments circling about, no one but Vincent seemed to note the earl's cryptic comment. *Specially prepared in what way?* Vincent wondered, but only for the fleeting space of a heartbeat. The situation threatened to go beyond control, leaving no time to spare on wondering how an exiled female had fared over the past few years.

"Hedgeford said he will see you rot in hell," remarked another advisor. He shot a glance at Vincent, and then sidled a step farther away, as if to place himself closer to the man who seemed to have gained the earl's favor.

"By God, so he did!" the earl bellowed, bringing silence to the room. He nodded his head decisively. "No man, dead or alive, will know the benefits of my friendship once someone in his family has cursed me. There will be no wedding."

The buzz of conversation resumed, turning the small chamber as raucous as a dining hall. The earl seemed to stand taller now that he'd declared his decision, and a half smile hovered over the face so recently ravaged by guilt and grief.

Michael of Hedgeford would not meekly accept the earl's decision. The earl's daughter possessed an enormous dowry, one arranged when Ardleswyck and Hedgeford were secure in their friendship. Recently, when King Richard had made an appeal for financial aid for his Crusade, the earl had made only the tiniest contribution, citing the dowry as the reason for his parsimony. He'd chortled with Hedgeford over the small sum handed over. They'd congratulated each other over keeping the fortune out of Richard's greedy grasp. "It stays in the family, Vincent," the earl had crowed.

Old King Henry, so recently dead, had been the first Plantagenet to sanction the betrothal. Richard had been fobbed off with his own reluctant acknowledgment that the betrothal was valid and would stand. Richard's fury would know no bounds once he learned that the money he had asked for, and been denied, had been placed beyond his reach, into the hands of the Church.

"My lord." Vincent was relieved to note his voice conveyed its normal, emotionless timbre. "Hedgeford will not meekly accept your decision."

"You shall deal with him."

"I cannot 'deal' with the king—"

"The king is in Sicily, mounting his Crusade. He thinks of nothing but fighting the infidels. By the time he takes an interest, 'twill be done."

The earl turned away. Now outwardly cheerful, he slapped a friendly hand upon the shoulder of the man who had suggested abandoning the betrothal. The counselor sneered at Vincent.

Vincent granted the counselor his moment of triumph. To his eye, the earl's smile seemed a little forced, his laughter a little false. Both nonetheless sounded in his head as clear as nails pounded into a coffin. The earl had declared his decision in public. He would not change his mind.

Vincent had fought unsuccessfully against this type of stubbornness before. No doubt he would face it again—providing he survived this task. When the punishments and penalties came due—and they would—the man responsible for carrying out the earl's order would be held to blame. Everything Vincent had attained could be negated.

Vincent bowed slightly from the waist. "A word alone, if it pleases your lordship," he said.

Ardleswyck humored him. With a regal jut of his chin and flip of his hand, the earl sent the others scurrying from the chamber. A servant was the last to step through the door, and he bowed low as he pulled it closed, sealing Vincent and the earl alone in the now-silent room.

The earl turned his back on Vincent. That meant, always, that the earl had something to hide, something that would have to be pried from him with tact and persistence.

"The dowry will not seriously deplete your coffers," Vincent said.

"No."

"The girl has lived apart from your household for years. She has never been home to visit, not even for Christmas. Her mother never speaks of her. She has not been missed to any great degree by her sisters—or by you, my lord."

"I think of her, sometimes."

Hardly a resounding declaration of fatherly devotion. Still, it represented progress since often the earl could spend hours reacting to Vincent's probing comments with little more than a grunt.

To Vincent's surprise, the earl whirled about. His arms were crossed over his chest. Although he glowered, his fierce expression contrasted with a hint of red cresting his cheeks, with something like chagrin stamping his features.

The earl—embarrassed?

"She has been . . . specially prepared," he said in an odd tone of voice.

"So you have said." The mild curiosity Vincent had dismissed when the earl mentioned this earlier now reasserted itself into a full-fledged need to know. His instincts settled on this as the key to breaching the earl's secrecy. "Your other daughters are betrothed, yet continue to reside here. I have noted no special preparations for them. Yet you sent this one—" He paused, groping for the name.

"Catherine."

"Catherine. You sent her away." Vincent wished now that he could remember the girl, but could conjure in his mind's eye little more than a wealth of light hair atop a slim supple frame common to most young females of gentle birth.

He tried to recall if she had been scarred by the pox, or perhaps born with a cleft lip, or maybe walked with a hitch in her gait. If she did possess a deformity, then it might explain why Ardleswyck had sequestered her in a foreign land, where she might bide unnoticed until the wedding took place. Most men were reluctant to admit they'd sired a grotesque, so he would broach the matter first.

"My lord, if she is flawed, then marrying her to your enemy would be a great revenge."

"Flawed?" The earl's mouth gaped; his eyes boggled. "Catherine is the most beautiful, the most perfect of all I've sired. No, Vincent, she is a beauty, and is now a treasure beyond compare. She has been in Italy. She has been specially prepared."

The earl stared at Vincent, seeming to silently beg for understanding while his flush deepened with true embarrassment. Try as he might, Vincent could not fathom what special preparations could be made in Italy that would turn an English heiress into a treasure beyond compare, or why the earl would grow so flustered simply by mentioning it.

He tried to recall what he knew of Italy. His knowledge came secondhand, from books and accounts of those who had traveled there. Religion. Artifacts. Sunshine. Good wine and fish.

"Let the marriage take place, my lord."

"Never."

The earl had hinted at some slight fatherly affection; perhaps, with the girl at his side, the earl would soften in his stance against her marriage. "Then bring Catherine home. We can negotiate with Hedgeford until you are appeased."

"Good God!" The earl's outburst took Vincent by surprise. "No. Never. Under no circumstances can Catherine be brought home. Not ever."

Exasperated, and yet intrigued, Vincent abandoned tact for bluntness. "If you are so set against Hedgeford taking her to wife, you must bring her home and keep her under guard. She is already his by law. The nuns in Italy cannot deny him if he simply goes to the convent where she resides and takes her."

"I . . . I had not thought of that."

Vincent's tact had not abandoned him totally. He managed to think, rather than say aloud, that the earl had not thought of anything at all before declaring the betrothal would not be honored.

"You must do something, Vincent."

"I am giving you my best advice, my lord. Let the marriage take place."

"Never."

"Then bring her home—or tell me why you refuse to do so. I cannot devise a plan to solve your problem if I lack the necessary information."

The earl raised his hands and clamped them over his head, rubbing as if to ease a raging headache. "Catherine does indeed live in seclusion, but not with nuns. Her mother would not have let her go to Italy if I had told her the truth."

Vincent felt like clutching his own head to ease the

thumping caused by the earl's convoluted evasions. "Where is she, my lord?"

"With Serena."

"Serena? You sent your daughter to live with your mistress?" Vincent did not even attempt to disguise his disbelief. The earl's long infatuation with the tempestuous Serena had disrupted the entire household. Nobody really knew the story behind the end of the affair, only that Ardleswyck had finally banished the dark-haired beauty and returned to his lady wife's bed. He had never seemed the same since, as if a heavy sorrow continually weighed him down. With his typical stubborn adherence to decisions once made, he had never called back the woman who'd infatuated him so. Nor, to Vincent's knowledge, had he ever taken up with another woman despite his unhappiness with his wife.

There was no denying the truth of what the earl had said. If she had known, the Countess of Ardleswyck would never have let her daughter leave her care.

"Why, my lord?"

Ardleswyck shook his head. His body hunched in misery. When finally he spoke, it was in low tones, as if talking to himself, reminiscing about the past. "It seemed like such a good idea at the time. Hedgeford"—the earl's voice broke over his dead friend's name—"Hedgeford was like a brother to me. He was the only one who could understand how I felt after Serena left. We spent many an hour simply talking about a man's heart. You cannot speak of such things to just anyone, you know."

Deep sorrow etched the earl's face. He scrubbed furiously at his eyes, as if they itched, but Vincent fancied he'd caught the glimpse of a tear.

"Hedgeford was no happier in his marriage than I

am in mine." The earl stated the fact simply, with no indication that he expected a contradiction from Vincent. Vincent would not have offered one in any event. He knew, more than most, that the earl and his countess barely tolerated each other's presence. "Like me, Hedgeford had known brief happiness with his mistress. It is the way of the world to arrange marriages for one's children. We yearned, above all else, for our children to find the happiness in marriage that ever eluded us."

"I do not understand, my lord." And indeed he did not. The lord's rambling did naught but confuse Vincent even more.

The earl cast him a glance. Vincent would have sworn he noted a flash of pity in the sorrowful man's eyes. "I do not expect you to understand. You care so little for pleasures of the flesh that you once sought to embrace the celibate life of a monk, as I recall."

Vincent did not know what shocked him more: that his lord remembered this about Vincent, or that he would choose this moment to fling his past in Vincent's face.

"I was not suited to a monk's life," Vincent answered in the same flat, emotionless voice he'd used to present his case to the bishop who had granted him release from his studies. "It had naught to do with my appetite for pleasures of the flesh. And frankly, my lord, I do not see what my past has to do with the matter at hand."

"Exactly." The earl's lip curled in the semblance of a smile, a smile of satisfaction, as if he'd expected Vincent to respond as he had done. "And so you will never be able to understand how two old men, maudlin and flown with wine, might think it the most sensible thing in this world to send an innocent young girl off to a courtesan to be trained to enjoy her own body, so that she and her husband might know joy in their marriage bed."

"My lord!"

"That's the problem, you know, with our wives. They detest their own bodies so much that they cannot take pleasure in them, and so deny their husbands."

"This conversation is taking an entirely too personal tone, my lord."

Ardleswyck continued on, ignoring Vincent's objections. "Hedgeford's favorite was a French girl. My Serena, an Italian. Oh, those lucky foreign men, to live among women who appreciate the joys their bodies can offer."

"My lord—the matter at hand." Vincent hated the desperation he heard in his own voice, but the subject they discussed was so troubling, so distasteful, and the earl so seemingly bent upon exploring it, that he could not see an immediate end to it.

"This *is* the matter at hand, Vincent. Catherine. Serena writes that my daughter must be kept under literal lock and key. She claims there are soldiers, knights, and ordinary men swarming all over Italy to join Richard's Crusade, making it unsafe to allow Catherine to so much as venture outside—but I believe Serena is not telling the full truth. My daughter must have displayed a startling aptitude for her studies, so that Serena cannot trust her. She keeps her locked in so that Catherine has had no opportunity to, shall we say, practice her lessons."

"My lord, I fear you are calling your daughter a . . ." Vincent could not say the word.

"Serena has been discreet. She calls Catherine enthusiastic. Impulsive and loving. She has begged me to hurry and see her married before something unfortunate happens to my daughter's virginity. So you see, I cannot bring her home, Vincent. I cannot have a nubile, lustful female prowling my hall. I cannot allow her mother to know the truth about what I've done or my life will become even more miserable than it is now. So, here is what you need to know: I will not let Michael of Hedgeford have her. She cannot come home. What can be done?"

Vincent let his mind have its way. Let it do its quick probing of the possibilities, let it filter back to him a handful of options to sort through. "I see no way to bring this to a satisfactory conclusion, in a strictly legal manner," he said eventually.

"I shall hear the illegal manners," said his lord.

"Marrying her quickly to another will not prevent the king's ruling later on Hedgeford's behalf, should Hedgeford lodge a royal appeal. If Hedgeford hates you as much as he claims, he could insist that any other marriage is illegal since his betrothal takes precedence. It would not matter to him that she comes lacking a maidenhead, if he gets his way and succeeds in tormenting you."

The earl nodded. "Nor do I know any man of sufficient influence to sway the king away from Hedgeford, who might also be free to take a wife so quickly. We must think of another way."

"If she died, there could be no marriage, and no way for Hedgeford to use her for revenge against you."

The earl's face creased with grief. "I must confess, arranging her death was my first thought. What manner of man am I, to contemplate the murder of my own child? I cannot do it, Vincent. I do love the girl, in my own way, and I regret the years we have spent apart. It is not her fault that she has become what I wanted her to be. I cannot have her killed."

Relief coursed through Vincent. The suggestion had been distasteful to make, but he'd had no choice, not if he meant to serve his lord to the best of his abilities.

"Then perhaps this would be best for all concerned: you could, in truth this time, place the girl in a convent. Someplace well fortified, capable of repelling a siege. Promise the Church her dowry when her final vows are taken. I say to you, my lord, that you will find no stauncher guardian of her person or virtue. I know a place that would suit our needs perfectly."

Ardleswyck nodded.

"Once she is locked away, we can make it known that she found religion and chose to take the veil of her own accord. Not even Hedgeford would dare flout the pope to steal a nun away from her convent."

The earl seemed to flinch at the mention of the pope. He took a shuddering breath, and then nodded again. "My poor Catherine. I will surely burn in hell for all eternity for doing this to her. Rousing her passions, only to lock her away forever in a place where she will always hunger for what she cannot have."

"She would be alive, my lord."

"Would she? I suppose you might think so, considering what you meant to do with your own life." The earl walked slowly to a chair and collapsed into it, a heap of finely clad misery. "See to it, Vincent."

Vincent inclined his head, accepting the charge. "I will select your finest men to carry out the task."

"No, Vincent. I want *you* to fetch her from Italy and see her safely installed where she will be best protected from herself and from others."

Of all the charges set by his lord, none had ever held less appeal. Traveling to Italy and back would give his competitors the advantage of proximity, and he knew they would exploit his absence. He would do no less, were the situation reversed.

He felt a curious repugnance, as well as annoyance, to think all he had worked for would be compromised for the sake of a female who could not control her own lusts. Vincent had no patience for those who allowed their appetites to carry them beyond the bounds of good sense.

He could not tell his liege that he held his daughter in contempt.

"My lord, I am a man of words and paper. Considering the circumstances, your daughter will require the protection of a military force."

"That is a problem, Vincent. You know my fees as well as I do."

"Aye, my lord. Ten horsed knights always at the ready."

"The king has already lured away more of my men than I care to number for his witless crusading. If he should call in my fee knights, I dare not leave my lands unprotected. Hedgeford can attack me here as well as through my daughter. I can spare none of my knights."

"Sergeants?"

"You may take a dozen."

"One knight to lead them, my lord!"

Ardleswyck shook his head. "You can lead them. You are more than capable. I have noted your strength and skill when you practice. You would make a fine fighting man, Vincent, if I did not have so much need of your lawyering skills."

Every able-bodied man on the estate was expected

to maintain fighting skills for defense of the homeland. Most men in Vincent's position begged off the practice, or gave it but cursory attention. Vincent, however, relished the hours of mock battle and riding. His youth had been spent in a physical manner, and though those days were long behind him, his body seemed to crave hard use. He never felt more clearheaded, more alive, than after a rousing session, when every muscle in his body ached and sweat streamed from every pore.

"I did not know you paid mind to the exercises," Vincent said.

"A man reveals something of his nature by the way he acts on the battlefield," said the earl. "I trust you in many ways. Dare I trust my daughter among a pack of woman-starved common soldiers? I shudder, Vincent, at the shame that might befall my name if I have created a wanton who would consort with the lower classes."

Since Vincent was himself of the lower classes, the earl had spoken an insult at the same time he'd dealt a compliment. But he'd extended a worse slur against his daughter: the earl appeared convinced that Catherine possessed no control over her lusts. Vincent said nothing.

"I can trust you with her, Vincent. You are immune to the lures of a woman, and you can keep the men from approaching her. See her safely locked away, and then we can return to normal, as if none of this ever happened."

Two

Genoa, Italy

Catherine sometimes wondered about the long-dead Italian princess for whom this tiny prayer room had been built. She hoped the woman had been fleshier. Catherine had grown tall with no fat to cushion her knees, and they ached abysmally from spending so many hours kneeling upon the *prei deiu*. She knew the woman must have been shorter, since Catherine had to hunch her shoulders to be able to see through the viewing hole cut through the wall in front of her.

She must not have minded being confined in such a dark, close space, for a stout hook enabled the prayer to fasten the door closed from the *inside* of this depressing little chamber—a lock Catherine never used. It was bad enough when the thick, paneled door swung closed on silent hinges behind her; with every stray shaft of light sealed out, save for what little filtered through the viewing hole, she would have to fumble like a blind woman to fasten the lock. She could not bring herself to fasten that hook to draw the door even tighter, did not dare try to imagine the panic of clawing for it blindly when the oppressiveness closed in on her, making her feel as if she were locked inside a coffin.

She hated the room, and yet she looked forward to the two or three hours she spent there each week.

Not because she shared the woman's faith or piety. No, she looked forward to these Sunday mornings because the Mass marked the passing of one more week of her exile, of her earth-bound limbo waiting for her real life to begin. Soon, soon, Michael would send for her, and each passing week brought that day closer.

But there were also times when hope flickered at a low ebb. Sometimes she overheard a remark about her age. Sometimes she had to offer good wishes and smile, smile, smile when a serving girl gave notice to quit her job to marry. Sometimes she spent hours sewing a gift for a woman who'd borne a child. She came to Mass on those Sundays with drooping spirits, which would revive after staring through the viewing hole at the priest performing the Mass, at the nuns who made up his tiny congregation. She would look at those people bound to God, and remind herself that matters could be worse. She could be doomed, as they were, to end her days vowed to poverty, obedience . . . and chastity.

She took heart, in those dark moments, by recalling the triumph of her personal heroine, the old queen, Eleanor of Aquitaine. Locked away in the severest circumstances by her husband, held prisoner for a full sixteen years, the old queen had emerged victorious. Still filled with a zest for life, strong and proud, she now served her son, Richard the Lionheart, with tasks normally handled by men. When despair threatened to overwhelm her, Catherine remembered the trials Eleanor had endured, and refused to succumb.

A stabbing ache speared her thigh. Grimacing, she shifted her weight to the other knee. The stout kneeler did not even creak, so heavy and sturdy had it been built all those years ago. The ancient carpenter had served his princess well.

Her architect had not been so masterful. The viewing window had, indeed, been a cunning idea, designed as it was so that from the chapel the rectangle, with a length of loosely woven black wool fastened over it, appeared to be part of the altar's embellishments. But the architect had failed to take into account that the priest performing the Mass would spend most of the time planted squarely in front of the viewing hole, denying the secret watcher the ability to see much of anything save for the priest's midsection.

Just now, Catherine could see nothing but the dirty cord knotted around the rough, woven brown wool covering Father Pascal's bulging belly.

Soon, soon, she would see the last of this place. Soon she could pray in a real church, with sun streaming through windows of colored glass.

Father Pascal moved to one side of the altar. Faint light filtered through the screened opening and eased, a little, her sense of confinement. She leaned forward eagerly for a rare glimpse of the nuns huddled in prayer. As always she felt sympathy mingled with relief. Catherine thought their knees must ache worse than hers, considering that they knelt directly on the chapel's marble floor. And with the stern eye of their Mother Superior upon them, they dared not slump at all.

No one could see her, of course, and so no one could

scold her if she abandoned the appropriate ramrod-stiff kneeling stance to ease the ache in her legs. She leaned back. Her bottom almost immediately came to rest against the door pressing behind her, reminding her once more how tiny, how square, how confining was this place.

Soon, soon, she would be free. Pray God, she would soon feel her husband's strong arms around her, his body melded with hers, his child stirring in her belly.

Had the Italian princess knelt here, ostensibly for the purpose of hearing Mass, but instead praying for deliverance from her situation? Maybe, like Catherine, she had taken to her knees to ask God to make her a wife, a mother. Maybe she had spent hours on her knees in prayerful attitude, pretending to pray for the forgiveness of her sins while inside she hoped to be delivered out of here so she might begin sinning with enthusiasm.

It could not be a sin, Catherine amended to herself, to look forward to bedding with her husband. Serena had promised there was much pleasure to be found when coupling with a man you loved.

And she loved Michael. He must come for her soon; he must. Each time a messenger came to the door, she hoped it might be word from Michael. Each Sunday she sealed herself in this room, privately bemoaning that yet another week of her youth had fled while she waited for the death of a man she barely knew, so that her betrothed would send for her.

The endless anticipation put a great strain on her nerves, but the hours she spent in the close-pressing darkness helped her by letting her see the nuns. She need only compare her situation with theirs to be reminded that while there was no reprieve for them from their vows, one day soon *she* would be released from here.

Father Pascal moved again, blocking her view of the nuns. She could see his hands moving across the altar, saw him pull the chalice from someplace above him, saw him pull a grimy cloth from his belt and wipe the goblet. Nobody but he drank from the vessel, but even so, the sight turned her stomach. She leaned back once more and closed her eyes. Strange, how with her eyes closed it didn't seem so dark. Father Pascal took a deep breath and launched into what she knew would be a lengthy, dull prayer. She allowed her mind to drift away from the nuns, from the Mass.

One day soon, Michael would come for her. Soon, soon. His father held to the old ways, of not trusting a son with an heir of his own to respect the will of the elder man. This was why, some claimed, the old king of England had never insisted his son Richard wed and breed heirs. Michael must be as impatient as she, and one day very soon he would come storming into the palazzo shouting her name. She had imagined that moment of her deliverance so often, she could almost hear him call to her from afar . . . *Catherine of Ardleswyck. Catherine of Ardleswyck.* And then louder, closer . . . *I seek Catherine of Ardleswyck.* A smile curved her lips.

"Catherine of Ardleswyck!" Very loud. Very close. So close it seemed only a wall separated her from the source of the call.

"Catherine of Ardleswyck!"

She bolted upright in astonishment.

She had not imagined the calling of her name. It rang out yet again, louder, and this time was followed by the splintering of a door. And again he called, this time followed by the hard clump and jingle of spurred boots striking against marble floors.

The chalice fell from Father Pascal's hand, clanging against the altar and then falling from her sight.

"See here!" Father Pascal abandoned the sacred words of the Mass and blustered a protest. "You cannot disturb the peace of the Lord's house in this manner!"

The priest's outrage did nothing to stop the men. Catherine could hear them, but she could not see them. "Move, move," she pleaded aloud to Father Pascal, but either he could not hear her, or he deliberately used his bulk as a shield in a misguided attempt to protect her.

She could not bear it—he blocked what she felt sure would be the first sight of her husband.

Michael. Michael had come for her. At long last, her prayers had been answered. She clutched her hands together and strained toward the small viewing hole. She briefly regretted the sacrilegious thoughts she had entertained while she should have been paying attention to the Mass.

God heeded her desires anyway. Father Pascal abandoned his place at the altar.

At first she could see nothing but the usual cluster of nuns. But the nuns no longer faced the altar. They remained on their knees, but had swiveled about to look behind them. A few cried out and raised their hands above their heads as if to ward off blows, and some crossed their arms over their breasts as if they feared being stripped naked. Their lips moved in prayer or alarm—or some combination of both, judging by the gabbled sounds echoing from the walls. As the encroaching party drew closer, several hoisted themselves to their feet and clumsily scurried away.

Catherine pressed closer to the viewing hole. She had never realized how little of the chapel had been revealed to her. She had never realized that she saw the whole of the nuns only because they were kneeling; when some stood, she could see only up to their waists. Now that some had run off, she could see into the empty space behind them, space that she had never suspected to loom so large. Space soon filled by dozens of booted feet marching with soldierly precision toward the altar. A few strides, and she could see up to their calves. Another stride, to their knees, and then to their waists. Soon, to mid-chest—but no farther. The men halted near the nuns who'd remained in place, and no matter how she bent and angled, the viewing window would reveal no more.

"Catherine of Ardleswyck?" someone demanded of the nuns. Those she could see shook their heads.

It had to be Michael. Something within her thrilled to the timbre of the voice, as if her body was able to recognize her true love simply by sound.

Sound. Serena had promised her that a soft gasp, a sweet moan, could stir a man's passions. Sometimes, at night in her bed, Catherine had practiced the sounds, but she had not truly believed a body could be set aflame without a single touch until this minute.

One man disengaged himself from the others. He approached the altar, stepped up onto the dais, and walked straight to Father Pascal's usual place in front of the viewing hole as if his body had been called to hers in the very same recognition of true love.

But no. He turned away to look out at the chapel.

He was not so wide as Father Pascal and so she could, if she chose, still peek around his midsection to see what lay beyond. But she was content to gaze at the

rectangle of man revealed to her. He wore a jerkin of
fine wool, soaking wet, that clung to supple, muscular
flesh that tapered to a taut waist. A wide leather belt
cinched his waist. Below the belt, she could see no
more than an inch or two of stout, clean, and wet
broadcloth breeches. She knew it rained outside, and
wondered why he had tramped through the downpour
rather than come to her through the palazzo where he
might have remained dry.

"I have come for Catherine of Ardleswyck."

His voice, deep and a little rough, again stirred that
nameless something within her. How she wished she
could see his face, to know if his expression matched
what she thought she heard in his voice—frustration to
match her own, and a tiredness, as if he'd traveled so
far and so fast he ought to be resting now, with his lady
wife's cool hand soothing his forehead, or traveling
lower, to ease him . . .

"You will not find her here," said Father Pascal.

Michael—it had to be Michael—who else would be
seeking her? He turned, revealing his middle to her
from the side. Lean and yet not spare. Flat. She almost
forgot to breathe for a moment, wondering how a taut
belly such as his would feel beneath her hand. Father
Pascal's bulging middle had never inspired such
thoughts within her.

"I was told she observed Mass in this chapel."

"Aye." Father Pascal cleared his throat. He shuffled his feet. He cleared his throat again. She fancied
he must be casting a guilty glance toward the viewing hole. He knew, of course, that she observed Mass
from the secret prayer room. The nuns did not, at his
suggestion, for he claimed they were timid creatures
who were instructed by God to pass unnoticed among

others. It would grieve them, he'd claimed, to think they were being watched. Their cringing reaction to Michael's arrival certainly seemed to confirm his opinion.

Now they would know. So, too, would Michael; and he would probably want to know as well why she was forced to observe as she did. Well, she would tell him. Later.

For now, she had no care for the nuns' gentle feelings or the priest's discomfiture. "Here I am!" she called, pressing her lips close to the tightly stretched cloth covering the hole. "Here!"

The magnificent torso in front of her bent one way and then the other, obviously searching for the source of the claim.

"Here!" she said again, certain that his heart must respond to her voice as hers had done to his.

She would make it easy for him. "Behind the altar."

He turned, moved so close that the altar's edge pressed into his belly the way she yearned to do. *Tap, tap. Thump. Tap tap.* She hoped he would not hurt his knuckles testing the construction of the altar.

"What trickery is this?" he demanded as he brought his curled fist down to pound against the flat marble where the chalice usually rested.

She could not bear to postpone their meeting another minute. She plunged her hand through the flimsy barrier provided by the tightly stretched cloth. Any other time she would have marveled at how easily it parted, at how it separated into shreds that clung like fine cobwebs to her fingers, hinting that this very same cloth may have served its purpose for centuries, from the first Italian princess to herself.

She doubted he noticed her hand at all until she

rested it gently against his fist before he could hit the altar again. Oh, God, just touching him sent a jolt of sensation so pure and fine through her that she all but swooned from her perch on the *prei deiu*. Surely he must feel it too.

He jerked his hand away, and he leaped backward as if he'd been stung by a bee.

At any other time, she would have welcomed the chance to observe the chapel without the cloth darkening the colors of everything. Her new view revealed mosaics, and frescoes, Stations of the Cross so beautifully sculpted that some famous artist must have done the pieces. Catherine so loved beautiful things that she could have spent hours studying them all. At any other time. For he bent to peer at her from the other side of the viewing hole, and at this moment, she cared only to look upon the bit of face revealed to her.

For all her remaining days, this face would greet her when she awoke, would be the last she saw before drifting into sleep. From now until she died, she would do all she could to bring a smile to this face, take every step possible to avoid causing it to frown.

She caught a glimpse of a strong angled jaw, lean cheeks, hair raked back to keep the soaking-wet strands from dripping water down his face. She could not tell if it was a light brown or a dark gold for all the water darkening it. And then he settled his position and she saw his eyes. Blue-green as the seas surrounding England, piercingly alert in the manner of a man who possessed much intelligence.

"I am Catherine," she said, her voice little more than a whisper.

"You? Catherine of Ardleswyck?"

He drew back, revealing more of his face. Such a

jumble of feelings rushed through her: delight, to find all of his face as handsome as his eyes, and dismay, to realize that she had not imagined having heard horror in his voice.

But she told herself at once that any man would be horrified to find his betrothed so secretively concealed. He could not see her as well as she saw him, so her looks could not have caused such a violent recoil.

And yet . . . he made no move to touch her hand, which lay with her palm pressed against the altar, where it had fallen when he had pulled his own hand away.

She turned her hand palm up, offering it to him.

He made no move to accept it.

"I . . . I am Catherine," she said, hating the halting way the words came forth. A chill overtook her as she withdrew her hand back into her prayer room.

She did not know if he meant to answer her, for just then the door behind her flew open, catching her square in the back and knocking the breath from her.

"Sweeting—you must come with me at once. Something terrible has happened."

It was Serena, dear Serena, who caught her by the shoulders and drew her to her feet. "Come, Catherine. Hurry. We have very little time."

"But he is here. Michael."

Serena muttered a curse so foul Catherine could scarcely credit it coming from her. "I had hoped to reach you before he found you. He is not Michael."

Catherine struggled to catch her breath. She suspected the blow to her back was only a part of her difficulty in breathing. Her mind's eye taunted her with the image of Michael's face—no, not Michael, if Serena was to be believed—recoiling from the sight of her in horror.

"Who, then? Why is he here?"

"Your father sent him. He has told me very little, but I do not like what I have heard. Come, we must hide you away from him."

Three

Vincent rammed the chamber door with the heel of his hand. He stepped through the doorway while the door crashed into the wall with a thud, bounced back to strike him on the arm, and swung slowly again toward the wall. The small chamber thus revealed to him boasted walls embellished with frescoes, their colors muted either by the dim light filtering through the windows, or by great age.

Frescoes could be easily damaged by stout oak banging against the painted plaster. He felt no pang of remorse. He meant to take control of the lady here and now, and it would suit him well if she feared his temper. If he damaged a portion of a fresco in the process, so be it.

Noise and foul temper might make up for what he felt certain was a decidedly nonthreatening appearance. Water dripped from his hair, from his clothes, forming puddles around his feet, and he had to fight the urge to shake himself like a dog. Rain, his nemesis from the moment this journey started, continued to plague him.

Behind him, the men who had marched with him through the rain to the chapel and back made the sounds common to all idled men: light coughing, feet shuffling, the musical clink of sheathed swords tapping against chain mail. He heard no muffled laughter, for which the women clinging together in one corner of the room ought to be grateful.

Vincent ran a sodden forearm over his brow, dashing away the water trickling from his hair.

"Where did you find them?" he asked the soldier he'd left behind to secretly watch Serena Monteverde while he'd led his men on the fool's errand to the chapel.

"She did just as you suspected, Mr. Kenby," said the soldier. "She ran off the minute you left, and fetched the lady from somewhere. I caught them just as they were about to run out into the stable yard."

Vincent studied the women. The older one still displayed the charms that had once captured the heart of an earl. Serena. Small, curvaceous, with the sun-kissed skin tone that bespoke her Mediterranean heritage. She wore a gauzy headdress that covered her hair with no more substance than a wisp of fog, revealing it to be a deep, rich brown only lightly speckled with gray. She glared at him with a malevolence in her dark, deep-set eyes completely at odds with the meaning of her name.

She had smiled so nicely at him earlier when he'd demanded to know Catherine's whereabouts. She'd told him Catherine of Ardleswyck observed Mass in the chapel, which was appended to the far end of the palazzo. She'd neatly avoided lying to him while misdirecting him.

"I know some lawyers who could learn a thing or two from you, madam," he said. She could not know that he seldom complimented an adversary. "I can only hope the lady did not absorb your skill with words as thoroughly as she learned . . . your other teachings."

Catherine appeared ready to challenge his statement, but Serena flashed a warning glance at the girl. Vincent noted the look, and decided Catherine had indeed been taught to bend words to her advantage. He warned himself to mistrust every word she said to him.

He studied the female placed in his charge.

Catherine. Catherine of Ardleswyck. Vincent would not have recognized her.

She had been sent to this place years earlier, a parting he vaguely remembered as causing nothing more than minor upheaval in the household's daily routine. He'd been busy in those days, settling into his position as a lowly scribe. A delicate balance had been required, for he was determined to rise in influence, and yet could not risk revealing his ambitions to the man who ruled over the writing room. He had learned much about political maneuvering while studying in the abbey; most men would be surprised to know that the religious orders were not immune to power struggles and greed.

The other scribes had gone to the window to watch the departure while he'd remained at his task. They'd jibed him, claiming that one so recently freed from the crushing vow of celibacy ought to relish a glimpse of a winsome lass. He'd ignored them and continued working. He was eager to lose the taint of the monastery, but ogling the earl's young daughter would gain him nothing, while turning out a perfect document for the earl's signature might draw some attention his way.

She might have been the mythical Helen of Troy, and he would not have spared her a second glance.

He had good reason to study her well now. She stood taller than Serena by half a head, slimmer than

Serena by a hand's width. From her head sprung a wealth of thick golden hair that she wore in the manner of an unmarried woman, pulled back straight from her forehead, tucked behind her ears to flow down her back.

When married, she would properly cover that almost obscene abundance of hair so no man but her husband could see it, and only then in the privacy of their own home.

But she would not marry. Not now. Her hair would be shorn when she took her vows, if not to the scalp then to no more than an inch of stubble.

Who would cut it from her head? A priest? A nun? Depriving the world of such luxuriant abundance struck him suddenly as almost a sacrilege—and then he did shake himself like a dog, scattering droplets of water throughout the chamber and casting his spellbound maundering along with it.

Regardless of the course Catherine's life had taken, her hair would be hidden away. It made no difference if she hid that hair from sight with a wife's silk headdress or a nun's headpiece.

His preoccupation with her hair was no doubt inspired by the sodden state of his own. He felt it lying plastered against his skull, and could not help noticing that hers tumbled in soft, riotous waves past her shoulders. Even in the room's murky light, with rain streaming down the window to further diffuse the dreary grayness that always marked a rainy day, her hair shone, rousing an uncomfortable urge to stroke it.

He clenched his hand into a fist. God's blood, not ten minutes in her presence and he itched with the need to touch her. The earl had been right to banish her from his hall. Vincent could not tell what wiles she plied as she stood there, silent, unmoving, but somehow casting a spell that riveted his attention upon her.

She said something to Serena. When she'd called to him from that cave of observance in the chapel, he'd found it difficult to sort her voice out from the others clamoring around him. Her voice had a slight lilt, a throaty fullness that was pleasant to the ear. So pleasant that at first it did not matter if her words were a babble, striking easy on the ears but a babble nonetheless.

The drenching rain must have lodged in his ears, the way water will do when a man tilts his head a certain way while swimming. He angled his neck to shake the water free when a stray word struck a chord of recognition, and he realized the girl spoke in a perverted form of Latin.

"Speak your natural tongue," he said. He assumed she would have grown up conversant in Norman French and Saxon, since her father spoke both tongues, and Vincent did now, too. He did not, however, understand Italian. Forcing her to speak the language of her homeland would jolt her out of the familiarity she felt in these surroundings that were so foreign to him.

"I would know why you have disrupted our household," she answered him in Norman French.

"Your father sent me."

Serena spat out words that sounded like a warning, but Catherine seemed not to hear. She wriggled free of the courtesan, movements that pulled her gown taut against her belly, and sent her breasts bouncing. Vincent's mouth turned dry and the chamber felt so hot and close of a sudden that he would not be surprised if his soaking-wet garments began steaming.

More temptress's tricks! He would have to take care to avoid looking at her unless absolutely necessary.

Joy lit her face. "My father! How fares he? And my mother—is she well?"

Questions bubbled from her while she moved toward him with a swift grace that made it seem she did not hurry at all. He'd noticed that fine ladies sometimes moved in that way, with a grace that must be born and bred in them. The women of his own class trudged, or more often grudged, every extra step.

"I feared your arrival meant something terrible had happened, the way Serena tried to rush us . . ." Her words drifted away, and she paused to glance back at Serena. "Oh dear, I have forgotten my manners in my thirst for news. What is your name, kind sir?"

Kind sir? And asking his name—nobody ever cared the name of the man who but carried out his lord's orders. Vincent's conscience stirred as he answered, "Vincent Kenby."

"And I am Catherine. As you already know." She gifted him with a wide, happy smile, a gesture that extended beyond mere politeness considering her excitement. His conscience stirred again.

"Why did you not want me to see Mr. Kenby, Serena?"

"He means you harm," said the woman.

"I mean to see her safely away from here." Vincent tamped down his qualms. He studied Serena with new respect. He had revealed nothing of his intentions toward Catherine, but somehow the woman had sensed his presence meant nothing good.

Catherine turned back to him, and if he had thought her alight with joy before, it had been as nothing compared to the radiance she projected now. "Then my prayers have been answered at last. It is time. You have come to take me home for my wedding."

Laughing, she shot back to Serena and enveloped the woman in an embrace not at all suited to their respective stations. She must have learned to show affection from Serena, for Vincent had never witnessed any evidence of such tendencies in her family. He remembered the earl had said she'd grown impulsive under Serena's care, and this certainly proved it.

"Oh, my conscience is tugging at me! The Earl of Hedgeford must have died to bring this about, and so I should not be quite so happy!" Catherine moved the two of them in an impromptu dance, her own movements carefree and excited while Serena Monteverde let herself be manipulated with the enthusiasm of a wooden doll.

And while Catherine frolicked, Serena kept her venomous gaze fixed upon Vincent with the disconcerting unblinking stare of a carved madonna staring down from the walls of a church upon a congregation of sinners.

He held himself impassive, refusing to let her see how the stare troubled him. He'd heard it whispered of Serena that she might be a witch, possessed of certain powers that had enslaved the earl and kept him yearning for her even to this day. The hatred with which she watched him hinted at far greater suffering for him, if it were in her power to truly lay a curse.

Catherine's delight troubled him as well. Although it might keep her amenable if he let her persist in believing she was soon to be wed, he could not in good conscience allow her to remain so deceived.

"Tell her," said Serena, seeming to eerily read his thoughts.

"Yes, tell me everything!" Catherine laughed again, a sweet trilling sound that would lighten a man's heart, lead a man toward indulgence, if that man had honestly inspired that laugh. Another thing to watch about her. "Can you not all see that I am bursting to know everything you can tell me, Mr. Kenby?"

Bursting seemed an apt description for her state. Her chest heaved from her exertions, calling attention to the way her pale-green silk shift molded her breasts and clung to her waist. Best not look there.

Diverting his attention upward let him linger upon lips full as ripe cherries, her skin soft and tinged with color like a late-summer peach. How odd that his farmer's blood should make itself known at this moment, reminding him that few greater sensory delights existed than those offered by fruits claimed at the peak of perfection.

Once her face was framed in the stiff cloth of a nun's wimple, her skin would no doubt assume the typical nunlike pallor, but those lips, those lips . . .

With a tremendous effort, he forced himself to stop looking at her at all.

"Yes, the Earl of Hedgeford has died."

She made a great effort to look solemn, but failed. "My father will sorely miss him."

"We leave at once," he said.

"Impossible." Serena shook her head.

"Immediately."

"No."

Catherine broke in to their verbal sparring. "I can be ready very quickly, Serena. Within a few days, perhaps even two, since I have been making ready for this journey all my life. And my father may need me."

Though she acknowledged her father might be

mourning, everything about her, from her trembling eagerness, from her unmasked delight, bespoke a woman eager to make the acquaintance of the man she expected to wed. A woman who had hoped and prayed she might be one of the fortunate few, who might find true love in marriage.

"Your father had a falling-out with Hedgeford before the earl died. He does not grieve."

"I would not have thought such a thing possible." She stared at him in puzzlement, and then her good humor was restored. "But then, it means he can enjoy himself at my wedding." She tugged at Serena's sleeve. "You must help me pack with care for the long journey. My wedding linens, my garments—"

"You will have no need of them." Vincent cut off her planning.

Her smile faltered, and then intensified. She must have an extraordinarily sunny nature, he thought, to persist in happiness when all he said ought to plunge her into gloom.

"Of course—my mother! I should have realized she would have provided for me. She no doubt spent these years preparing the things she knows I will need. I was not so handy with the needle when I left home. Michael and I shall treasure the work of my lady mother's hands even more than what I have made on my own."

Michael and I . . . The phrasing tripped from her lips so easily that Vincent knew she used it often. In her mind, in her heart, she and Michael of Hedgeford had been linked for years. Any fool could see she welcomed the linking. A willing wife, beautiful, trained in the arts of love . . . Vincent felt a sudden surge of sympathy for Michael of Hedgeford, who had been cheated of far more than a rich dowry.

What Catherine was being cheated of did not bear thinking upon.

Vincent could scarcely credit this tug-of-war within himself. In the overall scheme of things, the future of this almost insignificant female paled against everything else. What did it matter if she spent her days behind stone walls, clad in heavy layers of black wool, her unfortunately awakened appetites doomed to forever remain unsatisfied?

Her father would rest easy knowing she was safe and secure, and secretly gloat in knowing he had bested the son of the man who had gone to his death cursing his name. Vincent would be rewarded for carrying out this task, both with wealth and responsibility. No doubt he would have to roust out those who had taken advantage of his absence, others who had thought to displace him in his lord's affections. He had no doubt he would prevail. Once things were sorted out, he would live out his days in England, in the position he had fought and schemed to obtain.

Life would return to its comfortable, familiar routines. All would be as it should be. All, save for Catherine, would be content. One day he would take a wife, a meek, compliant girl who would do as she should in their bed, heedless of special preparations that might make the joining more pleasurable for both of them.

From nowhere came the uncomfortable thought that there might be times when he bedded his placid, dutiful wife, that his thoughts would travel back to the woman who had been locked away rather than allowed to indulge her passions. This woman who had set aside her own excitement for a moment to ask his name and smile at him. She looked so radiant, so lovely, that an inner voice warned that after only ten minutes in her presence he might be forever haunted by her.

Temptress. Wanton. He required no more evidence to know he did the world a favor by locking her away. She worked her wicked magic with her smiles, with her delight, and so for his own sake he must wipe that smile from her face, erase that delight from her heart.

"Your father has decreed that Michael of Hedgeford no longer has any interest in what you wear or what you have sewn."

His sharp comment found its mark. As her smile faltered and then faded, he unaccountably felt a sense of loss, and a surprising surge of guilt.

"I do not understand," she said.

"I knew he meant you ill." Serena curved her arm around Catherine's shoulders, as if that small defense could keep her safe.

Curse his commoners' blood, Vincent raged silently. One thing he had learned from living and working among the nobles was that they seldom let their conscience plague them when misfortune fell upon another. They could not, else they would never be able to demand rents from the starving tenant farmers who scraped their scanty living from the landowner's holdings.

Vincent had not caused Catherine of Ardleswyck's change in fortunes. He had only been forced into the middle of it. *What about it being your suggestion that she go to a convent?* taunted his conscience.

Vincent had thought he'd put these internal struggles behind him. It angered him to find them clamoring for attention again, especially now, when he found himself caught in an untenable situation. That anger had lain simmering from the moment the earl had decreed this course of action. He did nothing to tamp it down. Better anger than remorse. Better anger than guilt. Anger was a clean emotion, certain to carry him through the end of this unpleasant task.

Unfortunately, anger also led one to use abrupt declarations rather than prettying up a phrase the way his lawyer's training had taught him to do.

"Tell her," Serena challenged. "Tell her."

They waited for him.

"There will be no wedding."

"Has something happened to Michael?" She clasped her hands together while her eyes pled for him to deny it.

Her first thought was for Hedgeford's good health, rather than herself. The hot little nub of anger flared.

"To my knowledge, Hedgeford fares well."

"Did my father entrust you with the reason for changing his mind, or must I wait until I am home to find out why I am not to marry right now?"

"Your father trusts me implicitly. You are not going home."

Her face revealed everything: relief, confusion, hesitation. "Please do not torment me, Mr. Kenby. I must know."

"Very well. Your father has decided you will take the veil."

"No!" Serena cried out, and quickly pressed a fist against her mouth. It gave Vincent no satisfaction to see that her witchly abilities had obviously not revealed the full extent of his intentions toward Catherine.

"The veil?" Catherine's brow creased, and then her eyes widened in horror. "No." She echoed the denial in a bare whisper. "My father would not. Not that, of all things." A tremor coursed through her, and then she stiffened her shoulders. "He told you to say that to bait me. He has ever possessed the nature of a trickster."

Vincent almost smiled at the notion of the imperious Earl of Ardleswyck playing pranks. Almost. Vincent doubted that even the most callous nobleman could display humor in the face of Catherine's agony. He, with his farmer's blood, had to struggle mightily lest sympathy dampen the fine anger still fueling him.

He disliked causing her anguish. He would have to guard against this weakness, too.

"I brought a woman who will help you make yourself ready to travel. We leave in a quarter hour." He indicated his head toward Serena. "Make your farewells now."

He had feared tears, perhaps some wailing, but the two stood like statues carved to display horror and disbelief. He turned and motioned toward the contingent waiting outside the room. The well-armed soldiers separated from the others, and the lady's maid who had been biding her time in the hall while they had sought Catherine moved forward to join them. Vincent stepped aside so they could enter the room.

"Which one are we to guard, Mr. Kenby?" asked one of the soldiers. Vincent bit back an insult; given the way Serena had tried to forestall him, the question was not as witless as it first appeared.

"The one whose hair shines like gold beneath the sun," he said. The soldier's eyes sparked with interest as Vincent clenched his teeth and wondered where on earth such a poetic description had sprung from. He should have simply jerked his head toward Catherine. Or let the maid's common sense guide her toward the younger of the two women, and let the soldiers follow.

Instead, he had spouted nonsense.

"I will help my lady prepare for her journey." Serena stepped between Catherine and the maid.

Vincent shook his head. "No. I have witnessed first-hand evidence of your duplicity, mistress. From this moment, Catherine of Ardleswyck shall be accompanied by someone of my choosing, no matter how personal or private her task. My men will stand close to ensure nothing . . . happens to her."

Stony silence greeted his pronouncement. And then Catherine's shoulders drew back, and it seemed her eyes took on the same furor as the storm raging outside.

"I will not do this."

"Your father has ordered it so."

Women had no rights. When unmarried, they were ruled by their fathers. Once married, they were ruled by their husbands. She had no recourse but to honor her father's wishes.

"I demand explanations."

He felt a glimmer of appreciation for her strength. She had grown pale, and her excitement had subtly shifted into a fine trembling that hinted at her despair, but she did not resort to weeping. He tamped down his admiration, reminding himself of what he knew to be true about her, and suspecting it could all be a trick. She had spent the most important years of her life learning how to hide the soul of a harlot beneath the exterior of a lady. She might believe the skills she had learned at Serena's side enabled her to have her way with him.

The various weaknesses that had assailed him during this brief time he'd spent with her proved she was a menace. He must ever be on guard against her. She was not what she seemed.

"You would do well to acquaint yourself with humility and acceptance," he said. "From all I know of the life of nuns, they do not demand explanations."

"You are cruel, sirrah." Serena's eyes blazed with animosity, her whole being virtually crackled with distaste. "You have just destroyed my lady's dreams. Surely she may have a few moments to come to grips with the news you have sprung upon her."

Vincent's still-simmering anger again let him speak incautiously. "There is no time. As we stand here dithering about explaining something that needs no explanation, the Earl of Hedgeford's forces are making their way here to kidnap the lady."

They had sighted Hedgeford's banner on a ship following them at sea. Foul weather had slowed their own progress so much that what should have been a two-week advantage in time was now no more than a few days. Hedgeford's ship would sail into the port of Genoa very soon.

"Michael! You are saying Michael still wants me!"

Vincent's anger took an unaccountable leap when Catherine once more transformed with joy. Joy, at the very thought that Michael of Hedgeford wanted her.

"Aye, he wants you. Your father says he is not to have you. Lingering here can only expose you to danger, for a battle will no doubt ensue when his ship lands."

"He will not kill me," she said with confidence.

"Not a-purpose. It takes but one stray arrow to find its way into your heart." One arrow to still a heart that seemed to beat with love for the man she had thought to wed.

His anger surged.

"Gather what you need quickly, or I shall hoist you over my shoulder and take you away with naught but what you wear on your back at this moment."

He decided to offer one small concession and made a curt motion of his head toward Serena. "Show them all to the lady's chamber, and help make her ready. We leave in a quarter hour, no matter how she is dressed or what she has gathered."

Four

Catherine skidded to a stop just before reaching her private chamber. She did not remember how she had arrived here. Her mind had gone blank after Vincent Kenby had stated his ruthless purpose in coming for her. She must have walked, one foot in front of the other, led by blind instinct to the place that was her sanctuary, but she could not recall taking even one step.

If she could not remember walking here, then perhaps all of it had been a dream.

A nightmare. Yes! Perhaps she was only this moment awakening from sleep. She had never left the room, never witnessed a crowd of soldiers storming the Mass that morning, never raced through the palazzo's corridors with Serena, never heard a tall, disturbingly handsome man utter the words that destroyed her life.

But someone bumped into her from behind and knocked her forward by two steps. Crossing through the doorway moved her from nightmare to reality, straight into sensibility again.

"Forgive me, miss, I did not expect you to stop so sudden."

Catherine did not recognize the voice, and after so

many years of living in Italy the Saxon words struck harsh against her ears. She did not turn to see who followed so closely, and she did not move farther into her room. If she remained as she was, she might yet blink her eyes and find she had just awakened from a terrible nightmare.

And then Serena was there. "I know, sweeting, I know," she whispered. She closed the chamber door and, placing a gentle arm around Catherine's shoulders, led her into her room.

"You cannot know," Catherine answered, but as pain flickered through Serena's eyes, Catherine realized she had wronged her. Just so had a pronouncement from Catherine's father forever altered Serena's life and sent her into a sort of exile.

The old queen would understand, too. Eleanor had been locked away upon her husband's orders, and given no opportunity to protest, no chance to make a personal appeal for mercy. Men did these things to their women.

She stood paralyzed, still in that half-aware, nightmare state. She watched while the Englishwoman approached the ancient chest that was too heavy to ever be removed from this room, where Catherine had folded away the most precious of her wedding finery.

Opening the trunk's lid had always sent Catherine into a delightful reverie. She would touch the smooth silks, finger the intricate embroidery, and imagine a man's rough hand taking pleasure in doing the same when the garment rested against her warm skin.

A soft keening sound filled the room, and with a start she realized that the noise came from her own throat.

Serena's eyes filled with tears, and the sight of those tears, more than anything, told Catherine that this was not a nightmare from which she would awake.

"This must be a mistake," Catherine managed to choke, clinging desperately to hope that grew fainter by the moment. Speaking was better than betraying the depths of her pain through wordless anguish.

And movement was better than standing still as a rabbit held by a wolf's glare. She disengaged herself from Serena's worried embrace. Moving with the halting, uncertain steps of an aged crone, she crossed to the stacked boxes that held the efforts of years of sewing and dreaming.

She touched each one in turn, as if their solidity would validate her assertion. She rested a hand atop one of the boxes, and its solidity lent her a little strength. She stood taller and pointed across the room.

"Those brass-bound boxes are filled with linens destined for my marriage bed." She shifted her arm, and aimed at the next thing. "That cedar chest protects my fine woolens against moths. This Italian clime discourages the wearing of wool in all save the deepest winter months. I daresay I shall be glad of wool's warmth in England's damp chill."

"Catherine." Serena's voice quavered.

The English stranger knelt before the open trunk. Catherine, with a sound of annoyance, pushed the woman away before she could touch the jewel-toned garments heaped within. They were hers. *Hers*.

She dropped to her knees and drew out a gossamer wisp of nightwear. "Silk straight from China. My father spared no expense in providing the cloth." She laughed, a wild cackle. "He would not have ordered such luxurious colors for a woman destined for the convent."

She cast that bit of silk aside and delved deep into the trunk to pull out yet another delicate thing. "Do you remember, Serena, how we soaked wood balls with perfume and stored them at the bottom?" She held the garment against her cheek, and drew a deep breath. "Now all these things carry my favorite scent. The English would love to know how the Italians weave this cloth. This is so soft and fine, I sometimes take it out late at night and hold it against my skin and imagine . . . I can put it on myself and remove it myself but I am certain the way it slides against my skin will be far different when . . ."

"Catherine."

The heavy sorrow in Serena's voice struck Catherine like a hammer blow to the middle. She leaned forward and buried her face in the cool, smooth silks, retching with dry heaves while breathing in the scent of fine cloth and perfume.

Serena knelt beside her and drew her away from the trunk, back once more into her arms. Even the English stranger seemed affected. She sniffled, and gave Catherine's shoulder a quick, tentative pat. Catherine struck out at her. The maid avoided the blow, and moved away to stand with her hands clasped in an attitude of prayer as she gnawed her lower lip.

"Catherine!"

"I am sorry. I should not have struck at you," Catherine whispered. Embarrassed at having lashed out, at revealing the depths of her despair, she hid her face against Serena's bosom. How God had mocked her, giving her those moments earlier in the day when she had peered through the viewing hole at the nuns and dared to feel pity for them. Now she would be as they were. Meek and bowed and never knowing the joys of a husband, of children.

"I will not go. I will kill myself first."

She did not think anyone could have heard her utter the sacrilege, but Serena drew back and gripped her tightly by the chin, forcing her to look up. "Never, Catherine. Do not doom yourself for eternity. Do not lose heart."

"How can I not?"

"Think of Queen Eleanor." Serena knew the high regard Catherine held for the old queen, and, Catherine thought, Serena knew her as well.

Catherine always took heart from thinking of Eleanor. So many situations in the old queen's life paralleled her own, and Catherine had always drawn strength from knowing that Eleanor had triumphed over them all. Catherine struggled to find strength in the queen's history now.

"I do not know if I can be as brave as she, but I shall try."

The stranger snuffled aloud. "Lady, mayhap"—the stranger cleared her throat—"mayhap your old dad will change his mind."

She meant well, Catherine realized, but the woman had no personal knowledge of the Earl of Ardleswyck.

"My father never changes his mind, even when it would benefit him to do so."

The truth of her statement served to calm her, in a strange way. Her father never changed his mind. Even if she were by his side instead of half a world away, no amount of weeping or railing against the unfairness of his decision would sway him. He had decreed what would be done with her. He had dis-

patched his man to handle the affair. Her father's will
would be done.

She could lie to herself and pretend she had reason
to hope. Or she could accept—nay, never accept—she
could *acknowledge* what was to happen, and try to
make the best of it.

"I do not even know where he means to take me,"
she said. She found she wasn't even curious. Knowing
where she was to be imprisoned did not make it any
easier to accept.

"I will insist that this Vincent Kenby tell me where
he means to take you," Serena said. "I will use whatever influence I have with your father to press him for
a change of heart."

"If only I knew what brought about the falling-out
between my father and the earl."

"It must have been terrible, sweeting. Hedgeford
and your father were closer than brothers. This decision of his is not the act of a rational man. I fear your
father has lost his mind over this."

"You have taught me much about men, but not about
how to read their minds," Catherine said.

Serena gave her a tremulous smile. "Few men are
difficult to read. Most think of only two things: sex
and power."

"Then I must be the pawn sacrificed over whatever
wrong my father feels has been caused by the blood of
Hedgeford."

"It would appear so. If only we could ask the lout
who waits for you, but I would mistrust anything from
his lips."

"Why so?"

"I have seen his kind before. This Vincent reeks of
his hunger for power. He cannot claim it by right of

birth, and so must gain what power he can through your father's favor. Unfortunately, it means he will do whatever it takes to carry out this witless plan."

"Is it a witless plan, Serena?" Although she knew there was scant reason to hope, Catherine could not prevent a little flicker of it from flaring to life.

"You are a valuable asset to your father, sweeting. To lock you away in a convent seems an act of spite, nothing more. Your father is stubborn to a fault, but he always takes care to profit from situations. And I have always found him loving and generous to those he cares about—and he does care about you; there is no doubt in my mind of that. I cannot believe he was in his right mind when he ordered this done to you. There is hope that he might one day realize he acted in hot-tempered haste when ordering this to be done to you."

They were silent for a moment, allowing hope to blossom, but in the quiet Catherine recalled so many instances of her father's stubbornness that she could not sustain the hope.

"He will not relent," said Catherine.

"He will not live forever," said Serena.

The comment seemed to reverberate around them. Her father's death might set her free, the way King Henry's death had freed Eleanor from incarceration.

"It is so hard to bear," Catherine said. "For all these years I have been looking forward to the death of one man, so his son might be free to marry me. And now, I must look forward to the death of my own father."

The chamber door creaked open, startling her out of that bit of melancholy. A soldier poked his head past the door and scowled to see that she was not yet ready to depart.

"You!" he bellowed at the Englishwoman. "Mr. Kenby set you the charge of making her ready with all speed. One bundle cannot be so difficult to fill."

The reprimand wiped away the traces of sympathy which the woman had displayed. Her face hardened. "She's the dithering sort," she said to the soldier. She shouldered Catherine aside and commenced rooting through the garments in the trunk. "Nothing suitable for your journey in here. You'll be wanting one or two stout wool gowns."

Catherine bit back a retort, and was glad she'd held her tongue when the woman leaned back and glared at the soldier. "No need to hover. I know my job."

The soldier looked askance, but withdrew from the room.

"Thank you," said Catherine. The woman had shown kindness once; she might become friendly again. Catherine would have need of a friend.

She realized that she still clutched her favorite nightdress in her hand. Crimson silk, a shockingly wanton color that nonetheless delighted her. Its folds lay draped over the ancient trunk, vibrant against the age-blackened wood.

"I shall take everything," she said.

"Mr. Kenby said one bundle."

"Very well. One bundle it shall be." Catherine stood and yanked the counterpane from her bed, and then spread it next to the trunk. She scooped the full contents into her arms, and then dropped everything onto the counterpane.

Serena laughed.

The Englishwoman opened her mouth to protest, but then cast a glance toward the doorway and scowled, as if remembering the insult she'd taken from the soldier. She shrugged—and then she, too, smiled.

Catherine darted around the perimeter of the chamber. She pulled every garment from every peg to add to the heap. Serena and the Englishwoman upturned each brass-bound box to spill all the contents upon the collected stuff. As the crowning touch, Catherine dropped the red silk nightdress atop the pile. It took the three of them to gather up the edges of the counterpane and fasten the corners into a rough knot.

One bundle. Outrageously huge, but one bundle, as she'd been ordered.

The three women looked at each other, and though five minutes earlier Catherine would not have believed it possible, she laughed.

Vincent never paced. Doing so always revealed a man's inner turmoil: excitement, anxiousness, entrapment. Many were the times, though, when he had to forcibly hold his legs still to avoid revealing himself in such an obvious manner.

This was one of those times. He waited in the chill of the palazzo's hall, anxious for word from the soldier whom he'd sent to consult with the ship's captain . . . and feeling trapped by the situation forced upon him by the Earl of Ardleswyck.

His distraction differed subtly, and most troublingly, from the frustration that had gripped him from the moment he'd been handed the assignment. Then, he'd thought only of the inconvenience to himself. He'd calculated the time he would waste, and grudged every minute of it in advance. He'd taken what steps he could to protect his interests, but knew that the moment he

left England, his so-called colleagues would be doing
everything they could to erase every shred of his
power.

Then, he'd not considered at all that he might find
carrying out the assignment to be a loathsome task for
its end result, not for the time taken away from his
usual activities.

He moved toward a window and pretended interest in the glass pane. Curiosity in such a rarity could
not be questioned by even the most interested observer, and would betray nothing about the turmoil
he felt within. He rubbed a finger over the wavery
surface. The earl had lavished the best upon his exiled courtesan.

The rain pelted the glass so heavily it seemed coated
with a sheet of water. The narrow street outside was
scarcely visible, so distorted was the image. The hulk-
ing building directly across the way added gloom to
the already dark atmosphere, and the cobblestones lay
black from absorbing so much water, dark and dull as
the bottom of a grave. This palazzo lay so close to the
port of Genoa that one might smell the salt breeze in
the air, but the warrenlike maze of streets and buildings surrounding it provided a view as familiar, and as
dreary, as the stews of London.

Rangold, the soldier Vincent had been awaiting,
called out to him from the far edge of the hall. "Mr.
Kenby—the news is not good."

Vincent turned away from the window and motioned the man closer. Before the man could offer his
report, though, a commotion at yet another door leading into the hall announced the arrival of Catherine of
Ardleswyck.

He cast her the most cursory glance, and found himself so compelled to stare at her that he had to pretend indifference. Turning his head toward the soldier required a surprising expenditure of strength, and was accomplished only by scolding himself, reminding himself that the soldier's information required immediate attention.

"Captain says wind's all wrong, Mr. Kenby. Blowin' straight in to land. Ship ain't likely to move at all, do we set sail now." The man's teeth chattered—the storm apparently carried a bitter chill as well as torrential rain.

Vincent remained impassive while inwardly he cursed the weather. The wind had been against them for the first, important days of their voyage, slowing their progress sufficiently that Michael of Hedgeford's forces followed only a day or two behind them.

The soldier, heedless of Catherine's presence, or perhaps only eager to impress Vincent, babbled on before Vincent could warn him into silence. "Whilst our ship struggles its way out to sea, yon Hedgeford's ship can sail straight in to port slick as butter."

"You have sighted Michael's ship?" Catherine's question rang through the hall.

She stood with Serena, while in the narrow passageway behind her two of his men moved in an awkward, hunched-over way, dragging and tugging at something he could not see. Catherine wore a luxuriant wolfskin cape, with one hand clutching it close at her neck, while her other gripped a small satchel. She exuded hope, creating an aura of brightness in the dim, chill chamber.

Half an hour earlier, she'd stumbled in a sort of daze from this hall, shocked to the core by the news he'd brought. Now she smiled, heartened at the mere mention of Hedgeford's name. Decimated by Vincent; resurrected by Hedgeford.

Vincent decided his sudden fury could be blamed on the soldier's wagging tongue.

"When did you last see Michael of Hedgeford?" he asked Catherine.

Her smile widened, and his fury grew apace.

"When?" he demanded.

She shrugged, a graceful gesture that sent her fur cape rippling down the length of her. "We may have met as children, but I confess I do not recall."

"And yet you simper like a lovesick maid at the mere mention of the man's name."

Good Lord—he'd whined the accusation like a rejected suitor! What ailed him, to have lost such control over his words? He snapped shut his jaw so tightly that he hoped he had not cracked a tooth.

Serena Monteverde smirked at him.

"I love him," Catherine said simply. "And I know that he loves me. I heard your man say his ship is in sight, so it confirms the suspicion you admitted earlier. Michael comes to claim me against my father's wishes."

Vincent ignored her observation. "Hedgeford does not know what you look like. Nor would you be able to recognize him."

Catherine could not know the thrust of his statements, and she proved it by turning whimsical. Her eyes softened, darkened, and a dreamy smile curved her lips.

"I hoped he might have a gentle side, and would hold some tender feelings for me. I imagined him tall, lean, strong, and fierce. Somewhat . . . somewhat like you, Mr. Kenby." She seemed as surprised by her remark as he was himself, for she flushed a little.

Somewhat like him. She imagined herself in love with a man who looked somewhat like him.

The skin on his face felt hotter, tighter than usual. Perhaps it was because he was finally drying out after his jaunt in the rain. It could be nothing else.

He turned back to the soldier. "Have all the horses been unloaded from the ship, Rangold?"

"Aye." Rangold shifted, clearly unhappy. "That be the rest of my bad news, Mr. Kenby. Horse master says they ain't fit to ride yet. Need a day or two to get their legs back under them afore they carry a full-grown man. Horse master said 'twould be best to turn 'em out on grass and soak up some sun."

"Our stables can accommodate your horses, Mr. Kenby," Serena said. "I cannot conjure sunshine for you, but our stables are dry, and our hay is fragrant and fresh from this year's first cutting."

"How many horses in your stable?" Vincent asked.

"Two. All others have been confiscated by Tancred for the Crusade. There is plenty of room for your animals."

He ignored Serena's offer. "Return at once to the ship," he said to Rangold. "Choose the best fighting men and bring them back here with all of the horses. Advise the others to reboard, along with one of the women, and set sail for home, at once, despite the weather." He cast a glance toward Catherine. "When . . . *if* . . . Hedgeford's ship is sighted, tell them to make sure the woman is seen on deck. Tell the men to run about, using both stairwells to run from belowdecks to above to make it seem there is a full force on board."

"Aye, Mr. Kenby."

Rangold, a good soldier, asked no questions but made a quick bow at the waist and hurried from the hall.

"You're hoping Michael will turn and pursue the ship while my lady remains here," guessed Serena.

"It will not be so easy to fool Michael," said Catherine. *Michael.* She said his name with a sort of reverence, her tongue and lips lingering over the syllables. Her irritating, lovesick smile widened.

Michael, Michael, he was sick of hearing these women invoke Hedgeford's name, and credit him with knightly qualities, as if he'd impressed them on the tourney field, or somehow earned their affection and admiration.

Catherine dropped her bundle. "Then we stay after all. I packed for naught."

"We leave immediately," said Vincent. "We shall travel overland."

"You cannot expect my lady to travel in a litter all the way to England!" Serena protested.

"I said nothing about a litter. And we are not bound for England."

"Exactly where do you mean to take me?" Catherine asked.

He realized, as soon as she asked, how much he had been dreading the question. "The cloisters of Saint Justinius. In France," he said, hoping she would not probe for a more definitive answer.

He did not relish telling her that the cloister lay in the desolate mountains near the German border, so remote, so isolated, that she would never see anyone save for the women confined with her.

"What is it like there?"

"I have never seen it," he said, an honest response,

but he knew the answer to be an evasion of the truth nonetheless.

"It cannot be a place of quality," said Serena, "if you can expect to simply show up with a woman in tow and have her accepted."

"I assure you the cloister holds to the highest standards," said Vincent. "While we stand here wasting time, the details are being handled. Your father dispatched the Ardleswyck bishop to first gain the King of France's permission to lodge you in that country, and then to move on and negotiate the terms for your entrance into the cloister."

"Then I may hold hope that the king has denied his permission," said Catherine.

"King Louis will welcome the chance to keep Richard Lionheart's hands off your dowry. Richard has earned the king's wrath for failing to honor his betrothal to the French princess."

"I know all about Richard's betrothals," said Catherine. "I have studied everything written about the Queen Mother, Eleanor."

Vincent passed off her comment as typical womanish nonsense, for matters involving kings had nothing to do with women, even their mothers. But since Catherine had claimed some knowledge of the situation, he expanded his explanation. "Then you must know King Louis is renowned for his piety. It should please the king well to welcome a bride of Christ into his lands, especially since it will let him tweak Richard's hopes of getting his hands on your dowry. All will be arranged by the time we arrive."

"If I had some idea of what to expect . . ."

"I have never seen the place."

But he had chosen the cloister himself. When he'd

posed to the solution to his lord, he'd known exactly where Catherine could best be confined. Saint Justinius was the sort of place a counselor needed to know about when those they served found themselves saddled with a recalcitrant daughter, a hideous sister, a spinster aunt. Widows had willingly gone there rather than endure forced marriage when the deaths of their husbands left them with lands and wealth worth taking.

The cloister lay high on a mountain, where its inaccessibility and the difficult climate served to discourage casual visitors. Sheer rock walls edged the perimeter, fortifying the religious house more thoroughly than many castles. The cloister guarded its occupants well. No woman had ever been stolen away.

No woman had ever left of her own accord, either. The only way out of the cloister, it was said, was for the man who had installed her there to claim her back . . . or for death to take her.

"France," said Serena. "The climate is much like here, in certain parts."

"France," Catherine said. "Better than England, perhaps. The weather there is so foul. I have come to love the sunshine after living here for so many years."

Not so foul, Vincent thought, as the windswept cold that hovered year-round so high in the mountains. This woman who loved the sunshine would be locked within a great stone edifice where only the minimal number of arrow slits pierced the gloom. And he was responsible for taking her there; he would close the door with his own hand.

He seized the opportunity to turn the conversation away from the cloister. "The only weather that concerns us is the weather outside at this moment."

"Rain. And cold for this time of year," said Serena.

"The journey will not be comfortable, but perhaps it is not amiss for the lady to become accustomed to rigorous conditions."

He had best abandon all talk of weather. Vincent saw his men still struggling with something in the corridor beyond. "Walter—I have need of you. Drop whatever it is you're dragging and come to me."

At that moment, though, Walter and his partner succeeded in their task, which appeared to be squeezing an enormous bundle of bedcoverings through the doorway. Casting the bundle a look of disgust, Walter kicked at it. "At your service, Mr. Kenby."

Vincent pulled a leather purse from his jerkin. Hefting it, the sound of gold coins clinking together could be heard. He tossed the pouch to Walter. "I want you and two men to buy every available horse within easy walking distance of the port."

"You'll find none," Serena said. "Our king has thrown all his support to yours in his mad Crusade."

"Find horses," Vincent said.

The men left to do his bidding.

"I will have your animals, as well," Vincent said when he was alone with the women again. "Everything in this place was purchased with the earl's money and all belongs to him. You will manage despite the inconvenience."

"I must have a horse," Serena protested.

Vincent shook his head. "If Hedgeford manages to land and find out the deception, I want to make it as difficult as possible for him to follow us."

"You think you have an answer for everything," Serena said.

"I am a careful man, madam," he answered. He

prided himself on analyzing every plan, and planning
for every possible contingency. That was why he'd carried horses on a journey meant to be accomplished on
sea, over the protests of the ship's captain and despite
not-so-subtle mutterings of the crew. That was why
he'd insisted upon bringing two women said to share
Catherine of Ardleswyck's physical characteristics,
again over the protest of the captain and crew, who
held a superstitious fear of transporting female pas-
sengers.

"No matter how careful, you cannot anticipate
everything," Serena said.

"Perhaps not," he agreed, "but there is little that es-
capes my attention." He did not discount the whims of
fate, but all too often he had witnessed suffering
caused by nothing more than poor planning. He held
the firm belief that only those not intelligent enough
to foresee potential pitfalls found themselves blind-
sided by surprise. "Can you suggest an area where my
foresight appears to be lacking?"

"Aye." Serena caught Catherine's hand in her own.
"Sweeting—take care to suspect any feelings you
might develop for this man. You guard your heart as
well, Vincent Kenby."

The courtesan's warning struck so absurd that Vincent laughed aloud. Catherine shot him a look of such
utter loathing that it ought to have reassured Serena
Monteverde that her darling was in no danger of developing soft feelings for him.

Serena ignored both of their outward repudiations
of the warning. "It may be difficult to believe so now,
but the two of you will be traveling in close quarters,
with the weight of the future pressing down upon you."

"Which is precisely why I should never develop the

slightest bit of fondness for this . . . this . . . fiend," Catherine said.

Serena shook her head. "I have tried my best to fill a mother's role for you, but you have been love-starved all your life. You believe yourself to be in love with a man you have never met, and your heart can easily mistake this one for the other. Your hatred of him will melt at any kindness from him. Never lose sight of what this one means to do to you, Catherine. You will find yourself creating excuses for him in your mind; you will be most eager to embrace those excuses and forgive him."

"Ha!" Catherine's short laugh echoed through the hall.

"Ha!" He breathed out at the same time. He could think of nothing less likely, that he should show her kindnesses. He intended to hold himself as distant from her as possible, lest she seek to ply her seductress ways upon him. He meant to keep her frightened, alone, helpless.

"I caution you not to dismiss my warning," said Serena. "You, who think you can plan and control any outcome, will find that you cannot make human beings dance to the strings you pull—you cannot even exert complete control over yourself, no matter what you might think."

If these words of warning were an example of the knowledge Serena had taught to Catherine, then perhaps Vincent had credited her for more wisdom than she possessed.

"We go," he said. He plucked Catherine's satchel from her hands and tucked it beneath his arm. He caught her upper arm with his other hand, and found himself rooted to the floor by the jolt of sensation that coursed through him to find her so soft, so supple, in his hand.

Serena watched, smug and confident, with a crooked little smile that told him she knew exactly what he had felt just then.

"Remember my warning, Catherine," she said. "And you, Mr. Kenby."

Five

"The journey shall be difficult and tedious."

There was nothing in Vincent's voice to betray annoyance, but Catherine sensed it. Serena was right about so much, Catherine thought. Men were easy to read. Vincent Kenby loathed this task as much as she hated being its purpose.

"Do you have a favorite horse in yon stables?" he asked. "One capable of speed, and yet with gentle manners and—"

To her surprise, his gaze dropped to her legs, and she fancied he studied the length and shape of them through her gown.

"I do not ride, Mr. Kenby," she said softly. She had been forbidden the pleasure, for the very reason he had so subtly studied her legs, imagining them spread across the wide back of a horse when in truth her husband must be the first to part them in such a way.

She had often regretted the ban on riding, for she had enjoyed the few lessons she'd had as a child. Her early days in Genoa had allowed her a great deal of freedom, which she'd exercised in the maze-like warren of alleys and lanes that made this one city best traversed on foot.

But more recently, when the crusaders began

swarming through the town and she had been confined within the walls of the palazzo, she had yearned for some kind, any kind, of freedom. Perhaps knowing she would soon return to England, she had remembered the open spaces, the low hills and fields, and tried to imagine what it would feel like to race a powerful horse across valleys and up hills, imagined the wind in her face, the thrust of the powerful beast performing at her command.

"You must have planned for a litter," Serena mocked. "Any fool knows 'tis the only accepted mode of travel for virgins of gentle birth."

Vincent's hands clenched at his sides. "A horse, a litter, it makes little difference. We shall use your litter."

"We do not have one. I repeatedly advised Catherine's father that it has not been safe for her to leave the house with all these mercenaries roaming about."

"Then she will ride in your cart."

"Nor do we have a cart. We hire a cart and driver as needed."

"Fetch the carter."

"You cannot expect my lady to travel unsheltered from the elements. I do not think you would want to report to her father that she sickened from cold and wet while under your care."

Catherine suspected most men would have exploded in fury at Serena's goading. Vincent stood tense, practically simmering with anger, but not a word betrayed him, and save for the clenching of his hands he gave not the slightest indication of his annoyance. She realized why her father entrusted him with such a task—it would be difficult to know whether this man thought you a fool or an equal, or whether this man lied or told the truth.

He'd parried every one of Serena's thrusts, and now he drove the killing blow.

"A cart would slow us down too much, and would not protect her from the weather. The lady's virginity no longer has any value. She will ride like the rest of us."

Serena, who had been gloating, wavered. "My neighbor owns a strange little conveyance. I cannot vouch for its speed. He may be willing to loan it to us."

"Hire his driver as well, to return the vehicle to him."

"I shall inquire." Serena hastened away.

The guard and the maid seemed to fade into oblivion, for once Serena left the hall, Catherine felt so awkward and tense, it was as if only she and Vincent occupied the hall. She had no interest in easing the strain between them. Serena's warning, ridiculous as it had seemed, deserved to be heeded, for already Catherine found within herself distressing tendencies to do exactly what Serena had warned against.

No tender feelings for Vincent—never! But already her conscience whispered that he but did her father's bidding, and not his own. She wanted to hate him as the one who came between her and Michael, but her conscience whispered no, her father owned that responsibility.

She would have to guard against softening toward him.

Vincent helped. He motioned toward the bundle of things. "While we wait, sort out only the most important of those things."

"The bundle can ride in the cart with me."

"So much will only make the vehicle heavier to pull and slower. You shall discard the bulk of it."

"I see. You mean to punish me as well as lock me away."

The barest flicker of an eyelid hinted that she might have struck something soft within him. "If you are unable to choose what to take, I shall do it for you."

He would, too—she had already had ample evidence of his resolve. The memory of how she and the others had laughed while tying the huge bundle mocked her now. It had been a silly, futile gesture.

She angrily released the clasp at her neck and let the fur cloak fall to her feet. "If I am to become wet, why bother with a cloak? 'Tis nigh onto midsummer. This rain will cease and the heat will return."

"You will need the cloak."

"No."

"I promise that one day you will thank me for insisting."

"I will never thank you for anything."

He did not react at all to her sting. He nodded toward the maid. "Help her."

The woman slouched toward Catherine, and she thought she saw a regretful tear in the woman's eyes at the thought of so many fine things being discarded. Catherine understood. Maids usually had their pick of their mistress's discarded garments. This poor creature would be permitted to carry no more than she herself was allowed.

She let the cloak lay on the marble floor. Bending toward the bulging bundle she pulled a simple shift from it. Standing, she held the garment against herself and smoothed it down.

"'Tis a simple enough gown," she said. "A color that

should not be amiss in a convent. Finely wrought." Indeed it was; the wool had been so finely woven that it was a tactile pleasure to run her hand over it, and so she did it again. And again, flattening it against her belly while shooting a glance toward Vincent to see how he could possibly disagree with her choice of this garment.

His gaze seemed riveted on where her hand rested low against her belly. He stood rigid as stone, transfixed, and a jolt of pure sensation shot through her when she realized his man's blood had been roused by her simple movements.

She let the gown drop to the floor, to mingle with the fur already heaped at her feet.

She bent to choose another.

He did not say her nay.

"This one," she said, rising and holding it in front of her as if it were a towel she meant to step into after her bath. Then she drew it back against her breast and trailed her hand lightly from her neck to her middle, knowing the soft cloth molded itself perfectly to her form. "Linen, for hot days. I like to avoid becoming damp in the heat—it makes my skin glisten so."

He said nothing, but what she could see of his own skin seemed to develop a distinct shine, as if he'd grown quite warm.

She let the linen shift drop.

"This one, my lady." The Englishwoman shoved the red silk nightdress into Catherine's hand.

Her favorite, the one garment she treasured above all others and now would never wear. Whisper-light, cool and redolent with lavender, her favorite scent. She by habit rubbed it against her cheek. She closed her eyes, savoring the feel of silk against skin, enjoying the heady scent of lavender. How many times had she done this very thing, dreaming of the night when she would wear this and welcome her husband into her bed? Although anger and despair still held a grip upon her, the delightful sensations and dreams associated with the wisp of red silk made her smile.

"Not that one."

Reluctant to let go of her pleasant sensations, she opened her eyes slowly to find Vincent had stormed across the room, and before she could react he had plucked the nightdress from her fingers. He held it away from him as if it were a stinking shroud, and then flung it at the woman. "Not this one."

The Englishwoman caught the nightdress and turned away; from the corner of her eye Catherine saw her shove the red silk well down behind her apron.

"What would you suggest I wear to sleep, Mr. Kenby?" Catherine asked.

"You may go to your bed naked for all I care," he gritted.

"Perhaps I will," she said softly. "My fur cloak does make a warm cover, although I have found that my limbs stick out."

She knew this to be true, for she had on occasion gone to bed exactly in this way, and from the sudden rigidness in Vincent's posture, he had no difficulty in imagining how a woman might look lying entangled in thick, soft furs, with one leg, one shoulder, bared.

He bent and gathered her cloak and the two gowns she'd held against herself. He pushed them into her arms. A fold of her cloak brushed her cheek; without thinking, she rubbed against it, and to her consternation he tore the things from her hands to let them fall to the floor once again.

"Make one bundle of those things and nothing more." He inclined his head toward the heaped clothing at her feet. "I must go to the yard and hurry along the preparations. I expect you to join me as soon as you have this bundle packed."

When the door closed behind him, the English maid laughed, a low throaty chuckle that caused Catherine to look at her with new interest.

"You certainly got him all a-bother," snickered the woman.

"I did nothing to raise his ire. He has simply hated me from the beginning."

"I do not think he hates you, my lady. The opposite, I should say. And I am guessing 'tis not his ire that you have raised."

There was a twinkle in the woman's eyes, a genuine smile that led Catherine to respond in kind. "We are to travel together. Might we be friends?"

"We might." The woman sent a surreptitious glance toward the bulge in her apron, and Catherine remembered the red silk she had hidden there. She would not let a garment she would never wear cost her a friend at this moment.

"That was to be my bed wear on my wedding night," she said. "I ask that you treasure it and save it for an occasion of importance."

"I will—but 'tis yours, if you have need of it first."

Catherine warmed toward the woman. "Not very likely, I am afraid."

The woman nodded.

"What shall I call you?" Catherine asked.

"My name is Maisie. I know what I shall call you: Sister Catherine."

"Oh." Unbidden, tears welled in Catherine's eyes.

"Take heart," said Maisie, and with a surprisingly gentle hand brushed away Catherine's tears. "I shall call you that only to provoke Mr. Kenby. My guess is it will goad him sore."

The stable yard lacked the seething sense of urgency that usually preceded the imminent departure of a large party. Vincent, always cognizant that some of the men resented being ordered about by one who was not a soldier, motioned for Rangold to approach.

"Are we near to departing?"

"Beggin' your pardon, Mr. Kenby, but I do hope you might reconsider. Yonder are the horses brung from the ship."

The animals were a miserable lot. They stood with their heads down, legs quivering, not even nibbling at the hay that had been dropped for them.

"Have the men found any fresh animals to buy?"

"Not so far, Mr.—" Rangold's attention swerved toward the courtyard entrance. "Mayhap we are in luck. Here comes someone."

But guffaws, and then a wave of laughter, accompanied the man who trudged into the courtyard, leading a trio of donkeys.

"Oh, shut yer traps," he shouted, defending his find with red-faced fervor. "These be hearty little beasts with hearts like a lion."

True enough, a donkey would stagger along while bearing a man's weight—but not at any great speed.

Hard on his heels followed another soldier, leading

a pair of bow-backed horses that looked no more fit than their own animals. Again, laughter greeted the arrival, but it seemed a little muted, whether by the incessant rain, or by the realization that they would find no better, Vincent could not tell.

"Grain and water them all," Vincent ordered. "Quickly."

The rain drummed cold and sharp, and the men walked hunched over, their heads down, as they sloshed through the puddles carrying buckets. The drenching rain muted the clatter of bucket against feed bin, the wet clop of hooves, the shouts of approval when another soldier arrived leading two young mules.

"Mr. Kenby, I feel obliged to point out that the men, too, would benefit from a night of sleep before setting off," warned Rangold. "The horses can do little better than shamble along. One night of rest for man and beast! I promise we would make such better time that you will reckon the delay well spent."

"We cannot stay here, Rangold. I hope Hedgeford will fall for the trickery of the earl's ship setting back out to sea. But if he does not, we must be gone from here. We have only a handful of men, and no idea how many Hedgeford will bring to the fray. We must go, even if we gain only a mile of advantage."

Vincent had explained himself more than his wont, because he sensed that Rangold wanted to continue arguing, and held his tongue with difficulty. Vincent would—almost—have preferred to continue the verbal battle.

Or, at the least, engage in conversation. Anything to take his mind off those moments when he had been alone in the hall with Catherine. He realized he never

spoke to Rangold—or to any of the soldiers—save to
issue an order, lodge a complaint, ask for information.
So many years of keeping his own counsel, guarding
every word, had influenced his behavior with these
men on their sea voyage. Now it was impossible for
him to clap a hand on Rangold's back and cheerfully
say, "So much for Italy's vaunted warmth and sunshine!"

He welcomed the deluge pelting him, for the chill
and wetness worked almost as well as dousing his head
in a horse trough would, to wake him from the spell
that had caught him in its evil grip. The image of
Catherine of Ardleswyck smoothing soft silk against
her belly seemed almost like a dream that had visited
him after drinking too much wine, and everyone knew
a good soaking was a sovereign remedy for drunken-
ness.

Rangold jerked his head up. "Good God—what
might that be?"

A small, clumsy vehicle, pulled by an old mule,
trundled into the courtyard. It appeared to be an ordinary farmer's cart, with a tall, narrow enclosure built
onto the back.

Rangold shivered and fashioned a quick sign of
the cross. "Looks like a traveling coffin, sort of," he
said with a hint of imagination Vincent had not suspected.

"It must be the vehicle Madam Serena bespoke,"
said Vincent. She'd called it a strangle little conveyance, and it seemed an apt description. Squat and
heavy, it rolled on two rough wheels that would sink
deep into every hole and rut in the road. Such a conveyance would limit their speed to barely above a

crawl. Serena had most likely chosen it deliberately to thwart him.

The carter pulled to a halt in front of them, and tugged his forelock but did not dismount from his bench.

"Turn it about," Vincent said, to save time for later, and to save Catherine a few steps in the rain.

The carter said something that Vincent could not understand.

"Exactly what I needed, a carter who cannot understand my commands," he muttered.

Somehow, with hand signals and Rangold's hand on the mule's bridle, they maneuvered the cart so that the mule's head faced the gate and the enclosure aimed toward the door from which Catherine must eventually emerge.

The men still tended the animals, but even if they had finished it would not matter, for Catherine had not yet joined them. Vincent walked a circle around the cart, studying it, and paused at the rear. Rangold stood there, too, staring unhappily at the vehicle.

"We won't make any speed at all with this," he said.

"No."

"I do believe I would rather ride through the rain than stay dry inside there."

"The lady does not ride," said Vincent.

The enclosure had been constructed with long, wide slabs of wood, probably oak, well-grooved and tight as any finely paneled wall. Vincent doubted that a single mote of light could penetrate those seams. The builder had, however, shaved away a rectangle measuring about an inch wide and a foot tall just above the leather door pull, almost like an arrow slit, so that whoever rode within would not be completely sealed in the dark.

He pulled open the door and could not prevent a shudder at what he found. Despite the door being flung wide, it was so dreary within that he could not tell if it was clean or foul, but since no odor came forth he hoped for the best. Two slabs of wood had been affixed like benches on either side of the small space. No cushions or padding to offer a bit of comfort or guard against splinters.

Something inside him stirred with protest at thinking of Catherine sealed up inside that wooden enclosure. He would put her there. He had found her inside the confines of the tiny prayer room, and meant to deliver her to a convent where she would spend most of her days and nights inside a small cell. He would put her there, too.

"I've never seen its like," said Rangold. "At least two can ride within, and the lady shall have the company of her maid to distract her."

"She rides alone," said Vincent.

He had not missed the camaraderie that had sprung up so quickly among the women. He intended to keep Catherine frightened, friendless.

"That seems cruel, Mr. Kenby."

Rangold's censure took Vincent by surprise. He'd known the man chafed at taking orders from him, but never before had Rangold so bluntly criticized him.

"I did not bring the woman to keep the lady company," said Vincent. He pushed the door closed so he did not have to look inside the dismal little enclosure.

Rangold stared stolidly at the closed door, saying nothing.

Vincent had explained his purpose in bringing women along at the beginning of the journey. He'd thought there might be reason to need an imposter or two. He'd already dispatched one to the ship in the hopes of tricking Hedgeford, so he'd already been proven right—but Rangold gave him no credit for it.

Cruel, Mr. Kenby.

Vincent let Rangold stew. Perhaps, given enough time, the soldier would remember that these females had jobs to do. The women resembled, somewhat, the way the Earl of Ardleswyck had thought his daughter might look. Nobody had seen Catherine for eight years or more. The earl thought she might have matched her lady mother's height and shape, since the girls who remained at home did appear to be younger versions of his wife. All the women in his household had yellow hair, and he'd remembered Catherine's had been golden when she was a child, so it ought to still be so.

The impostors were the right height, their hair the right color, but no man who had ever set his eyes upon Catherine of Ardleswyck could mistake either of those wenches for her.

Blood prevailed, for Catherine did favor her mother and sisters. And yet, she did not. Something about the way Catherine moved made the Countess of Ardleswyck seem a stiff, clumsy hag in comparison. Somehow the thick, soft waves of her hair caught the light and invited a man to touch it, so that her sisters' yellow tresses seemed no livelier than broomstraw in retrospect.

Rangold be damned for not remembering what he'd been told about the women! All this blathering about them did nothing but torment Vincent. Why did every thought have to turn to the temptress who was the cause of all his troubles? He had never before wasted one minute comparing one woman against another.

Vincent bent his head so that the rain drummed hard against his exposed neck, relishing the coolness, hoping it would wash his mind clean.

"Women like to chatter," Rangold said, stubbornly following the course he'd begun.

Vincent sighed. It seemed he would have to enumerate his many reasons for his harsh handling of Catherine.

"Aye, they like to chatter. All the more reason to keep them apart. You noticed, I trust, the way the maid Maisie conducted herself on board ship?"

Rangold grinned broadly.

"I thought so," said Vincent. "Those women proved themselves possessed of strong appetites for food, for drink, for keeping *company*"—he laid a little more emphasis on the word—"with men behind stacked casks and belowdecks."

"Truth to tell, Mr. Kenby, we did not think you noticed."

"I notice everything." Something about Rangold's tone of voice compelled Vincent to defend himself. "The lady is unwed," said Vincent, choosing his words carefully to avoid revealing too much to Rangold. The manner in which Catherine had been confined within the palazzo, for example, had been both a surprise and a relief. Serena had kept such close watch upon the girl that there was every chance Catherine's appetites had been whetted, but not yet slaked, and if he could keep her away from the men, they might never suspect what she really was.

"My lord's daughter is an innocent, Rangold, who might faint from shock or swoon with dismay if Maisie speaks too frankly of her adventures on board ship."

"I . . . I did not think of that, Mr. Kenby."

Good. He had Rangold on the defensive. "Maisie makes a good impostor. She can lend a hand to the lady, and help her with her needs while we travel. But she is not fit company."

Slowly, Rangold nodded his agreement, and in the way of one who'd had his opinion swayed, he offered more reasons for supporting his change of mind. "The men have become overly familiar with that Maisie wench. You are right, Mr. Kenby, 'twould not do to set her alongside the lady in this cart and over-hear the arrangements sure to be whispered betwixt that wench and any soldier who has a fancy for her. Also 'twould not do to put the two of them side by side for the men to compare. From what I've seen of the lady, her charms very much outshine the wench's."

"Aye, that they do," muttered Vincent.

Rangold dashed some of the wetness from his fore-head. "Well, I do thank God for your agreement, Mr. Kenby. No sooner had I said it than I worried you'd think ill of me for speaking so familiarly of the earl's daughter."

"She's a lovely lass," said Vincent. "Pretending she is otherwise will not change that."

"Aye, there be something about her to fire a man's loins."

Vincent gave him a sharp look. Rangold had spent even less time in Catherine's presence than he had, and somehow the seductress had spun her web over him, as well. What might happen when she was living and traveling among them all, if she graced them with her smiles, with flirtatious words from those red, full lips—any doubt he had about isolating her dissipated.

"She is the earl's daughter," he said. "Any man who thinks to touch her, or approach her in any way, does so at his peril."

"So you shall be the only one to deal with her, then, Mr. Kenby?"

"It is perhaps best so."

"Aye, you are the next best thing to a priest," said Rangold.

Vincent gave a short laugh. He could, in England, produce any number of women who would swear with assurance that he'd abandoned all thoughts of celibacy.

"Well, you never availed yourself of Maisie's pleasures," Rangold said, seeming to smart over Vincent's amusement. "Women ain't the only ones who chatter, you know. More than a couple of the fellows claimed you had inclinations in another direction, if you get my meaning."

"If the men have so much spare time to discuss my personal tastes, then perhaps they have need of more tasks set to them," Vincent said mildly.

Rangold scowled and turned away, putting distance between them as clearly as if he'd stalked across the courtyard. He stared at the cart as if regretting his previous capitulation on its use. Belatedly Vincent realized he'd missed an opportunity to break down some of the man's defenses. He thought he'd made some progress in that regard. Apparently not.

He'd expected the soldiers' aloofness during the sea voyage, for he seldom found it possible to mix easily with men who had been born into circumstances similar to his own. Some of those men could rightly consider themselves successful, but few had attained the social leap that he'd managed, which for some reason made them dissatisfied with the way things had gone for them. From them, he expected either resentment or envy. Those who had been born above him in status likewise held no affection for one who had clawed his way to a level they believed belonged to them by divine right.

He'd grown accustomed to feeling like an outcast in the midst of a crowd. He didn't allow himself to think much about it, but the sense was always there, like an invisible cloak of chain mail. He'd been lonely during the sea voyage, and the balance of this journey promised no end to his solitary state.

He hadn't realized, until Rangold turned away, that he'd held out some slight hope that things would be different. That here, in this land so far from their own, where no man among them was truly master over another, they might set aside their mistrust and wariness, and for a time he might be . . . less lonely.

He saw it all so clearly now—the men taking up Rangold's declaration of *Cruel, Mr. Kenby.* Catherine, the only one who'd within recent memory offered him a genuine smile, locked in that upright coffin of a cart, rightfully despising him for doing this to her.

Catherine—the only one who had let him forget, for a moment, the ever-present sense of isolation that pressed down on him.

A chill that had nothing to do with the rain pouring down ran through him. Serena's warning about falling prey to Catherine's charms suddenly struck him as a real possibility rather than a foolish woman's maun-

dering. He stood there in the rain, pining for a warm
smile, a friendly touch, like any green boy spending
the first day at work away from his mother.

He must take care to mistrust every one of Catherine's smiles, must be sure to look beneath the surface
of every word she said. She had been specially prepared to tempt and tantalize a man, and he must not
allow himself to fall prey to her wiles.

She came into the courtyard at that very moment.

Flanked by Maisie and Serena, she stepped away
from the palazzo but remained sheltered under the
portico. Vincent noticed she carried two bundles with
her rather than the one he had ordered, and despite
all his firm resolutions of the past moments, he found
himself unable to order her to abandon half her possessions. Despite his silent reminders to hold himself
immune from her, his mouth ran dry, his skin felt
hot, to think of her yet again going through her garments there in the yard in front of the men, smoothing
the fine cloth against her skin for all to see.

He would have to indulge her in this small rebellion.
He would hold her accountable for it later.

He crossed the yard, intent upon escorting her directly into the wagon so they could be on their way.

She did not seem to notice his approach. The miserable little wagon held her full attention.

"I will carry these for you," he said, pulling the bundles from her hands. She let loose of them with no
resistance. He nodded at the two servants hovering behind her. They held a roll of oiled cloth between them,
its corners fastened to sticks. They hoisted the sticks
high and took places on either side of her to form a
canopy over her head to shield her from the rain.

Vincent had intended to catch her by the arm and

pull her toward the cart, but saw that to do so he would have to walk bent over to fit under the canopy alongside her. He had not realized there was such a difference in their heights.

Serena, watching unhappily, was of a size to walk along with her. Vincent gave her a little push to urge her beneath the canopy. "See to it that she makes straight for the wagon," he said.

Vincent went first, slogging through the puddles toward the cart. He'd closed its door firmly just minutes earlier, and he had to give the leather pull a hard tug to open it again. The confined space seemed to have grown darker and closer during the intervening time. There were advantages to riding within, he told himself. It was dry. And . . . it was dry. He could think of nothing more.

He congratulated himself for decreeing she should ride alone. It was true that two could sit facing each other, provided one angled toward the right and one toward the left. Knees would knock frequently, though, and any passenger chancing to stretch out or shift for a more comfortable position would no doubt collide with the other passenger.

His whole being rebelled at the notion of being shut up inside such a place.

The small entourage arrived at the cart. He was grateful that the canopy shielded her from his sight, for he did not want to see the expression on her face when she looked inside the cart for the first time. He stood aside to give her a moment's privacy.

"No—'tis like closing you inside a grave!" Serena broke into sobs.

"How am I to get inside?" Catherine asked after a long moment.

It was a reasonable question, spoken in a calm manner. If the interior of the cart dismayed her as much as it did everyone else, the canopy hid her reaction from him, and her voice gave no sign.

She possessed courage. Her father would be proud of her.

The cart offered nothing in the way of steps or mounting block. He quickly assessed the options. He could keep her standing there, staring into that dark hole while he summoned the necessary items to let her climb inside herself, or he could lift her. Each minute that passed would no doubt increase her aversion to entering the miserable place. Lifting her meant touching her, meant gripping that small supple waist between his hands . . .

"Perhaps I might ride, after all," she said.

Riding meant providing her with one of the animals, meant continually looking to see that she didn't fall off, to note the way her legs gripped the beast and remember that he should have known virgins of gentle birth never rode astride . . .

"I shall hoist you in," he said.

He shot his hands under the canopy, to where he judged her waist would be. He misjudged her height; his hands settled firmly against rounded, supple fullness that sent a jolt of delight spearing straight into his nether reaches. She made a sound, half moan, half gasp of pleasure. The sound jerked his thumbs as if they'd been attached to strings, like puppets, and they pressed and caressed taut little nubbins of flesh poking through her gown.

He forgot to breathe, and a delight unlike anything he'd ever known shot through him.

Good Lord, he was fondling the breasts of the earl's daughter, and she did not say him nay!

He jerked away as though he'd been scalded.

Serena left off with her sobbing and said something in her tongue. The servants made no response, but Vincent could see that they strove to contain their mirth. Fortunately, the canopy they held had shielded his accidental groping from the rest of the yard, or else they all might be shaking with laughter over what he'd done. *Look at our monkish Mr. Kenby.* They would laugh. *Does he know what to do with what's in his hands?*

With a wordless curse, he knocked away the canopy. The rain found her at once, but so did he. He caught her properly around the waist and hoisted her up and into the cave-like darkness so quickly he scarcely had time to register how light, how slim, she felt in his hands.

He set her down with a thump. The air stirred through her hair and her garments to release a waft of lavender scent that surrounded him despite the rain, hinting at sunshine and warmth.

A man could stand there all day, in the wind and the rain, if he had a woman like her to look upon, to sweeten every breath he took.

Temptress. She had probably chosen that gown, that scent, deliberately to provoke him.

"Give me your word that you shall not try to escape. Otherwise, I warn you—if needs must I shall order a man to fasten a latch on the outside of this door."

Her look of puzzlement made it clear she'd not given one thought to escaping. He had only himself to blame, now, if she tried.

"How am I to escape, Mr. Kenby? Will you not notice if I crawl over you?"

She assumed he meant to ride inside with her. A natural assumption, he supposed, considering the foul weather, considering his role as her jailer. She thought he would ride in there, in the dark with her, with the feel of her breasts still tingling upon his hands, with every breath he took scented with lavender and pampered woman. The scent would swirl and eddy all about, heightened because the small space would be warmed by her. *Crawl over you to escape* . . . her silken hair, slipping down over her shoulders to brush against his face, her skirts lifted so as not to tangle her legs, sliding one across his middle . . .

He swung the door closed in her face.

Six

Catherine's eyes struggled to adjust to the sudden dark.

She could tell, before she could see, that the top of her head almost brushed the roof of the enclosure—she could feel the little prickle in her scalp where the hair springing from her crown was slightly flattened. Her breathing bounced from the walls, telling her the sides lay so close that she need not spread her arms wide to touch either side.

But so far she did not feel trapped or frantic to escape . . . So far she felt oddly grateful for this quiet, dark place where she might bide quietly for a bit to regain her peace of mind.

She burned.

She burned with a fire that shook her with its ferocity, a fire that had its kindling point at her breasts, with lingering heat smoldering at her waist, where she could still feel the strength of Vincent's hands gripping her.

She burned.

Letting loose a shaky breath, she rested her forehead against the rough wood door. He had touched that door, to close her within. She pressed her palm flat against the wood, as if touching it would let her thrill to his strength again.

She could see again within a moment, even though the scant light seeping through a small vertical slit at the door admitted less brightness than did her viewing hole in the prayer room. Fine spray from the rain misted through the space, enough to make her wish, then, that she might step out of the wagon and let the deluge cool her of this strange, unseemly heat.

He would fasten a lock to the door if she did so. He had promised he would do it. With the heat coursing through her, she could not summon outrage or hatred over his declaration.

"Sweeting."

Catherine angled her head so she could see Serena peering at her through the slit. The inner fire ebbed a bit, smoldered.

Catherine could tell the older woman stood on tiptoe, while rain cascaded down her face and washed away the careful artifices she always applied to look her best each day. With her view of her so utterly focused, Catherine could see the fine age lines surrounding Serena's eyes, could see the loosening texture of skin no longer young. While Catherine had fretted over losing weeks of her youth, Serena had lost years.

Serena had already lived an endless span of years without the comfort of the man she loved. She might live many years yet, alone. But Serena had known love, if only for a brief while.

"Do not succumb to despair," Serena pleaded, seeming to have read Catherine's thoughts. "I shall write to your father at once, imploring him to change his mind, and I will not give up until he calls you home."

"I know you will," Catherine whispered. She slid

her hand through the slit, and Serena's fingertips met her own. "I feel . . ." she began, the way she had initiated so many whispered confidences, but found herself unable to continue. She had never kept secrets from Serena; if anything, she had been shockingly, appallingly forthright in her confessions and questions.

Not now, though. She could not bring herself to talk about the way her body had reacted to Vincent Kenby's touch, the way it still clamored. It seemed right, somehow, that she should be isolated, given this place in the dark to silently puzzle over the sensations that had leaped to life within her.

"Remember all I have taught you," Serena said.

"I believe I know next to nothing," Catherine said. A calm, firm new knowledge whispered silently that everything Serena had told her only hinted at the reality of what could be.

Serena had taught her many things about herself, and many of those lessons explained the ways of men and women together. She had promised Catherine that she would find delight and fulfillment from a man's touch. But nothing Serena had taught her even hinted at the turmoil, the giddy sensations Catherine was just now managing to place under control.

"Remember most of all how I warned you against developing soft feelings for this man."

"Aye," Catherine whispered.

If she burned from the brief, accidental touch of a man who was her enemy, what awaited her at the hands of the man she loved?

Michael. She loved Michael. She would melt from the flames his touch roused. This sensation she felt was but a prelude to what she would know with Michael, a curl of smoke rather than a full-blown flame.

But she had to struggle to fix Michael's name in her heart, Michael's name in her mind. Her treacherous body yearned toward the one who stood right outside this miserable cart. She had another reason to be glad of her confinement, since it hid her flush of embarrassment from Serena's wise eyes.

With that flush, reason flowed through her once more. How could she have allowed her body's sensations to let her forget, for one single minute, what Vincent Kenby meant to do to her?

If he ever touched her again, if that inner flame ever again leaped to life because of him, she would pretend it was hellfire licking at her vitals.

"I will remember," she said.

With a shout and a jolt, the cart began to move. She shot out her arms to brace herself in position; otherwise she might have tumbled to the floor. In a way, she was glad Vincent Kenby showed so little regard for her that he'd failed to warn her of their imminent departure.

He had not even allowed her a moment to say a proper good-bye to Serena.

This lack of consideration was one more cruelty she could add to her list of things to hate about him, and she would recite them all if that fire started burning again.

A small, weak animal would fight nigh unto death when attacked by a creature larger, more powerful. If the little one survived, it took to the ground while it healed. There, in the shelter of its dark den, it would curl up, nose tucked to tail, while nature worked its miracles.

Catherine's body showed no bruises, her limbs remained sound and whole. She knew, though, that Vincent's attack had caught her by surprise, and though she'd lashed out, she had lost the battle. She'd been wounded at a level that felt mortal. She could not bear to think about the reason she was riding in the cart. She did not want to acknowledge the way her body had welcomed Vincent Kenby's touch, wanted nothing more than to erase that from her mind. She longed for the blankness, the emptiness of unconsciousness.

While the uncomfortable wagon lurched through the rain and the mud, she wrapped her arms around her knees as if to protect her vitals, and lost herself in nothingness.

From time to time an exceptionally rough bump would jolt her out of her daze, and she would shift about on the uncomfortable slab seat, chastise herself for wasting away the time doing nothing when she had so much to ponder. She blinked, she yawned, she stretched, she berated herself for not making plans.

She ought to at the very least pray for deliverance for what was certain to happen. The rain beating against the wagon, the dark dim enclosure, the utter solitude in which she was confined offered the perfect opportunity for contemplation. But no manner of physical movement or silent scolding shook away her lethargy, and in no time she would drift into that nameless, timeless place again.

Queen Eleanor would be ashamed of her, her conscience mocked her.

What whim of fate had led her to follow so closely the life of Eleanor of Aquitaine? Her lifelong fascination now seemed to have risen from a premonition that certain aspects of her life would mimic those of this woman she most admired in the world. Impossible. What girl could ever, in her most imaginative moments, expect to be exiled from home, or bundled into a prison on wheels bound for a prison behind walls. And yet . . . Eleanor had married the King of France when she loved another. She had once been forced to travel against her will, and had later been cruelly incarcerated at the cost of some of the best years of her life.

Many years earlier, when the Christians of Europe had last mustered a Crusade, Queen Eleanor had promised the strength of her warriors from her lands of Aquitaine. The queen had been married at the time to King Louis of France, who had heeded too closely the advice of an avaricious priest and had grown to mistrust his beautiful bride. The king had confined his queen to a litter and forced her to travel concealed and isolated all the way from France to the Holy Land.

When the Crusade met with failure, it had been due in part to Louis's failure to heed the queen's advice. Eleanor had successfully petitioned for divorce after the misadventure. She must have been planning and thinking the whole time she'd been held against her will, not lying about like a lump of suet the way Catherine was doing.

Catherine knew that the old queen was at this very moment traveling through Italy. Her son Richard, now King of England, had made the isle of Sicily his headquarters for the new Crusade, and Eleanor traveled overland to join him. She accompanied the Princess Berengaria of Spain, who would wed Richard, and the betrothal had been arranged by Eleanor herself.

Eleanor remained as vital and influential at seventy

as she'd been in her youth. Aside from arranging the betrothal, which was a task ordinarily entrusted to men, she would travel with the army on this Crusade. Catherine's own father, younger than Eleanor, had fought during the previous Crusade, but stayed at home for this one. Eleanor's courage dwarfed his.

What if by some chance the queen's party passed hers? Catherine had never dared dream she might one day meet this woman who had inspired legends. What did one say to a legend? How she would treasure the chance to hold Eleanor's hand in her own, to exchange a warm kiss of friendship with someone who inspired her so much! How cruel to think they might pass on the road, with Catherine locked up like an animal, unable to convey her admiration, unable to even see the woman whose courage outweighed that of most men.

Perhaps, considering her state of dullness, it was best she would not see the passage of the old queen. Eleanor could feel nothing but contempt for a woman who let circumstances rob her of all spirit.

Catherine had not cried since curling up inside this cart. She did now, though, to think that she had somehow let down Queen Eleanor.

She must have cried herself to sleep, for without her ever noticing that the cart had stopped, that the door had been flung open, she lifted her head from the pillow of her arms to find Maisie, her face creased with worry, calling her name and shaking her hard about the shoulders.

"Come, lady. He has given leave for you to step out for a moment."

"I am fine."

"No, lady—we have traveled the day long. You must

needs move your limbs and attend other matters. Come along, now." Ignoring Catherine's protests, Maisie forced her to her feet and out of the wagon.

The rain had slowed to a mistlike drizzle, which nonetheless soaked Catherine through while they left the road and found a place deep in the dripping foliage to tend to their personal needs.

Maisie kept up a steady chatter. "Men! They can drink ale the night long without ever once visiting the necessary. For them 'tis not even a necessary, eh—they can whiz where they please without worrying about hems and skirts."

"I've had no ale," Catherine muttered. Such lethargy gripped her that it seemed more of an interruption than a relief to leave the wagon.

"No food, either, for more than a day. For all his masterful ways, Mr. Kenby makes a poor guardian. Did I not protest to him, he'd leave you shut up in that cart until we reached France, and then be angry with you for dying of thirst and starvation."

France. Another instance of her life following a parallel route to Eleanor's.

She did not want to think about it. She did not want to think about anything.

Maisie bullied her into a thicket. It seemed easier to do what Maisie told her to do rather than argue. Her body did what needed to be done without any thought from her.

While Maisie ushered her back to wagon, she noted with dull disinterest that the soldiers who accompanied them had made a small camp some distance up the road. One man stood midway between the camp and the wagon, in the middle of the road, watching, with his arms crossed.

Vincent Kenby, standing guard to see she did not escape.

If she were not so mired in apathy, Catherine would have laughed. No woman, even one whose wits and limbs were not deadened by malaise, could hope to outrun such a superb physical specimen. He stood so tall, broad of shoulders, his long legs encased in hose so soaked that she could see faint flesh tones and corded muscle where portions lay plastered against his skin.

She wondered if her own gown clung to her in such a manner, if her skin showed pale and pink through the water-darkened blue.

Any kitchen wench who chanced to use a wet cloth to protect her hand when lifting hot pots knew that wetness rendered cloth useless for protection. If Vincent attempted to lift her into the cart now, her rain-soaked gown would provide no barrier at all from the warmth of his hands.

Her body turned traitor, shedding the peaceful numbness to remind her how she had burned from Vincent Kenby's touch the first time. If he lifted her now, if his hard, muscular legs chanced to brush against her as he lifted . . .

"Here we go, my lady. Up with you." Maisie, unaware that she had interrupted the waking dream that had roused Catherine from oblivion, caught Catherine by the elbow and gave her a little push at her bottom. "There."

Catherine looked back at her. She saw the concern writ plain upon the maid's face. Perhaps it had been there all this while, and Catherine was too mired in self-pity to notice. She wavered, not knowing what she preferred—a return to that oblivion, or to set it aside—

but setting it aside only made her think improper thoughts about the man who was responsible for all her problems.

Oblivion, she decided, and stepped back into the cart.

"I'll fetch water and food."

"I don't want anything."

"You must sustain yourself, my lady."

"I hear good nuns develop abstemious habits regarding food and drink." She slumped back onto the bench. "Close the door. The light hurts my eyes."

"Lady, it is near dark."

"Close the door."

With one final frown, Maisie stepped back and slowly swung the door closed, sealing Catherine once more inside her snug little den. But something had changed. She did not find it so easy to sink back into the blessed oblivion. Her gown and hair lay wet and chill against her skin.

Though it was June, the cold brought by the storm threatened to freeze her to death. That would put an end to her suffering! She resolved to sit quietly until the cold stole the warmth from her blood. But no. Despite her craving for emptiness and oblivion, her mind tormented her with the knowledge that Vincent had stuffed her cloak into one of her sacks, and the thought would not go away. Stirring herself, finding the cloak, wrapping it around her shoulders, exhausted and warmed and infuriated.

With a rap at the door, Maisie announced her return. "I brought water and stew, lady."

Perhaps she could starve to death.

"Go away."

"But—"

"Go away."

She huddled into a corner, grateful for the quiet and the warmth of the cloak. She tried to recapture the dreamlike state that had let the hours pass. Instead, more often than not she found she'd opened her eyes to stare at nothing while her mind conjured again and again the unwelcome memory of Vincent Kenby standing in the road, watching her.

Something about the way he'd stood, the way he'd watched her, had unsettled her mind, so that oblivion eluded her yet again. She turned one way and then the other on the comfortless slab, the way one might twist and weave in an attempt to evade a pursuer. Though she wrestled with it through the long night, she never conquered it.

When birdsong and faint sunlight streamed through the slit in the door to herald dawn's arrival, she sat bolt upright. It was as though the light and sound had illuminated for her the reason why Vincent's watchfulness haunted her so.

He had expected her to try to escape.

Through her apathy first seeped shame, and then amazement, that she'd spent unknown hours huddled there like a wounded sparrow who did not even try to flutter away, so certain was it that it could not escape a hungry cat.

Vincent Kenby had expected more of her. He'd expected her to be strong.

How strange. She found herself sitting straighter. She rubbed the sleepiness from her eyes.

Nobody had ever credited her with possessing strength. For good reason—she'd never shown a modicum of it. She'd been a loving, dutiful daughter. A willing, apt pupil. She'd dreamed of the day when she would become an obedient wife to a man she'd never met. Nobody had any reason to expect her to do anything other than meekly follow her father's commands now, to let herself be hauled overland through the mountains and byways of Italy to meet a fate few women would ever willingly choose.

And what had she done? She'd made a few token protestations, and then she'd let herself be propelled into this cart where she'd promptly collapsed into a motionless heap of nothing, so complaisant that she'd had to be coaxed outside to relieve her most basic needs.

But from the first moment he'd seen her, Vincent Kenby had treated her with a wariness a soldier might show an enemy. He struck her as a man who could not be easily fooled, a man who understood human frailties and human strengths.

And he fancied she was strong.

How odd. Odd that he would credit her with a quality nobody—including herself—had ever suspected she might possess. Even now, wondering about her own abilities, she did not know if she was strong or weak.

Lolling about in this cart, as befuddled as someone who'd tipped an entire skin of wine into her gullet, did not seem particularly brave. Nor did her courage appear any bolder in looking back upon how she'd spent all the days of her life, doing exactly as she'd been told.

But . . . always, within her, had been a voice whispering, *This is just the beginning. Someday, all shall be as I wish it to be.*

A weak person would not think such rebellious thoughts. When a weak person bowed her head, it meant that she accepted her fate. Either way, the person stood outwardly bowed, but within there was a subtle difference between weak and strong—and somehow Vincent Kenby had noticed that in her.

It didn't seem like much. But it was enough to rouse Vincent Kenby's instincts. His noticing was like the sun striking down on a radish seed. If that seed had been sown but denied the light of the sun because it lay hidden beneath a rock or a mat of wet leaves, then that seed would forever lay dormant, a dried husk of nothing. But if someone chanced to remove the obstacle, allowing the sun to shine full on it, the seed would sprout.

She laughed, a strangled-sounding little giggle that rang off the close walls. She clapped her hand over her mouth, though it seemed unlikely the small sound could escape the rough enclosure.

The sound of laughter might not escape, but *she* could. Vincent expected it of her, after all. And if she tried, even if she failed, she could hold her head high if she chanced to meet Queen Eleanor.

The queen had not tried to escape her prison, because she had sons and a daughter who would incur her husband's wrath for any attempt she might make. Catherine had no one to worry about except herself.

The pang of loneliness that accompanied that realization threatened to send her swooning. Her mother, her father, had made it clear they did not want her. Her sisters had probably forgotten all about her. Serena could do nothing, and was lost to her. Catherine was alone in this world, a loneliness so profound that nobody could possibly understand.

Except, perhaps, a man who always found himself not belonging in one place or the other.

She set all thoughts of Vincent Kenby aside, remembering how Serena had warned her to be wary of developing feelings for him. Here she sat, with her own problems to mull over, and unbidden came thoughts of him. Not anymore.

She would end up no richer in loved ones than him if she let herself be locked up in the convent.

She was suddenly ravenously hungry, thirsty as a smith after a hot day working over the forge.

She pushed through the door to find Maisie waiting outside.

"My lady! I had just come to fetch you in hopes of convincing you to break your fast."

Her self-imposed fast took on new meaning. That, too, hinted at the strength within her. A weak-willed female would eat when instructed, would actually make a great show of it in an effort to please.

"You tried to urge food upon me earlier," Catherine said with a grateful smile.

"Now it is a day and more since you ate," said Maisie.

"Close on to two," Catherine mused. No good Catholic ate before Mass, even when one did not anticipate taking communion, and so her last solid meal had been the night before Vincent's arrival. Small wonder she'd been so lethargic! "I would enjoy a bite, now that my temper has settled."

"I'll fetch a portion for you at once," said the maid. "I am happy to see you doing better, my lady."

"I am better," agreed Catherine. "Better than I ever thought."

Seven

Vincent watched the maid carry a water skin and bowl of stew back to the wagon, and then a few moments later return with the bowl empty.

"Sister Catherine ate it," Maisie said, waving the bowl to prove it held nothing.

He scowled at her, and she in turn glowered at him quite fiercely, as if he'd tried somehow to stop her from taking food to Catherine.

She stomped to the cook fire, casting him vicious glances over her shoulder. She handed over the empty bowl to one of the men who helped the cook, glared at Vincent, then paused to joke with those who performed the tidying up chores around the camp before glaring at Vincent again.

He thought she might resume the inappropriate frisking that roused his men's lust, but instead she marched back to him with her eyes narrowed.

"I've known many a man in my day," she said, "but you are the cruelest I've come across."

The second person in so many days to call him cruel. Vincent folded his arms across his chest.

"Sister Catherine—" she began.

"Do not call her that."

She smirked.

"Sis—my lady tries to put a bright face on matters, but I see how she droops. Locking her up as if she is a common criminal!"

"What do you mean, she droops?"

"Like this." To his amusement, she bent and picked a buttercup and waved it beneath his nose. "Lest I put this in a bowl of water straightaway, the petals will curl and darken, the leaves fall off. That is what you have done to my lady."

Before his eyes, the flower's stem lost its strength and bent beneath the weight of its head, wilting into a half-dead imitation of itself. He couldn't bear to look at it for long.

This was exactly what he had intended to happen to Catherine—to render her weak and spiritless, less trouble to handle.

"Catherine of Ardleswyck is not a wildflower," he said somewhat stiffly, for the maid had, in her rough way, perfectly illustrated how damaging something beautiful cast a pall over everything that surrounded it.

"Sister Catherine—"

"I told you, do not call her that."

"My lady sent me away the moment she finished her meal. Said she craved a bit of privacy. Humpf! I don't mind telling you, I fear for what she might do to herself when she's alone, and you'll have only yourself to blame."

There was no mistaking Maisie's sincerity despite her annoying habit of referring to Catherine as if she were already a nun; she truly feared for Catherine's personal safety. Vincent ought to be congratulating himself for succeeding in so thoroughly demoralizing Catherine, and yet his conscience stirred, chiding him for destroying something that should be treasured rather than ruined.

His lawyer's mind, trained to probe every word and action for hidden meaning, reminded him that Catherine was not to be trusted.

"I believe the lady possesses more resilience than you credit her with," he said. "I will see for myself."

The rain, blessedly, had ceased. Back in England one rainy day usually led right into another just as gloomy, but here in this strange land the day dawned with a glorious clean-washed beauty that made the sky seem impossibly blue, the air impossibly sweet. Birds trilled, and leaves rustled in a light breeze.

This was the sort of day to inspire hopefulness rather than despair. If Catherine had meant to do herself harm, it would more likely have occurred in the rain or the night, rather than now. She had nothing but more isolation to look forward to, so asking for privacy when she had company at hand hinted at deviousness.

He listened carefully for anything that might betray someone sneaking through the brush. Nothing. Surprisingly, he found himself disappointed.

Perhaps she'd really wanted nothing more than a little privacy to sniffle into her handkerchief. Thus far Catherine of Ardleswyck had proven to be far less troublesome than the wench and soldiers he'd brought along to guard against her hysterics. Her father had called her a good, compliant girl, but Vincent, knowing her bloodlines, had expected more spirit.

He found her outside the cart. She basked in the morning sun. She leaned back against the wagon bed, her head tilted back, her eyes closed, a half smile curving those lush, red lips. Her hair had escaped its neat tie. It still hung down her back, but here and there strands had curled toward her face, lifting gently in the breeze, glinting with golden highlights.

No weeping, no ranting, no attempt to run away. If she continued behaving so meekly, so agreeably, this task would be no more onerous than delivering a sack of flour to the nunnery at Saint Justinius. Michael of Hedgeford might owe him a debt of gratitude for locking away a woman who would, as wife, be no more interesting or resourceful than a head of cabbage.

He saw no evidence of the decline Maisie had claimed.

His temper, unaccountably quick to rise these days, leaped for no good reason.

"We leave in a few moments," he said with a sharpness to his voice that caused her to start.

"I will have need of Maisie for those moments." Just as she spoke, the wench's laughter came to them, joined with bawdy male shouts.

"I will send her to you," Vincent said.

"No—let her enjoy herself. I can manage."

She moved toward a gap in the tangled vines and brush at the edge of the road. She lifted a low-hanging branch and glanced over her shoulder—not at him—but toward the camp where Maisie stood surrounded by a cluster of men who had better things to do than flirt with a woman. A wistful smile played about her lips. *Let her enjoy herself,* Catherine had said, as if she knew exactly what went through a woman's mind when men sniffed about her skirts.

She did know, Vincent reminded himself.

She entered the woods and let the branch drop down behind her. He could see the blue of her gown through the leaves as she slowly picked her way through the growth. She had not bade him to look away, as any woman of modesty would do.

He looked away.

He could hear her progress through the brush, the crackling, the snapping, and then nothing. Not two minutes earlier he had been congratulating himself over a job easier than expected, but all of a sudden the memory of that long look toward the soldiers and Maisie reminded him that there was an indefinable something about Catherine that told him she was no head of cabbage content to roll this way and that according to her father's whim. She might, at this very moment, be bolting for freedom.

The day seemed to brighten a bit, again.

He would have to explore these strange emotional surges of his, anger waxing for no reason, waning for no reason, and why he had suddenly found himself interested in whether or not a woman lacked spirit. He would think these matters through later, when he was back where he belonged. For now, he had a bit of stalking to do.

Taking care to make as little noise as possible, he found another path into the woods and began creeping along a circuitous route that would bring him slightly beyond where he'd last seen her. If she returned at once to the cart, she'd never know he'd suspected her, and there would be no harm done in himself finding a bit of privacy amid the trees. But if she thought to escape him by creeping through the brush . . .

And that's exactly what he found her doing. She was moving with as much stealth as he, stepping lightly over fallen limbs, ducking low to avoid overhead branches, watching her feet to avoid stepping on a sharp-cracking twig. So intent was she that she almost walked straight into his chest before she noticed him.

"Oh!" She came to a stop. He strained to hear disappointment in her voice, or find disappointment slumping the line of her carriage, but could detect nothing. She gave him a wide smile made all the more dazzling by the lushness of her lips. Her features lit with delight and something more—a strange sort of satisfaction that took him aback. "You came looking for me!"

"I feared you might have lost your way," he lied.

"Perhaps."

And perhaps the lady was insane, Vincent found himself thinking as he led her back to the wagon. She followed obligingly, making no comments, light on her feet, graceful, managing to look as if he'd done her a great favor by suspecting she would try to escape. Could it be that she was dim-witted and had truly lost her way and was glad to be found?

He curbed his desire to shout a denial.

He berated himself for a fool as he bit the inside of his cheek. The wench worked sorcery on his mind. From this point on, he would atone for any uncharacteristic flight of fancy by spending an hour on his knees, praying the rosary. If the men caught him at it, they'd credit his penance to monkishness. Little would they suspect the real reason behind his praying.

"I'll help you into the cart," he said when they regained the wagon. At once he assigned himself an hour at prayer, for he was instantly tormented by the memory of lifting her into it the first time, and how good she'd felt in his hands.

"The day is fine and I relish the sun," she said. "I

shall just walk alongside for a bit. I am familiar with this road, and enjoy the sights."

"How do you know this road?"

"Serena hails from these mountains. Her sister's husband rules a remote village. We would visit, sometimes." She waved a hand in the direction of the peaks that marched north toward France. "I always loved the wild places, more than Genoa."

On its surface, her desire to walk sounded logical enough. The cart lumbered so slowly that a half-lame grandmother would be able to keep pace. The men would no longer have to walk, since the horses had recovered after the night resting in camp. They would have to set their pace to match the cart's, so they wouldn't move any faster. Rangold had given him sound advice about waiting to set off; he should have paid closer heed.

Just as he ought to pay heed to the familiarity she claimed with the lay of the land. She might believe she knew enough to enable her to escape—the little diversion earlier might have been her first attempt. He hoped that his ease in finding her had proven to her that she could not succeed. If she took it into her head to try again, despite knowing she couldn't win, they would waste valuable time hunting her down.

A burst of laughter from the almost cleared camp drew their attention. Catherine watched with interest as Maisie frolicked. She held her skirts up to mid-calf and with intricate dancing steps used her feet to send gusts of dirt over the campfire pit. The soldiers lounged about, watching the woman with hungry eyes.

They would watch Catherine that way, too, if she walked outside in the open for all of them to ogle. And judging by the interested way she marked the men's behavior, she would welcome the stares, the suggestions. Catherine was by far the more attractive of the two women, and in no time at all every soldier would be vying for her attention, and jealous of whomever she deigned to glance upon.

Vincent would have to resist the urge to pummel to a pulp any man who drew her regard. His lord had bade him to do so, which might explain why he knew he would eagerly use his fists on any man who caught her eye.

He'd never entertained any fantasies of violence toward his men while he'd been on board ship. Only here. Only now.

Smothering a sigh, he assigned himself another hour on his knees, even though his urge to beat any man who looked at her certainly stemmed from his role as her guardian, nothing more.

"You cannot walk," he said. "You will ride inside."

"Mr. Kenby, look about you—this Italian countryside is a feast for the eyes. This may be my last chance to enjoy it." The road they traveled cut through a wide valley. All around them rose towering mountains that threatened to pierce the sky with their snowcapped tips. The sky loomed a glorious shade of blue unlike any he'd ever seen in England's far more dreary clime.

"I was just a little girl when we left England," she mused, as if she'd read his thoughts. "I do not remember the scenery there being so breathtaking."

"I will not deny the beauty of this land. But it is not safe for you to walk," he said.

"I am quite sure of foot. Maisie can walk with me."

"That would be worse. Between the two of you—" He clapped his mouth shut.

"Between the two of us, what?"

"She might encourage you," he said.

"To do what?" Her beautiful eyes seemed almost a match for the sky as she cocked her head questioningly.

"To be as she is with those men."

"As if I—"

"I know the truth about you, Catherine of Ardleswyck."

"Oh, you do . . . ? Enlighten me."

She stood with her chin lifted, proud, defiant, and still with that strange sense of being pleased that he held her in suspicion. Very well. There seemed to be no point in avoiding the truth, no sense in pretending he did not know what she was, no sense in her pretending to be something she was not.

"I know you spent these past years with a notorious courtesan."

"Serena lives an exemplary life. One that many women would do well to emulate."

"Exactly why your father sent you to her, hmmm?"

She flushed at that. "I do admit I was somewhat puzzled by it at first . . ."

"And then, when the courtesan taught you all her wily seductress's tricks, you understood."

"I did not learn 'tricks' from Serena, Mr. Kenby."

"Did you not? Then tell me, mistress, why is it that when you walk, no man can keep his eyes from the sway of your hips?"

"Because looking hungrily at women is part of a man's nature," she answered.

"I assure you it is not. I myself am never drawn in by female posturing, and yet I find I cannot stop looking at you!"

The declaration seemed to reverberate around them.

Her eyes widened. Those lips that held such fascination for him parted, and with the tumbled softness of her hair wreathing her face she looked more luscious than any woman he'd taken to his bed.

What did she see when she looked at him? He'd never before felt the slightest curiosity about a woman's impressions of his looks.

"I am doing nothing to draw your untoward attention," she said, making mock of his inability to look away from her.

"Madam—every move you make is designed to call attention to your charms. You move with an uncommon grace. Your face and form are very pleasing to the eye."

Rather than taking offense, she smiled.

"I do believe you are paying me compliments, Mr. Kenby."

He'd done worse than pay compliments; he had spoken aloud to her things he'd not dared admit even to himself. He could not stop looking at her. He was conscious of her presence with every breath he took. Conscious, too, of his iron control slipping farther away the closer they stood.

It worried him to recognize that the shield he had forged so long ago and had served him so well could be breached so easily. He lashed out, knowing anger was his only defense, knowing that hurting her might make her withdraw those smiles and teasing words.

"No, 'tis not a compliment to admit that a woman trained to be a harlot acts like a harlot."

She paled. She swayed. She lifted a hand to her mouth—and that, too, was an elegant, graceful gesture that could drive a man to his knees to thank God for creating the female form. To thank Him for embell-

SCHOOLED FOR SEDUCTION 117

ishing woman with the ability to make a simple movement a thing of great beauty. Beautiful enough that he had to fight the urge to take that trembling hand and press it to his lips; had to fight the urge to gather her into his arms and hold her close and tell her he wished she did not have to go back into that hole of a cart, that she did not have to spend all her days in a nunnery.

Something terrible had happened to him. Something that defied explanation.

Sorcery might explain it, but Vincent did not believe in sorcery. His studies of the priesthood had convinced him that ordinary man was more than capable of causing the havoc often attributed to Satan and his minions. So since sorcery could not be responsible for Catherine's strange hold upon his attentions, it had to mean that the skills she had learned from Serena Monteverde were what held him in thrall. There could be no other explanation.

Even as he knew this, even as he recognized his susceptibility to her, something within bled to know he was the cause of her obvious pain. His conscience stabbed at him, too, for being so deliberately cruel. He could never apologize without weakening his authority over her, but he could grant her a small boon to make up for his lapse in manners.

"You need not travel alone. I will send Maisie to ride with you."

She gave a short laugh. "You speak as if you are doing me a favor."

"I am."

"No, 'tis I who do you the favor by removing Maisie from your sight. She seems happy moving about as she does. Perhaps it is the idea of women enjoying themselves that you dislike, Mr. Kenby."

He did not resent women enjoying themselves, but she had hit upon a partial truth. He would be glad to have Maisie out of sight, happy to remove that aura of lust and play, for his men had shown a distressing tendency to be drawn away from their true purpose in being here.

And with Maisie closed up in the cart, he might not be continually reminded of how men and women naturally gravitated toward one another, would not be lured into thinking what it might be like if a woman's gaze chanced to meet with his, and if the smile she gave him meant something more than a polite sign of acknowledgment.

"I shall send her to you," he said.

Eight

"No reason why we can't allow a little air and light into this hole," Maisie said. "Do you mind, my lady, if I use one of your sacks to fix this door open?"

Catherine shook her head. Maisie shook Catherine's things out of one of the woven bags.

"Be careful," she urged, as Maisie inched carefully along the slab. "This wagon lurches so, you might topple straight through the door if a jolt catches you off balance."

"Aye."

Maisie reached her destination without incident, and wedged her feet firmly into the corners as she stuffed the stout cloth into the joint between door and frame. She scooted back to a more secure position, and the two of them watched the door swing to and fro, as if they'd never seen a more interesting sight in their lives.

And in a way she had not, Catherine mused, for the light seemed exceptionally beautiful, the sun's warmth exceptionally welcome, in a way neither had until she'd been denied them.

The sack would not let the door go far enough either way to open or close fully. The leather hinges protested the added strain with a groaning creak that hinted at stretching, but there was no sound of door smacking against frame, for which Catherine was grateful. She had no doubt that if Vincent Kenby found out she was a tiny bit more comfortable, that she could at least breathe in some fresh air and see a little of the glorious Italian countryside, he would put an end to those small pleasures.

"There." Maisie heaved a sigh of satisfaction when it became certain they would not be closed in again. "Lest Mr. Kenby deigns to drop back and ride in our dust, he'll not know we've lightened things up a bit."

"He hates me," Catherine said.

Maisie chuckled. "I rather think he likes you a little too much, my lady. Do you know, I did as I promised and called you Sister Catherine in his hearing."

"Oh, did you?" Catherine pretended disinterest, but had to forcibly stop herself from demanding to know Vincent's response.

"He bade me not to address you in such a manner." Maisie giggled.

"He has no problem addressing me in a worse manner. He called me a . . ." Catherine could not bring herself to say the word that Serena had never allowed to be uttered.

"A whore?" Maisie guessed. "I'd not take that too deep to heart, mistress. Men like to think well of themselves, and so it suits them to call us vile temptresses and pretend we women have nothing better to do than plot their downfall. That way, they can pretend it's not their fault when they do exactly as they please, and things go wrong. Monkish men like Mr. Kenby be the worst for callin' women whores when they don't want to blame themselves for thinking lustful-like."

"Monkish?" Catherine laughed shortly. She contrasted the memory of Father Pascal's soft round belly against Vincent Kenby's taut, ridged middle; she remembered Vincent standing in the road, wide-shouldered, his thighs straining against the wet chausses. Father Pascal had often touched her head in benediction, or patted her shoulder with kindness, and never once roused the fire that leaped in her blood when Vincent Kenby touched her.

"He is, you know." Maisie's smug look told Catherine she knew more than she told. Quelling her curiosity, she recalled Serena's warnings and reminded herself that the less she knew about Vincent Kenby, the better.

It was better by far if she concentrated only on what she did know about him—that he meant to ruin her life.

But Maisie seemed inclined to blabber. "Came this close, I'm told, to taking his vows." She held her thumb and forefinger a scant inch apart. "He's still a monk in all that matters. I saw for myself. When we were all roistering on ship, he took himself off—no doubt to pray for our souls. The men call him Brother Vincent behind his back."

Catherine remembered him standing in the road, midway between her and the camp. She'd thought then that he'd often found himself in such a position, nei-ther belonging in one place or the other. "Then there is no hope for me. He probably thinks it's a fine thing to be forced into a convent, to take vows."

"I wouldn't be so sure, mistress. He did not take his, after all."

"I wonder why?" Catherine mused, and caught her-self before she allowed her curiosity to overcome her cautiousness. She shook her head. "It does not matter.

He holds a horrible opinion of me, and now I think I understand why. He thinks that just because Serena was . . . Oh, she was my father's mistress; there is no getting around that. He thinks she has, well, taught me the ways of a seductress."

"Did she?"

"Of course not!"

"That be a shame."

"Maisie!"

"What I meant is, did you know a certain way to seduce him, then you might convince him to run off with you rather than do what he means to do."

Run off with Vincent . . . An unwarranted excitement coursed through her, to imagine herself riding pillion with him, her legs wrapped around a straining horse, her arms wrapped around his strong stomach, her head pressed tight against his back.

She shook her head, dispelling the idea and the fantasy at the same time.

"My father loved Serena because she did not use her influence to gain favors."

"Well, excuse me for sayin' mistress, but 'tis uncommon strange for a man such as your father to send his daughter to one like her. He must have had in mind that you could learn *something* from her."

Catherine found she could not give a definitive answer. "I don't know. The whole thing happened rather suddenly, and was never clearly explained to me. But my mother certainly would have never agreed to send me for training as a . . . a . . ." She remembered the derision in Vincent's eyes and could not complete her thought.

"Your mother's letters must have asked you to tell

her what you were learning here in Italy. What did you tell her?"

"My mother cannot read or write. I wrote often to my father, long letters filled with details of my days. I hope my father read them to her. He always included her loving wishes in his letters to me. She was far more affectionate in her messages than she ever was in the flesh."

Catherine had taken great pride in learning to read and write under Serena's care—skills she knew her father would approve, since he'd so admired them in Serena. She had never before considered that such knowledge was a great advantage for someone who chose to keep motives secret from another who did not possess those skills.

"How convenient," Maisie said, eerily echoing Catherine's sudden suspicion.

"What do you mean by that?"

"Could it be that your mother didn't know what your father was up to when he sent you here?"

"He could not have kept such a thing a secret from her."

But now that she thought about it, there was something of a mystery about the situation. Catherine's mother had always been so remote, so wrapped up in her own interests that she'd never paid much attention to her children. She'd spent most of Catherine's last year at home secluded by choice within her own spacious apartments in the manor.

Catherine's father had decided she would be sent away for fostering, and he had broken the news to her himself, but had not revealed her destination, calling it only a surprise. If Catherine's mother had objected over his decision or his methods of handling it, Catherine never knew about it.

"She did come to say good-bye, but in thinking back, her sentiments do seem surprisingly . . . pious," Catherine remembered.

"Do you remember what she said?"

"Every word—she so seldom spoke to me. She urged me to hold true to my beliefs, to do nothing to disrupt my bond with God, and to pray often and well."

"Aha!" cried Maisie. "Those do not sound like the words one would say to a girl bound for a wonderful surprise."

"No, they do not. But I was too upset over being sent away to wonder about what she'd said, for she also mentioned she was pleased to have borne a daughter who would dedicate her life to good works and the care of the sick. Those are all the sorts of things that befall the lady wife of an important man such as my betrothed."

Maisie raised a brow and looked smug.

And now Catherine had to wonder—did her mother really know where she had gone?

How strange, to think of her mother's parting words in a new light. The Countess of Ardleswyck might have been sending her away to be fostered by her husband's mistress . . . or just as easily could have been dispatching her to the convent.

Just as was happening to her now. Perhaps her mother had believed her ensconced in a nunnery all those years ago.

"Why did he send me to Serena?" Catherine wondered aloud.

"Just what did you learn from her?" Maisie leaned

forward, obviously eager to hear all Catherine was willing to say.

"I don't know how to begin, there was so much." From the first, living with Serena had opened a new world to Catherine—a world where her curiosity was encouraged, where her interests were explored. "Little things, mostly. For example, we talked at mealtimes. At home, women and children held silent while men discoursed on the most mundane topics."

Maisie nodded. "Courtesans are known for their conversational skills."

"She taught me to write, and then to write less; what I mean is, never to use ten words if three would do. She showed me how to find humor in the most dire situations, and how to convey the humor."

"Aye, that's important. Men lose their patience quickly, and the lady who can make them laugh makes things easier for everyone."

Alarm began creeping through Catherine. "She helped me determine which foods put fat on my waist against those I could eat with impunity."

"Men claim to like a woman with a hearty appetite, but they dislike a fat wench."

Maisie's comments disturbed Catherine. Reading, writing, laughing, talking, taking pride in one's appearance—such small accomplishments, but did they as a whole make her something a woman of her kind was not meant to be? If so, she was truly doomed, for those qualities were such a part of her, she could see no way of turning back. Nor would she want to, considering the contrast between Serena and her mother.

Oh, she respected her mother—all daughters must—but respect was all that she felt for the cold, haughty woman, so stiff with pride, so wrapped in her own concerns that she'd had none to spare for anyone else. Catherine had learned how to love from Serena, whose warmth and gaiety, whose generosity and caring, had provided an example of another way of approaching life.

"If I had stayed at home, and gone straight to Michael from there, I should have been just like her," Catherine whispered.

And she knew, in that moment, that her mother would never have taught her the things Serena told her every woman must know if she wanted to keep her husband's love.

"What about the good bits?" Maisie asked, as if she'd sensed Catherine had more to reveal.

"Good bits?"

"You know." Maisie winked, and then made a rude gesture by shoving the forefinger of one hand into the curled fist of the other. "Did she teach you how to touch a man?"

Catherine's face warmed.

"She did!" Maisie crowed. "Do tell, my lady!"

Catherine's mother would have quelled Maisie's overly familiar interest with one scornful glance, and then spent the balance of the journey in tense silence. Catherine longed, suddenly, for Serena, for the chance to tell her how Vincent Kenby's touch turned her knees weak, to ask for reassurance that nothing was wrong with her. Lacking Serena's presence, Maisie proved a welcome, and friendly, confidante.

"She taught me how to touch myself, so that I might be able to tell my husband where it pleased me to be touched. She said he would want to please me, and that I would be more willing to touch him in return if I knew how good it felt. Is it true, Maisie?"

"Aye. It is true, providing the man is the sort who realizes his own pleasure is all the greater when the woman finds her release, too."

"You mean some men are . . . not that sort?"

Maisie gave her a rueful nod.

"How do you know what sort he is before you, well, before?"

"Oh, a merry man who likes his food and ale, who likes to tease and fondle, can usually be counted on to give a girl a rousing good romp."

"So a sour, spare man . . ."

"Sour and spare with his kisses, most likely."

"And what about . . ." Catherine paused, her throat suddenly dry. "What about the monkish sort?"

Maisie gave her a sharp glance, and then shrugged. "They can take you by surprise. Some go at it like each thrust is a bead on the rosary; all that matters to them is getting to the end, with no worry for whether the, um, rest of the congregation has kept pace or not."

"Oh."

"But, as I said, they can surprise you," said Maisie, almost reluctantly. "I've known one or two who bring a kind of, oh, I don't know how to say this, my lady . . . a kind of reverence to the deed. For them, it's like the woman is a rare old manuscript, or a special fine wine—they can't help running their fingers over every inch, they want to taste, they want to absorb you through their very skin. Those are the best."

Which one would the monkish Mr. Kenby be? Catherine wondered.

Their eyes met, and Catherine knew her own cheeks were flaring with the same bright color as Maisie's.

"Serena said I should always feel free to express my

innermost thoughts, unless they would hurt someone," she said to ease their mutual embarrassment.

"Yon Serena sounds like a wise woman."

They sat in silence for a moment, and then Catherine could not help asking, "Does knowing these things make me a courtesan, Maisie?"

"I'd say they make you a good companion, my lady, and truth to tell, from what I've seen over the years I think a man finds himself drawn to a woman first for lust, and then for companionship. I'd say your Serena did you no harm, and possibly did you a great deal of good."

"Except none of this will matter in a convent," Catherine said.

"Aye." Maisie drooped with sympathy. "Aye."

Earlier in the day, Vincent had looked ahead and chosen a landmark as their first resting place. Despite four hours' traveling, it seemed no closer. He knew distance skewed perception, but he also knew that walking horses moved little faster than men afoot, and a man on foot could walk from sunup to sundown and travel no more than twenty miles.

And they had hundreds of miles to cross.

He also knew that the dust cloud roiling far ahead, but moving in their direction, meant a party of mounted riders approached from the north, and that they were not hampered by gently born virgins and slow-rolling carts.

"Rangold," he said, inclining his head toward the disturbance.

"Aye, Mr. Kenby. I've marked them. Pilgrims in an uncommon hurry, let us hope."

They'd crossed paths with pilgrims several times already. Italy had always been a lure, with its rich religious history. These days, though, the pilgrims were more apt to be fighting men making their way toward Sicily, where Richard Plantagenet was gathering his great army to launch his Crusade against the infidels.

Common men, scantily armed, seldom mounted, were no cause for concern. One such had passed them earlier in the day, and quietly asked for some bread, which Vincent had allowed. The others had simply shuffled past with the most cursory of hails, sometimes giving Catherine's wagon a curious look, their faces lined with fatigue but lit with the inner fervor that united rock-slinger with knight on this quest for God.

They didn't pause for conversation, didn't slacken their pace. They hurried, anxious to reach their destination before Richard's army left without them.

Vincent understood, for he, too, was all but consumed by a need to hurry, but his stemmed from illogical reasons. Unlike the crusaders, he had no specific date whereby he must deliver Catherine to the convent. He had no specific proof that Michael of Hedgeford had failed to be tricked by his deviousness and might be following. And yet, with every slow pace of his horse an inner voice whispered, *Hurry.* With every urge he squelched to look back at the rough lumbering cart, that same voice whispered, *Hurry,* and not from eagerness to finish, or from fear of being attacked. He simply wanted the task to be ended.

He wanted her away from him. His peace of mind had deserted him and would not return until he was rid of both task and woman.

He'd long savored that calm, safe peace of mind. He ought to look forward to its return. And yet in the midst of all the inner urging to hurry, something else didn't mind at all that their pace was so slow, that Catherine's date of incarceration was postponed hour by hour.

Perhaps he had been too hasty in discounting sorcery. The strength of mind that had let him rise from freeborn farmer's son to monk-in-training, and then to willingly abandon that position of pride for the less certain but more lucrative position of lawyer to an earl, had deserted him. What but witchcraft could account for his thoughts turning to her again and again, when so many other things ought to occupy his mind?

He realized with a start that he could not recall the last time he'd stewed over what might be happening back in England. Something had driven his concerns over his place straight out of his head.

Dismay over his lapse of concern must have led him to forget to blink, for it pained his eyes when sunlight reflected against something inside the approaching dust cloud.

"Armor," he said. "Knights."

A loud, boisterous group of Burgundians, judging by the words he could make out as they drew near.

Vincent counted eight mounted knights, six mounted squires, and two more squires who ran alongside their masters' horses with one hand gripping the stirrups.

It was impossible for two mounted parties to pass on the narrow road without slowing. Vincent, chafing at the difficulty in communicating his wishes, made it known to the carter that he should pull the cart up onto the verge to make way for the horses. With the cart off to the side, the knights might pass without pause.

They did not.

"Ho! Honor and God's glory lie in the other direction!" called the lead knight as his party drew their horses to a stop. They carried the banners of France and Burgundy, and wore the white cross of the crusaders upon their breasts.

"Not for us, this time. Lop off a Saracen head for me." Vincent hoped to discourage conversation by guiding his horse past the knights.

Some chuckled, but one knight, whose squire had bent at the waist and stood heaving for breath during this stop, reached to touch Vincent's arm as he passed. "A word about your extra horses, if you please."

Vincent could not pass without insulting the knight. The only thing worse than a curious knight was an insulted knight. Swallowing his dread, he pulled up. "A sorry lot."

"Better than having none. We must needs ride fully armored in this heat, lacking pack animals. Have a look toward my squire—he fares to run his heart into bursting for want of a mount. And I see you have extras."

"Only as many as we need, considering the poor health of some."

"Where are you bound?"

The very last thing Vincent wanted to do was name their destination, for if these knights came across Michael of Hedgeford, they would be able to tell the man exactly where to find them. And yet he could not tell these crusaders a story that might let them decide their own purpose was nobler than his. Knights they might be, but here in this strange land they were not bound by the same codes as they would accord citizens in their own land.

They meant to fight the Saracen infidels, but their mercenary natures also craved the looting and pillage the fighting would afford. His little group, with no knight to protect them or demand their respect, with two women belonging to none of them in particular, might seem an interesting diversion, a chance to gain an early taste of plunder.

"You serve the Lord in one way," Vincent said. "We serve in another. Yon wagon carries a noble lady who has been promised as a bride to Christ."

He'd chosen right; he saw the disappointment flicker through some of them and knew Catherine, at least, was safe. And then he thought of something that might help.

"We could spare a mule to carry your armor," he said. "And donkeys for your squires."

"At what cost?"

"Someone who would deny the lady to God might be following. If you happened across such a person, your silence would cost you nothing."

"The lady has a true vocation?"

"Would she be traveling in such mean circumstances, with no sign to herald her status, otherwise?"

"'Tis true." The knight nodded. "Let us have done with the bargain, and we shall be on our way. We shall avert our eyes as we pass, so we can in truth say we saw no lady should someone ask."

"Well done, Mr. Kenby," Rangold said later, when the squires were mounted bareback on their bony-backed little donkeys and the knights had continued their progress. Vincent made some wordless acknowledgment as he watched them ride away. He felt no confidence that the knights would uphold their bargain; nor did his mood improve when the knights all ostentatiously turned their heads away from the wagon as they rode by.

He could not, obviously, see into the back of the cart from where he sat, so he could only pray that none of the knights caught a glimpse of silk skirts covering long legs, of golden hair tumbling free and glinting in the sun. While most men revered a woman who'd devoted herself to God, Vincent knew there was another type of man who thought celibacy a crime against nature, and would feel it his manly duty to acquaint her with the pleasures of a man's body before she locked herself away in service to God.

"You do not trust them?"

"Tonight, when they gather around their fire, when their honesty is blunted by wine, they will remember how few we number, and how poorly we are armed in comparison to them. They will remind themselves that they are Burgundians, while we are English, and though their king and ours might be allies for one cause, we are all in a land where neither king can mete or demand punishment."

"Aye."

"We will travel through the night."

Rangold nodded. "We should post some sentries here. They could sleep for a few hours, until nightfall; then they can keep watch until daybreak and catch up with us, trading off with another group who can do the same."

"Excellent, Rangold."

The man looked pleased at the compliment, and seemed to thaw a little toward Vincent. All because Vincent had paid him a small compliment, something he would not have done if his worries had not over-taken his usual reserve.

"I will say this for you, Mr. Kenby. For a man who has done no soldiering, you have mapped out a fair strategy thus far, and even now have placed us in as good a position as possible. Save for the cart."

They held their mounts and watched as the carter whipped the mule into motion. The hardy animal leaned into its harness and dug its hooves deep into the dirt, and eventually the cart rumbled down off the verge and onto the road.

They maintained their positions as the cart rumbled past them. Vincent noticed that the door wasn't closed properly, and his concerns over the knights increased apace. They'd turned their heads as they passed the wagon, but he'd seen in tourney how knights fooled their opponents with their eyes; more than a few champions had been unhorsed by misreading their opponents' intentions.

"You have not welcomed my recommendations before, Mr. Kenby," Rangold said, "but I would venture to say that it might be a good idea to abandon the cart. We would make greater speed without it."

"The lady does not ride," Vincent said. He regretted he could not give Rangold a full explanation, but could not bring himself to discuss the state of Catherine's maidenhead with the man.

"If she cannot ride, perhaps you could give her a few lessons," said Rangold. "She might gain enough ex-pertise in a day or two to let us abandon the cart."

To think of himself alone with Catherine, hoisting her into the saddle, helping her to arrange her legs, placing his hands over hers to grip the reins . . . no. Im-possible.

And, unnecessary. She had never said she could not ride, only that she did not ride.

"I will think of something," said Vincent.

Nine

The cart lurched and Catherine braced her feet to keep from tumbling headfirst to the opposite side, where Maisie dozed, unperturbed by the shift. Then, with loud groans of protest, the cart angled, as if the wagon master had driven it straight up the roadside embankment. No amount of bracing could hold Catherine back, and she almost fell into Maisie's lap.

"Something has happened," she said when Maisie's eyes popped open. She levered herself away and hunched into a sitting position on the bench next to the maid.

Maisie made a small sound of acknowledgment. "We're lucky this thing doesn't topple over."

She'd spent less than three days on this journey, and yet she could sense a difference in the general noise made by their party. This unsafe shifting the cart, too, struck her as something Vincent Kenby would not permit under normal circumstances.

She tried to heave herself to her feet. "I am going to see what's going on."

Maisie shook her head. "No, lady, let me. Mr. Kenby would have my head if you slipped and hurt yourself."

Maisie edged toward the door, and then hand over

hand pulled herself up. She clung precariously to the door frame and craned her neck, trying to see beyond the edge of their enclosure.

"Can you see anything?"

"No. I can't see around the corner. Hold tight to my waist, lady, so I don't fall out. I need but another inch or two." Catherine braced her feet and then wound her hands into the loose cloth, pulling back as Maisie leaned forward. "Nothing unusual," said Maisie, and then, "Wait! There is something." She held her uncertain perch for another moment, and then with a little squeak of alarm flung herself back into the enclosure.

A thundering, a clinking, first sounded faintly and then increased to a frightening din. Catherine went to her knees and crawled to the door, and Maisie hung over her to do the same. A small contingent of mounted knights and men-at-arms trotted past. They all looked away from the cart as if offended by the sight of it. Two boys mounted on donkeys brought up the rear, losing ground quickly despite the twigs they used to swat the little animals' rumps.

"A rescue party?" Catherine asked hopefully.

"They be headin' the wrong way, my lady. Those knights are aimed back toward that place we left. Genoa."

Catherine leaned back against the bench. True enough, the knights rode away from them, showing nothing but their backs to a lady who was in great need of a knightly rescue. They couldn't be Michael's men, anyway, for the banner they carried was all wrong, bearing the French king's colors. Even so, they were knights and bound to come to a lady's aid.

"If I had known they were here," Catherine said thoughtfully, "I might have made an appeal."

"You couldn't have known, my lady."

"I *should* have known. Queen Eleanor would not have let such an opportunity slip by her. Did you know that when she was imprisoned, she managed to smuggle messages through an ordinary peddler?"

While Maisie stared at her in confusion, Catherine took herself to task. She had allowed herself to become acclimated to her circumstances. While Maisie had slept, she had slouched. Serena had never permitted her to slouch, claiming the lazy posture encouraged lazy thoughts, and this proved her right.

Catherine straightened her spine, squared her shoulders, folded her hands in her lap. A person's spirit and will should not succumb so easily to what was forced upon it.

"What does the old queen have to do with us?" Maisie asked.

"More than you would expect. I will tell you all about her, but not now. For now I will just say that I would do well to model my life after hers," said Catherine. "She never grew complacent. Do you know, after only three days of traveling in this horrible little wagon, I have grown *accustomed* to it? If I can slip so easily into this routine, then I am in danger of growing accustomed to life in a convent—"

The wagon jerked into motion again, cutting off Catherine's musings and sending them both sliding the short length of the bench. They lay tangled in a heap as the cart slowly regained the relative flatness of the road, and only the usual ruts and holes disturbed the ride.

"We shall both be black and blue with all this tossing about," complained Maisie as they each retook their bench seats.

SCHOOLED FOR SEDUCTION   139

Maisie showed no interest in continuing the discussion about staying alert for opportunity. She yawned, sighed, squirmed like a bored child. Catherine thought about the knights and vowed to never let apathy or despair overwhelm her, never let her spirit be cowed. Any turn in the road, any knock at the door, might bring opportunity—and might as quickly carry it away. She would have to be ready to act when chance presented itself.

Up to this point in their journey, the wretched little cart had rolled along at the rear of their party. Within a few minutes of the knights' passing, though, two mounted soldiers fell in behind the cart.

Vincent must have sent them there, to watch for Michael's men, to watch against the return of the knights. He never grew complacent. She could learn from him as well as from Queen Eleanor.

The men's hats shaded their eyes, but she could tell they stared inside, watching her, watching Maisie. She didn't like it, and wanted to tell them to watch the road instead, but that would only seem to indicate she approved of Vincent's precautions. She tucked the folds of her gown demurely beneath her legs, and was about to ask Maisie to close the door when one of the soldiers hied off toward the woods.

The one who remained called in to Maisie. "Mr. Kenby means to travel through the night. We're to sleep in shifts. Care to join me?"

Maisie darted a look toward Catherine and then giggled. "Just how much time do you have, mister?"

"Two, three hours."

"And just how much time do you plan to spend sleeping?"

"Depends whether you come with me or not, miss."

"And what happens if you don't get any sleep?"

"Then I shall be the tiredest but happiest soldier in Mr. Kenby's command."

Catherine found herself spellbound by the bantering. The man, his eyes ringed with road dust, with lines indicating great weariness, nonetheless smiled with genuine delight. Maisie, who had been slouching and fidgeting, now sat as straight-backed as a princess upon a throne—all because a man flirted with her.

Maisie looked at Catherine, not asking, but with such hope and anticipation on her face that she did not need to say what she wanted to do.

"Go," Catherine said. "I'll be fine."

"You're sure?"

"Did I not just finish saying that we should watch for opportunities and seize them?"

Maisie giggled again. She rose, and then gathered up her skirts, paused at the edge of the cart, and hopped down. She stumbled slightly upon landing, but soon had her feet under her and darted into the woods. With a whistle and a shout, the man spurred his horse and followed after her.

Catherine found herself standing at the door, holding tight and swaying with the lurching of the cart. Something within her longed to follow Maisie—not to do as she intended to do, and certainly not to watch their intimacies, but to gain just a little more knowledge of the things that went on between a man and a woman.

She had to know if the things Serena had promised could possibly be true.

The thud of fast-approaching hoofbeats seemed to match the beat of her heart, and she dared to think that perhaps someone had come for her the way they had come for Maisie—and then Vincent Kenby reined his horse toward the back of the cart.

Like the soldiers, weariness seemed stamped all over him. But he had bade the others to get their rest first. She wondered if he knew that at least one of his men meant to spend his time roistering rather than resting.

He quirked a brow to see her standing at the open doorway, her legs braced wide for balance. She knew that even though he could not see beyond her, he knew Maisie was gone from the cart. But he did not remark on Maisie's deserting her.

"I would not advise jumping," he said. "If you land badly, you could break a leg, and you would not get very far."

"I might manage to crawl to the woods, which is as far as I intend to go," she retorted. She felt heat climb from her neck, and knew she could not bear to tell him exactly why she had wanted to follow Maisie into the bushes. She took refuge in an excuse that held some merit. "Really, Mr. Kenby, if you mean to travel through the night, you might spare a moment's consideration for our personal needs."

To her astonishment, he nodded. "Aye. I have not been considerate. Please sit, my lady. I will have the carter stop so you may descend safely."

He called out the order to stop in Latin, which the wagon master apparently understood. She gripped tight to the edge of her seat so she wouldn't pitch forward. He pulled up his horse, and began to dismount. She knew he intended to hoist her out of the cart, which meant his hands around her waist again. Oh, God . . . not just now, when she'd been on fire with curiosity about the way of things between men and women. Before he was aground, she jumped the short distance to the road.

She thought he would also halt the entire progression, which would be a mortifying thing since all and sundry would see her make for the bushes and know what she was about, but to her surprise he simply nodded at finding her already standing on the road. Nodded . . . and did she imagine it, or did disappointment flicker ever so briefly across his features? He tied his horse to the back of the cart and gave the wood a smart slap. The cart creaked back into motion.

"But I haven't . . ." she began a protest.

"You mentioned a while ago that you wanted to walk. Tend to your needs. We can catch up with the wagon soon enough."

Her limbs, aching for a good stretch, quivered with gratitude. She was about to thank him for his kindness when she remembered Serena's warning. She must not let herself develop soft feelings for this man who doled out privileges that were hers by right. And, now that she thought about it, there was something decidedly suspect about his pleasant behavior. He was not a pleasant man. She cast him a sharp look.

"I thought you would enjoy walking," he said.

"'Tis not a privilege you have the right to grant or deny. A woman has the right to walk. I will not stand here all atremble with gratitude because you deign to 'allow' me to do something that the most base-born serf can perform without permission from his liege."

He had nothing to say for himself, not even an apology; more surprisingly, not even a curt retort.

She lifted her hem, tilted her chin upward, and proceeded to the bushes with as much dignity as she could muster.

When she reemerged, he had turned away to watch their party of soldiers and cart up ahead. She was surprised to see how close they still were. If this was the extent of their progress beneath a clear sky, in full daylight, then Catherine reckoned they'd put very little distance between themselves and the city of Genoa they'd left days earlier. Small wonder Vincent continually fretted at their lack of progress.

If she had more durable shoes, she could just hitch up her skirts and no doubt run back to the city in a couple of hours . . .

"The road is rough," he said.

She laughed. "Maisie just said we would no doubt be black and blue from being tossed to and fro inside the wagon. You have no need to tell me the road is rough."

"I merely thought to offer my arm if you thought you required assistance," he said without looking at her.

Both of them stood in the road looking down at the ruts and bumps. The rains that had soaked them days earlier had seeped deep into the dirt. The sun had dried the surface of the road somewhat, but now that the cart had gone on ahead she could see that its weight cut through the crusted layer to the moist ground below, leaving great furrows in the road. Walking could prove treacherous. But, she knew, so could clinging to the strong arm of Vincent Kenby.

Her body had never settled from the uproar that had started when first he'd touched her. Those embers showed a distressing tendency to flare up at the least provocation. And it seemed she'd had provocation after provocation, between discussing matters of men and women with Maisie, with the soldiers leering into the enclosure, with her curiosity piqued and demanding to know what Maisie and that man were doing back along the road right now . . .

No, the last thing she needed was to touch Vincent Kenby.

"I shall manage," she said.

She'd given him a tongue-lashing. He'd been reminded, in that moment, of the wide gulf in their status. She, the daughter of a nobleman; he, a farmer's son. Her father had granted him the right of putting her in her place, and yet he'd done nothing but stand there and accept her barbs, for he'd been silenced by admiration. He knew the strength of will it took to fight against the inevitable.

"It is no admission of weakness to accept an offer of help when circumstances are truly treacherous," he said.

His argument was proven when at that moment her toe caught against a clod. She did not stumble but did throw out her arm for balance, and her hand came up against his upper arm. He continued walking, acting for all the world as if her warmth did not penetrate the good wool from which his sleeve and tunic had been fashioned and strike hot against his skin.

"The footing is difficult," she admitted.

She let her hand rest against his arm for one more step, for two, and then it stroked down, slowly, and curled under to tuck into his elbow. Proper, very proper, the way they walked, with only her fingers and a bit of her palm pressed lightly against the joint of his elbow. He wished he could withdraw his offer to lend his arm, and at the same time wished she would once again make that light stroke from shoulder to elbow. Thank God for the sun that could excuse the sweat that had sprung to his brow; thank God for the breeze that cooled his skin.

"Am I permitted to talk?" she asked.

"When I forbid something, it is only because your safety is at stake. There is no risk to talking."

"Truly?" She seemed amused at his remark. "Well, I do enjoy talking, and since doing so cannot make you angry . . . I have been thinking back to my days at home, and I cannot remember your family, Mr. Kenby."

One pace, two, while he cursed himself silently for giving her permission to talk. Serena's confident assertion that he could not expect human beings to behave according to plan came back to haunt him.

"You would not remember them, my lady," he said.

"Why?"

Odd sensations coursed through him—reserve, for he never discussed such matters with anybody, and had no urge to do so. And something else, indefinable, that seemed oddly pleased that she had been curious about him.

"My history is a dull matter, and not worthy of discussion."

She laughed, a pretty, tinkling sound that blended with the birdsong trilling about them. "We have a long journey ahead of us. I truly doubt your story would be more dull than making this walk in utter silence would be."

Dismay held him silent for a few paces. Well-bred people did not pry. That she continued to question him was a shocking breach of manners that could not be excused even by her status as daughter of his lord. Ordinarily he would stop such an intrusion with a harsh comment, but somehow he could not take offense at Catherine's questioning. She looked up at him, her eyes lively with genuine curiosity, and no hint of malicious intent. She seemed so . . . interested. Interested beyond the mere filling of an uncomfortable silence.

"My father was a farmer."

"I knew it!"

"My lady?" Had he given himself away by act, word, or deed?

"It's your size. Your strength. Your intelligence. You were well-fed when young, but made to work hard."

"Aye." His acknowledgment sounded little better than a gasp. To reach that conclusion, she'd studied him, measured him, thought about him.

"From planting to politicking." She rapped him playfully on his upper arm with the back of her free hand. "And you said your history is a dull matter? Do go on, Mr. Kenby."

He shrugged to cover the pleasure that blossomed and bloomed everywhere she touched him. He'd been resented, and outright snubbed, in his struggle to gain his place. She was the first, to his recollection, who realized the extent of his accomplishment and remarked on it with something like approval.

Even so, the habit of holding himself aloof would not be so easily broken by a woman's curiosity.

"I assure you, the story is dull beyond belief."

"Then let me spin the tale. Let us a say there was a little boy so high"—she leveled her hand at waist height. "His father says, 'Ah, here I have a boy with a head for learning—'"

"My father never held with book learning." He could not allow that sour-hearted man to reap the credit that belonged to another, no matter how uncomfortable he felt at revealing information about himself. "No, 'twas our parish priest who fancied I might make a better scholar than a farmer."

"There must have been something about you, even then, to draw the priest's attention," she said.

Even then. His heart gave an odd lurch at the words. Even then, she had said, as if to say there was something special about him now. "Nothing remarkable. I just managed to remember the shape of the letters from one Sunday to the next."

He sounded gruffer than he'd intended, no doubt because his throat had gone a little tight. "Old Father Fanshaw held the theory that all children—girls, boys, it was of no matter to him—could learn as well as those of the better classes. Every year he would gather a batch of us together and show us the letters. I was the first in many years to remember all the shapes."

He had learned one of life's most valuable lessons that first day with Father Fanshaw—the letters that had danced so sharp and clear in his mind had done the same for other children. The priest had warned that unless they took care to remember, over the course of a week the letters would dance straight into oblivion. And so each night of that week, when he'd finished his chores, Vincent had taken a stick and copied the letters over and over again in the mud, familiarizing himself with them so thoroughly that they danced for him rather than away from him.

His father had caught him at it, and angrily stomped the rude tracings into muck. "Do something useful," he'd roared, and set Vincent to cleaning out the pigsty. Vincent had later learned that many illiterate men were like his father, outwardly derisive of what they called clerkly leanings, but inwardly intimidated and frightened of those who possessed the ability to read and write.

Father Fanshaw—old, half blind, and yet desperate to at last prove his theory—had used that intimidation to coerce Vincent's father into allowing him to attend a weekly tutoring session with the priest. The world thus opened held great appeal for Vincent. Somehow he'd managed to handle the work expected by his father and still find a little time for study and practice.

"Do you have many brothers?" Catherine asked.

"Two."

"Older?"

"Aye."

"So no land for you! Your father must have been very proud that you were able to find a living off the land."

"No, my father wanted nothing more than for me to spend all my days slaving alongside him in the fields, and then to do the same for my brother."

She stopped walking. "Then how . . ."

Never before had Vincent revealed so much to another. By rights he ought to forestall her curiosity now with a curt comment and enforced silence. Was this another of her temptress's tricks?

He had hesitated too long. "My turn to take up the story again?" she asked, peeping mischievously at him from the corner of her eye. "Very well! Your mother took a broom to your father and—"

His laugh rang out so loud and merry that some of the men far ahead twisted in their saddles to look back to see the source. One man gaped and almost fell off his mount, then swiveled about to gape again from the opposite side, as if unable to believe what he saw and heard.

Vincent had not laughed like that for . . . he could not remember ever having laughed so full, so deep.

"Shall I go on with the story?" she asked.

"No—please do not. I had not realized laughing was such an exhausting business, and I am tired enough as it is."

"You do look tired, Vincent," she said.

She had never said his given name before, always "Mr. Kenby," with sharpness overlaid with pain. But his name tripped from her lips with a softness warmed by the Italian sun, and struck something within him that had been let loose with his own laughter.

It was probably one of her temptress's tricks, his mind scolded—but hard on that warning came another thought, that he was too tired to suspect everything she did, and that not even the most cautious of men could fear telling her anything of import, since she would soon be locked away where nobody could possibly be interested in anything she might know about him.

He wondered if she would think of him, sometimes. He wondered if he would ever be able to *not* think of her.

Maybe someday she might find it in her heart not to hate him, if she understood a little about him.

"Father Fanshaw enlisted the aid of our bishop. They gained a place for me at the abbey, and then the two of them approached my father and declared I had a devout vocation and belonged to God. My father could and would keep me on the farm for any reason, save even he would not dare flout God."

"But you are not a monk."

He glanced down, and fancied he saw a blush cresting her cheeks.

"No. Although, to be rid of the farm, I would've agreed to anything. I began the studies, and might have completed them and taken my vows, except that Father Fanshaw died and there was no further need for pretense."

"Gratitude held you to your studies."

"Aye."

He'd never admitted that to a soul; never to Father Fanshaw, to whom he owed everything. Never even to the abbot who had released him from his studies after Father Fanshaw died.

He, who had grown up surefooted, and took care to never appear bumbling, stumbled. It was as though telling so much about himself had drained him somehow, for he felt loose-limbed and curiously tired—tired in a pleasant way, the way his father had sometimes claimed a farmer would feel after completing a task long dreaded. "Now, that one is off my shoulders," his father would comment on those nights, and he'd be sleepy and smiling and pleasant to be with for a few hours.

And as Vincent stumbled, Catherine's hand tightened, to steady him.

Exhaustion, he decided. He'd slept so little since fetching Catherine from the palazzo—a few moments snatched while on horseback. He'd not dared to do as he'd instructed the men, and curl up in a blanket at the side of the road and catch up with the contingent later. He was responsible for Catherine of Ardleswyck and would not entrust her into the care of anyone else, not even Rangold.

"Then you can understand why I dread with my

whole being what is happening to me. I have no vocation, and no reason to take up a religious life."

Her remark snapped him out of his strange mental
lull. He silently cursed his loose tongue, and specifi-
cally most regretted mentioning his religious studies
and his relatively easy escape from vows. He could not
blame her for grasping at the opportunity to test his resolve in this matter.

"What could my father have been thinking?" She
stopped again, and he took one quick glance at her
eyes, dark with confusion and pain. He had to look
away, for it had not been her father's thinking that
brought this about, but his own mind that concocted
the plan.

Perhaps it was his reminiscing about the past, rousing all the guilty feelings he'd had about deceiving
Father Fanshaw over the matter of his vocation, that
made it so easy for him now to feel plagued with guilt
over his part in this. Now was the perfect time to admit
the truth, that installing her in a convent had been his
idea first. Eagerly adopted by her father, but nonetheless Vincent's idea first. Left to his own devices, the
Earl of Ardleswyck would have never thought of such
a solution to his problem.

Somehow, he could no more bring himself to admit
that to her than he'd been able to tell Father Fanshaw
he had no deep-seated faith.

By then they were nearly caught up with the cart. It
lurched and wobbled ahead of them, so close he could
touch it simply by taking a few quick steps and reaching out his hand. He had good reasons for locking her
in there. The ever-present threat of Hedgeford's forces
finding them, the newer threat of the knights deciding
to return and claim all their animals and whatever

plunder caught their fancy. Aside from her safety, his indiscreet babbling meant he had to somehow keep her away from everyone so that she would not reveal things about him he did not wish them to know.

It was all right if she knew, but not anybody else.

Exhaustion swept through him at the thought of juggling so many responsibilities. Maybe it wouldn't have been so bad to have remained at the farm, where his biggest concerns would be whether to let the peaches ripen on the tree for another day, or whether to mate the black bull or the brown one to the golden heifer.

Fruitfulness. Mating. Spilling his innermost secrets to a woman he could not trust. Nothing could explain his strangeness except for the lack of sleep. If he did not manage to get some, he would go off his head again, and God alone knew what foolishness might then occur, what lapse of will would result.

"You look tired, Mr. Kenby."

"I'll manage."

"You gave leave to some of the others to sleep for a couple of hours."

"I am responsible for you, my lady. I cannot simply go off into the woods and take a nap while who knows what might happen on this road."

"You cannot stay awake forever."

"You are taking an uncommon interest in my rest. It makes me wonder what you might be planning to do when I do close my eyes."

That worry must have been lurking deep in the recesses of his mind, for he had not given it any conscious thought. But now he could not dismiss it.

Especially as she made no effort to protest his suspicion.

He called out to the carter, and when the wagon wobbled to a stop he pulled open the door and boosted her inside so quickly that he could not revel in the feel of her between his hands.

He'd tossed her in with a little more vigor than required, and she landed against the far wall and slid down at once to the bench.

That left a deal of space next to her, and the whole of the bench across from her, and without thinking he hopped into the enclosure himself.

"What are you doing?"

He did not know. But his body did. His eyes burned so much that he could scarcely keep them open. A huge yawn threatened to split his face asunder.

"I'm taking a nap."

"In here?"

"In here."

He wedged himself onto the bench opposite her, with one foot atop the bench next to her and the other firmly planted on the floor. If she wanted to climb out, she'd have to crawl over him. Just as she had said she would have to do in order to escape.

"I am a very light sleeper, my lady," he said.

"I pray you do not snore."

He chuckled, enjoying the pert tilt of her chin, the sparkle in her eyes, even as he quelled the inner voice that wondered where or when she might have heard a sleeping man snore.

Ten

Vincent rested for no more than a moment when Catherine saw him frown. He flung an arm over his eyes, and she realized that the sun streaming through the open door bothered him.

"The door will close if you pull out the sacking," she said.

"Would you mind?"

The request made sense, since the joint where the sacking was wedged was on her side of the cart. But she could not reach it without leaning over him, without pressing her upper body against his legs. "Well . . ." she said.

He sighed. He lowered his arm and took in the situation at a glance—and then she fancied he blushed. "I shall do it," he said, rising.

He could not stand fully erect inside the cart. Not surprising—she had noticed when they had walked side by side along the road that she'd had to tilt her head back at quite a sharp angle to look up at his face. Once, while walking, she'd bumped into him and found that the top of her head did not clear his shoulder. Since her crown did just brush the ceiling of this enclosure, that meant he had to stoop low indeed.

While tending to the cloth, she realized for the first

time exactly how wide he measured at the shoulders. He blocked the doorway completely. Though light filtered around and past him, she could not see one thing beyond the stretched cloth of his tunic. He was as effective as a closed door in sealing her inside, and yet she did not feel confined at all.

He finished, pulled the door closed, and then lowered himself back onto the slab of seat opposite her. Though the amount of light entering the enclosure was greatly reduced, limited by the slot cut in the door, there was enough to reveal how little space remained with the two of them sitting within.

"'Tis closer in here than I thought," he said.

"Your eyes will soon adjust," she said with familiarity. "And, it feels closest of all, when you sit in here alone."

"Surely you feel more cramped when someone else sits in here."

You would think so, she silently agreed, and yet the opposite was true. Particularly now, where having him lounging across from her lent an unusual excitement to the space, the way an impending thunderstorm caused one's skin to tingle.

"When Maisie is here, we talk. Talking relieves the closeness, somehow. And, we kept the door propped open."

"I mean to sleep," he said. "And I have ordered two men to take up position at our rear. 'Twould not do for them to follow and see me snoring—it might set a bad example."

"But sealing yourself inside here with me will not set a bad example?"

He sent her a mirthless little grin. "For various reasons, my being inside here will not compromise your reputation in the eyes of my men, my lady."

Various reasons. His own reputation for monklike tendencies, she supposed, protected her reputation. She wondered at the foolishness of men, who could look at this man, spend one minute in his presence, and think him the least bit monkish. Restrained, to an inhuman degree. Solitary, by an extreme force of will. But monkish—never. Impossible. Even she, who had so little personal knowledge of men, knew that few of them had to work so hard to hold their appetites in check.

He closed his eyes, and she knew he wanted to end their conversation. She wanted to prolong it.

"You did not set a rear guard until today. I expect that means you fear my betrothed is hard on our heels. I am sure that is so."

She found herself curiously ambivalent over the prospect of rescue, and more excited to think Vincent would react to her jibe and continue talking to her. Thank God Serena had warned her against this weakness, so she was able to recognize the melting of her will in the presence of this man.

She did not, however, know how to put a stop to its happening. Even as she was cognizant of her distressing weakness, she understood that her need to talk to him, to hear his voice, to learn something more about him did not abate.

The enclosure had been *her* space for all these days, and after only a few moments of sharing it with him, it felt like *theirs*. Her and Vincent's.

He sent her a hard look, but did not rise to her remark. He settled back against the wall, and propped his feet on the opposite slab. He twisted and turned and then sighed with so much pleasure that one would think he'd landed on a down-filled mattress rather than rough, hard oak.

He closed his eyes again.

"I must warn you—this cart can jostle you right out of your seat with no warning."

"I've held my own under worse conditions."

Catherine doubted it. She wanted to tell him about the mishap she and Maisie had shared, in a light and amusing way that would bring a smile to his lips and at the same time warn him of the precariousness of his position. Well, she had tried to warn him. If a lurch sent him sprawling to the floor, it would be no fault of hers.

She could not really move at all without some part of her coming into contact with some part of him. If she lifted her hand to smooth her hair, then the back of her hand would brush against his boot. If she stretched out a leg to ease a tight muscle, then her thigh would rest against his hard-muscled lower leg.

She certainly could not move to the other side, for his upper half sprawled more widely on that side of the enclosure, taking up nearly all the space along the slab. If she tried to wedge herself into the narrow gap that was left, all of him would be right up against all of her.

The thought made her shiver, in a pleasant way. Not from cold, for the cessation of rain had ended the unseasonal chill, and Vincent's bulk further warmed the small space. Nor did she shiver from fear, although there was an element of the unknown in the shivering.

She had given herself away, somehow, for he opened one eye and then the other, and frowned at her.

"I have taken too much space," he said.

"No—no, I am comfortable enough." Mindful of Serena's warning, she decided it best not to tell him that his presence did not overwhelm the space so much as make it feel safe, a nice cozy nest for a woman to curl up and enjoy. Better not to dwell on such thoughts!

"Then why do you wriggle so?"

"I am not wriggling! I merely . . . I simply enjoy talking when I have company, nothing more."

"My lady, I am near faint with tiredness, and besides, I think enough words have passed between us." He closed his eyes again, and crossed his arms over his chest as if to seal all his words inside. In less time than she would have believed possible, his posture softened, his breathing changed, and she knew he'd fallen asleep.

So much for Maisie's belief that a woman trained in the art of easy conversation had learned something of value to a courtesan. What use was such a skill if the man would prefer sleeping over discoursing? And what a poor job she must have done in learning, to be unable to keep him sufficiently interested in what she had to say.

The sun pouring through the slot in the door brightened the space enough to allow her to study him. There was so much of him, and with no talk to distract her, nothing else to do but look at him. With his declaration that they should not talk, her mind perversely called up all the words he had spoken on their brief walk along the road.

It was easy to see the farmer in him. Not in his speech, which was impeccably proper, and not in his demeanor, which was carefully circumspect, but his size and shape gave away his breeding. People came in all sizes, of course, but over the years Catherine had noticed that there were three basic frames that revealed a person's start in life as clearly as if they'd written out their history for her to read.

She could tell when a lad or a lass who worked on her father's estate came from an overcrowded cottage, where a permanent state of semistarvation meant the mother herself could not produce the milk that would get her child off to a good start. A regular diet of nothing but gruel and bread stunted height, so that sometimes it could be difficult to tell the three-year-olds picking rocks in a field from the boys of six who ought to be taller, but seldom were. She'd seen how some with this thin-boned, stooped frame turned out spindle-shanked and emaciated, while others grew overly fat in a flabby, weak way, as if their flesh always put too much of a strain on their bones.

Her own kind, well-fed and never working at hard labor during their youth, turned out with what she thought of as the normal sort of shape. They were usually of a height to equal one of the parents, with flesh in proportion to their appetites and exertions.

The third sort she saw least often, for those who possessed that frame usually need not seek serving positions at the earl's estate, nor were they welcomed through the door as guests. These were the relatively prosperous freehold farm families, who could afford to feed their children well, and who expected them to work, but not beyond a body's endurance. The children of such farmers usually towered over those who should be their peers, whether the child be male or female; their bodies grew tall and lean, and possessed a unique athletic grace that came from being familiar with one's strength and confident of how to use it.

Men of her class always sought the ranks of knight, and some, through sheer physical effort, managed to change the shape of their flesh. But never did they seem so comfortable in their own skins as one who had grown into massive strength by exercising it since childhood.

Vincent Kenby possessed the body any knight would envy, that any woman would desire. Much as she despised the man, she could not let pass the chance to study him while he slept.

In his height she could see a hardworking family's sacrifices and efforts to provide for their child. In the firmness and contours of his flesh she could see the solid strength built up working alongside his father and brothers. By his own account, he had not done such work for many years. Apparently the shape, once forged, could stay with a man for the balance of his days.

If he'd completed his religious studies, a monk's robes would not have concealed the width of his shoulders, the breadth of his chest, the flat plane of his belly.

How happily she would have sealed herself into the palazzo's prayer room, if a priest shaped like Vincent had been the one to stand with his belly pressed against her viewing window. She would have stared and stared, and not been so resentful as she'd so often been while Father Pascal's belly had blocked the light.

She could stare at Vincent's belly for as long as it pleased her to do so, now that he slept right next to her.

Her heart beat a little faster.

He would not allow such a leisurely, assessing perusal if he were awake, she knew. Some men enjoyed being the object of attention and would pose and posture. Vincent had a way of shuttering his expression, of holding that fine body like a shield. She knew somehow that it was his size, his manner of aloofness that had allowed him to rule the soldiers who traveled with them as easily as he did; such men did not accept orders lightly from one who was not one of their own.

And now, she was alone with him, and could see her fill of what he tried so hard to hide.

But in no time at all, she had to admit that looking did not satisfy her curiosity. She should have known. She had never been able to visit a market stall and simply say, "I choose that one." No, she must always lift the thing that had caught her eye, and weigh it in her hand; she must stroke it against her finger, or her cheek, to judge the quality, to feel if it was well made or if a lovely exterior covered inferior goods. With fruit, with scent, she had to move it through the air and then inhale to assure herself of its perfume.

But if she meant to be truthful to herself, she had to admit her usual shopping habits were not all that was behind her almost unstoppable urge to touch him. She could not still the little voice inside that repeated some of the things Serena had told her about men. How their skin was the same to look at as a woman's, but different to touch. How the fine hairs that sprung along a woman's arm were as nothing, while hairs sprung from a man's skin with vigor and wiriness that were rough but somehow felt pleasant against a woman's skin.

She could see dark, curling hairs peeping out through the open neck of his tunic. Serena had promised she would relish the feel of a man's chest hairs against her own bare breasts.

She would never know.

She might never again have a chance to study a man close-up. She might never again be afforded the opportunity to touch a man. Her hand drifted toward him, and then she snatched it back, mortified. How could she contemplate doing such a thing? She would not want someone to make free with her body while she slept.

She would not want to be oblivious to a caress.

He was utterly unaware, deep in slumber in the way the truly exhausted slept. He would never know if she touched, with the very tip of her finger, just one of those curling hairs.

She gripped her hands together. They shook from wanting to touch him. She could not.

But she could, and did, open one trembling hand flat and pass it above his leg, ran it along the length from knee to ankle. Warmer at the knee, cool as the ambient air at the ankle, where a stout layer of boot leather held in the heat of his body.

Her hand drifted back to the knee, and then a couple of inches higher. Warmer.

She shifted forward on the bench, taking care not to brush up against his propped-up foot. A couple of inches farther along his thigh . . . warmer yet.

His breathing did not change. He did not move. Still asleep.

She leaned forward as far as she could without coming away from the bench, leaving her awkwardly balanced, but she could draw back in the blink of an eye if need be. Her hand hovered over his loins. Her nervous trembling stopped, so surprised was she by the heat emanating from that area of him.

The cart lurched, and in her unbalanced position,

she went toppling onto him, with her outstretched hand leading the way.

Somehow, she knew not how, she managed to shift her hand a scant couple of inches higher so that when she landed against him, she did so with one hand pressed into his belly and one against the open neck of his tunic.

She had no time to whisper a prayer of gratitude that she had not ended up lying there with her hand buried in his loins. His eyes flew open at once and held hers in a challenging stare. With reflexes so quick she doubted a cat could best him, one of his arms trapped her about her waist, and his other hand caught hers, near his neck, so tightly that if she had been attacking him with a knife it would have clattered from her fingers, which had gone numb beneath his grip.

The rest of her was not numb.

The rest of her was molded like a second skin against his midsection, where the heat that had so fascinated her seemed to throb and burn even hotter, straight through the folds of her gown to tantalize the skin of her belly. The arm clamped around her middle all but ground her into him. She drew a breath, and that slight expansion of her belly meant she pressed against hard contours so unfamiliar, and yet so exciting, that she forgot to take a second breath.

"What are you doing?" His voice was hoarse with sleep, and with something more.

She could not think of a single thing to say that would excuse her position.

The cart shifted again, sparing her the need to lie, for this time the lurch came from his side of the cart. In less time than it took to blink an eye, they were tossed the opposite way, so that she found herself with her shoulder blades uncomfortably wedged on the bench beneath her while his weight held her down. The heat she'd thought could not possibly grow without setting him afire at his middle flared so high that she fancied her bones might melt, it felt so good.

He wedged an arm beneath her back to spare her against the rough wood, started to pull away and then came another lurch, and he let out an "oof" of dismay as they were sent spinning again. With his arm behind her, she found herself pressed nose-first into the open neck of his tunic. His scent filled her and her cheek slid against the fine, curling hairs there. Everything Serena had told her about the way a man's body hair felt against a woman's skin was true. She turned her head lest she be overcome with sensation, but it only made matters worse for her lips—accidentally, she hoped—then brushed where her cheek had rested.

Without thinking at all she darted out her tongue. The very tip touched his neck for an instant, a mere instant, so she was certain he did not notice. She tasted him, warm and salty, firm and earthy. A small sound of delight escaped her.

He must have thought she'd cried out in pain. Cursing, he maneuvered them about roughly, making no attempt to spare them harm. In short order they ended up separated as before, one on either side of the cart. Her knees and elbows smarted from knocking against the wood, and drove that mindless pleasure from her, leaving her somewhat breathless and blinking and wondering if she'd imagined it all.

"I will have a word with the carter," he said, seeming to have as much difficulty in breathing as she did. "He could avoid the worst of the ruts if he drives with attention."

He rose and moved toward the door. As before, he could not stand fully upright, but this time he curved his hands in front of him as if it were another part of him that risked banging into the oak.

"You cannot speak the language," she reminded him.

"I can make my orders known."

He could; the carter seemed to understand him, and she'd been able to tell, almost from the first, what he expected of her. Right now, she knew he wanted her to hold her tongue and let him leave the cart.

"You did not sleep very long," she blurted out.

"Enough."

"No more than a nap."

"A good, sound nap can refresh a man more thoroughly than a full night of restless sleep."

"If it is sound, yes."

"I napped with the utmost soundness."

"I am happy to hear that."

He pushed open the door, and after a moment to judge the cart's movements, he jumped from the enclosure.

All at once, it felt small again, and stifling.

She licked her lips, tasting him once more, and then angrily rubbed the back of her hand over her mouth to rub everything about him away.

She hated him. She really did.

Vincent stood in the middle of the road, breathing harder than any exertion warranted, and watched the crude cart, holding her, roll forward along the road.

His body, from head to toe, tingled with sensation. He stood beneath the warm Italian sun, feeling alternately heated and then chilled, and then flushed with warmth again, all the earmarks of a fever and yet nothing ailed. Nothing save his peace of mind.

What tormented him was not the memory of holding her in his arms. No, what bothered him most was that of which he was not truly certain . . . the half-formed image of her leaning over him, her eyes hot with hunger and need, while her hand hovered and yet did not touch . . .

Could he have dreamed it?

Most likely. For all his days his dreams had centered around him reaching out toward something that always eluded his grasp.

When he'd been a child, those dreams had been mysterious and lacking a clear goal—he had not known what it was he reached toward, only that it was something beyond the scope of barnyard and stable. Then later he'd dreamed that the letters and numbers he studied so assiduously would one day settle into things he could understand and put the world of literacy at his command, and they had, but not in the way he'd imagined. Mastering them had only revealed how little he truly knew and how much more there was to discover.

He'd dreamed of escaping the farm and he had, but only so far as studying for the priesthood. Then he'd dreamed of escaping the cloth without hurting the old priest who had brought him so far. And he had, into the earl's service where all those yearnings of the past served him well, and he'd enjoyed tremendous success. Yet his accomplishments had not been, had never been, enough.

How could it be that he'd always accomplished what he set out to do, and still found himself dissatisfied?

The only possible explanation was that he reached for the wrong things, while something inside secretly yearned for something else. Something that all his work, all his success, fell short of finding.

So perhaps that dreamy, not really seen so much as felt, sensation of being reached toward by Catherine was no more than another manifestation of his dreaming. She had reached, as he always did in his dreams, and he had ached, as he had always done in his dreams, but this one was different in a way that was subtle and yet not subtle. For this time, he had not been the one doing the reaching. He had not been grasping toward something unobtainable—he had himself wanted to be obtained.

Was that what he'd been seeking all these years? Someone who would reach toward him, take him and say, "I want you just the way you are?"

Abruptly the heat deserted him as chill doused him with the thoroughness of a rainstorm.

He had wanted her to touch him, to desire him as a woman wants a man.

He forced himself to take one step, and then another, while the weight of his realization threatened to root him into the ground. A man might dream anything. He might lust after any woman, but never after the daughter of his lord.

In fact, the mere thought of lusting after the earl's daughter so thoroughly threatened everything he had ever accomplished, that his logic and intelligence would never have allowed such lust to develop. Impossible.

It had to be her fault. Hers.

She had, after all, been trained to fire a man's lusts. She had been sent to this land of uncommon beauty, where one's senses were all aswirl with light and colors so intense and pure that artists spent their lives trying to capture them with paints.

His soldiers had proven to lack immunity to the lures surrounding them. Even now, he knew at least one of them dallied far behind with the wench Maisie. The wench herself had succumbed to the land's siren call; she'd been a mild distraction in England while preparing for the journey, and on the ship while traveling here, but nothing compared to the way she'd behaved in Italy. The lot of them had gone so far off their heads that they would rather fornicate than rest, while he . . .

He had not gone off his head. He stood here, alone in the middle of the road, proving that he'd held on to his sanity.

But in that cart, moving so slowly, lurching from side to side, he had just narrowly escaped debauchery himself. She had been so close, so willing, he had only to grasp her hand with gentleness rather than alarm, and lead that hand to where he ached for her to touch and things would have gone rather differently.

He stumbled over a clod and nearly fell, and then realized where his thoughts had drifted. He stopped again, and shook himself angrily, as if he could shake the inappropriate ideas right out of himself. The ideas she, with her seductress's ways, had planted there.

He had allowed himself to be swayed by pity for the girl. By guilt for the part he had played in where she was bound. By relief that she had not put up more of a battle over her fate. He had grown lazy and confident when he should have taken care to remain sharp and wary.

She could not be trusted. She had lulled him into

such a confident state that he had actually fallen asleep—asleep!—in her presence. If his iron-clad will had not let him repel the advances she made, she would have been deflowered and despoiled in that crude cart, and no doubt supremely happy about it, no doubt have done so to further lull him into dropping his guard. Perhaps she had hoped he might be grateful and let her escape her fate.

The cart, so heavy and rough and dark, taunted him with the knowledge of what it hid within. Her—her beauty, her hunger, her zest for life—sealed up and taken from the world, because of him.

No. That this guilt should plague him so was just further proof that she was an accomplished temptress, capable of twisting a man's heart and mind into any shape that suited her. He must be on guard, always, until he had handed her safely over to the abbess at Saint Justinius.

Eleven

How could she have done such a thing?

Catherine did not know how long she sat, her hands clutched in a knot on her lap, shivering first with the cold of abandonment, then with the heat of mortification, as she remembered how he'd caught her indulging her curiosity, how he'd slammed out of the cart as if all the demons of hell had been unleashed within.

How could she have behaved so wantonly?

She'd confirmed Vincent's poor opinion of her.

He would not believe her now if she told him that she'd never before felt such an overwhelming urge to study, to touch, another human being. She could sit across from sleeping men every day for the rest of her life and never feel that same compulsion. His being a man, and her being a woman were surely a part of that urge, but not all of it. Some deeper, specific need demanded to be fulfilled, something else, and she did not understand what it could be.

She would never know now. He would not ever again willingly make himself vulnerable to her. Nor would she ever again put herself in a position to be scorned, to be held in contempt, just because she wanted, she needed . . . she knew not what.

While she tried to sort out the muddle in her mind, she'd been aware of a minor commotion outside. This business of traveling overland was noisier, more fraught with interruptions than one would ever expect. She craved quiet so she might think, and so she deliberately tried to close her ears to the sounds. She could not block out a loud, hoarse shout, however, especially since it immediately brought about a stoppage of the cart, and she had to brace herself to keep from falling yet again.

The next moment, after a furious pounding on the back of the cart, the door was flung open from outside to reveal the man who'd earlier encouraged Maisie to run off into the woods with him.

"My lady! Come with me at once. You are urgently needed."

"What is it?"

"Please, lady—just come. You shall see." His face was mottled red with emotion. She knew his sort, rough, uneducated men whose words came hard and seldom conveyed what they meant to say, and so she did not torture him by demanding further explanations.

He helped her from the wagon. "Can you ride or will you run, my lady?"

"How far must we go?"

He screwed up his face, figuring. "A quarter hour on horse. Longer on foot." He shook his head. "Might be too late, when we get there."

"Too late for what? Please tell me."

"Please do not make me tell you, lady." He looked so miserable that she knew she would have to pry the information from him, something that could take a very long time.

"I will ride."

He lifted her high to sit in the saddle and climbed up in front of her. He spurred the horse into a gallop. She clung tight. How odd, she thought, that holding onto this man, feeling him so close, roused no heat in her blood. Just looking at Vincent had been enough to set her aflame.

Perhaps her lack of response to this man merely meant she was too mired in shame from what she'd been caught at with Vincent to feel these things for another.

Within the promised quarter hour, they reached the place in the road where Maisie had jumped from the cart to go into the woods with her soldier. Now Maisie, with the neck of her gown all askew, with her hair hanging tangled and tumbled over her shoulders, knelt over what looked to be a bundle of cloth lying in the road.

Several soldiers, their mounts standing near with heads hanging down in exhaustion, stood with Vincent Kenby. They were her father's men, judging by the clothes they wore, though she could have sworn Vincent had not left so many to rest back here. Vincent stood so absorbed in what they had to see that he made no indication he noticed her arrival.

Maisie looked up, and Catherine saw her face was streaked with tears. "My lady! Thank God you are here." She stood and stepped gently around the heap in the road, and ran to await Catherine's dismount. She caught Catherine by the arm, as if to fortify her, and then led her back toward the bundle.

As they approached, Catherine realized the cloth tatters fluttering in the breeze were the edge of a sleeve, a bit of lace, a trailing scarf. She recognized the color of the sleeve, the pattern of the lace. Dread coursed through her, and she gathered her skirts to run.

Serena.

Swallowing her cry of distress, Catherine dropped to her knees alongside the woman. Serena lay with her eyes closed. She panted, taking short sharp breaths as if it hurt her to fill her lungs. Cuts and bruises marred her lovely face. No wonder the soldier had not wanted to tell her why she was needed.

Catherine placed a gentle hand against Serena's arm but snatched it back when Serena cried out at the touch. To Catherine's horror a bright red blossom bloomed just under Serena's left breast. She realized then that the bodice of Serena's gown was not rust colored, but that the reddish-brown color was dried blood.

"Serena, 'tis Catherine."

Serena's eyes fluttered open, and the barest hint of a smile quirked at the edges of her lips before she gasped out a shuddering breath.

"Close your eyes," Catherine whispered. "Rest."

Murmuring words of comfort in Italian, in French, in the senseless babble of those who hoped sound could soothe, Catherine used the most featherlight touch to stroke the beloved face that lay almost impossibly pale beneath the obscene marks of violence.

"What happened?" she asked one of the soldiers. Maisie knelt at Serena's opposite side, wringing her hands with uselessness.

The soldier glanced toward Vincent, as if he required permission to speak with her, and then gave an almost imperceptible shrug. "Mr. Kenby's ruse did not work. Well, it might've worked but the weather was against us, has been from the start. Try as the captain might, he could not sail the ship out of the bay before

Hedgeford's ship came sailing in smart as a racing vessel, with the wind going the right way into its sails."

Michael! He had truly come for her. His arrival was not a half-formed fear in Vincent's head, but a real rescue party mounted by the man she loved! She would soon see the man whose image she had created in her mind, had held so dear. And yet it was not that imagined visage that filled her thoughts now, but the memory of Vincent's face as he'd slept. She shook it all away.

"Hedgeford's forces boarded our ship and learned straightaway that the impostor was not you, my lady."

"How was Serena injured?"

"Ah—Hedgeford's men attacked the palazzo."

Hedgeford's forces? Hedgeford's men? "What of Michael of Hedgeford himself? What part did the earl play in this attack?"

"Far as I can tell, my lady, the Earl of Hedgeford did not accompany his men on this quest."

Michael had not come himself to rescue her. He'd stayed home.

Her heart gave an odd little lurch, a sensation that hurt. She told herself Michael's decision to stay away meant nothing. He was, after all, but newly installed in his father's position and felt it more important to tend to matters at home rather than rush off on a rescue mission that might not be successful. Her father had done much the same in sending Vincent to handle her.

At that moment, Serena stirred and moaned. The movement caused the torn edges of her tunic to part, and revealed a horrendous gash in her side.

Catherine bit her lip to avoid crying out her dismay. If Serena had been gored by a bull, the wound could not be more severe.

"Lie still." Catherine tried to soothe with a tender touch but her hand trembled so, she was afraid she would accidentally cause Serena more pain.

"Can you help her, my lady?" Maisie whispered.

Catherine shook her head.

Serena had taught her much about the healing arts. The wife of a man who ruled a vast estate would often be called upon to provide remedies and palliatives for the villeins and others under her husband's protection. She had been taught to recognize those illnesses and hurts where her herbs and tinctures could be effective, and also taught to recognize those that were beyond her skills. She knew, with agonizing certainty, that Serena's injury was so severe that nobody could help her.

One could not say everything would be all right; it was plain to every eye that Serena's wound was mortal. One could not say they would soon have her fixed and feeling better; they traveled with no medicines, no physician, no barber-surgeon, no hope. The words one used to console the sick could not be said to Serena, for the usual platitudes would be lies, and she would know it.

With another moan that ended as a wheeze, Serena drifted into blessed unconsciousness.

Catherine glanced at the small party that had brought Serena. She counted one horse for each man, and no litter, no litter bearers. Her friend, struck with this mortal wound, must have ridden pillion while her life's blood soaked her gown.

"Why did you force her to travel in such condition?" Catherine demanded fiercely through her tears.

The soldier shifted and looked embarrassed. "Well, lady, we didn't have much time to think matters through. Yon lady was sore injured, and if we left her behind, Hedgeford's men would have been able to gain information from her—she made no secret that she is dead set against Mr. Kenby's plans."

"You did the right thing," announced Vincent.

Catherine whirled about, maddened into incoherence, to glare at Vincent for making such a cavalier statement.

He ignored her venomous regard. "Madame Monteverde is the only one who knew we were bound for Saint Justinius. Genoa sits like a spider at the edge of a web of roads. It will take Hedgeford some time to sort out which direction we've traveled, and with us buying up all the spare horses he will have to rest his own before he sets out. By bringing her along with you, you gained us a day or two."

"And cost Serena her life," Catherine added bitterly. As well as her own, she thought, but did not say aloud. Vincent looked away as if he had heard the words she had not spoken.

"'Twas your precious Hedgeford who dealt this death blow," said Vincent.

"He did not. He is not in Italy."

"Is he not? Interesting."

The observation hung in the air between them. She fancied she could read his thoughts—*The man you claim to love cared so little for you that he could not be bothered to make this journey.*

"Think on this, my lady. His men attacked the palazzo with no care for whether or not you still resided within. I warned you that stray blows could strike the wrong target. It could just as easily be you lying there mortally wounded."

Vincent's observation jolted Catherine a little. He'd clarified two matters of concern: Michael's failure to come after her himself, and Michael's men seeming to think they would not incur his wrath over besieging the place where his betrothed was supposed to be.

"No doubt those men knew more than you give them credit for," she came to Michael's defense. "Your own man told me that they boarded the ship and discovered your ruse. One of the men aboard ship may have mentioned that I had been forced to leave Genoa against my will. They merely sought to gain information when they attacked the palazzo."

"If it suits you, continue to think thus," Vincent said. But he seemed distracted, and completely unaware—and uncaring—that she waged her own internal battle over Michael's absence and apparent disregard for her safety. He did not even spare a glance for Serena, but kept his attention focused on the road they'd already traveled, as if he believed Michael's men would appear at any moment despite his brave words about being several days ahead of them.

"Bring water, and some clean cloth," Catherine said. She would keep her doubts to herself, and worry over them later. For now, she must devote every ounce of her being toward easing Serena's final moments. She smoothed Serena's hair back from her face, crying inwardly over each mark of violence on the skin Serena had tended so carefully.

Someone brought her a bowl and a clean square of linen. She wet the cloth and wrung a few drops from it to fall upon Serena's fever-dried lips, and the water seemed to revive her a little.

"Bring wine!"

Serena stirred, and Catherine shushed her into quiet, and tenderly dabbed at the dried blood and road dust on her face. Someone handed her one of the small wineskins the soldiers kept tied to their saddles. She cupped Serena's head and held the opening to her lips, urging her to let a little trickle down her throat.

Serena's eyes fluttered open, and tears brimmed within, but somehow Catherine knew these did not stem from physical pain.

"I would have told them where to find you," Serena said, her voice little more than a hoarse whisper. "I missed the chance."

"You have the courage of a tigress," said Catherine.

"Do not lose hope," said Serena.

"I have not."

"Be ever alert, and seize any opportunity."

"I will."

"They will find you. And *he* will lose."

Talking so openly about escaping Vincent and her fate right beneath his nose seemed to restore Serena— or perhaps it was just the wine that had fortified her. She struggled to sit up a little, but gave up with a gasp. "Be proud of yourself," Serena said. "Never let him or anyone make you regret what you are."

Vincent said nothing, but Catherine could read in his expression, in his stance, exactly what he thought she was. Heat coursed through her at remembering that just a short time ago she had given him ample reason to believe he was right about her.

"He holds a very poor opinion of me," said Catherine.

"He is the worst sort of fool," said Serena. "I know his kind. Filled with pride and the belief that they understand human nature—and yet so blinded by their own ambitions and prejudices that they cannot see the truth in front of them."

The outburst weakened her; she seemed to settle

more deeply against the earth, as if her body already prepared to return to that state. Catherine's tears flowed and she did not try to stop them—she did not care if everyone could see her grief.

"Take a little more water," she urged. She set aside the wineskin for the water bowl, and tried dribbling a little liquid against Serena's lips, but Serena could not, or would not, swallow. The water produced a paroxysm of coughing that caused her once more to cry out in pain. Heartsick at having her good intentions cause more hurt, Catherine flung the bowl aside and carefully gathered the woman into her arms.

"I am here," she said. "I am here."

She sat in the dirt, holding Serena for a very long time, on one hand praying for a merciful death to ease her friend's agony, and on the other selfishly praying that she might hold on for just a bit longer, for once she was gone Catherine would have no friend in the entire world.

Even Hedgeford's men who followed had no care for her as a person—to them, she was a thing to be hunted down and handed over to its rightful owner. A tourney prize would be afforded better treatment.

And then, quite clearly and with something like contentment in her voice, Serena said, "These olive trees were growing here before I was a child, and they will live on long after all of us are gone."

Ancient, gnarled olive trees grew among the others lining the road they traveled. They were easy to spot among the others, for their leaves had a distinctive surface that looked dulled and grayed against the shiny deep greens of the other trees.

"Yes," said Catherine.

"I used to pluck at the leaves when I walked this

road. I like the way they feel against my fingers, so soft, like fine leather."

"Go—get me some leaves," Catherine said to Maisie, who ran off and tugged a cluster from a low-lying branch.

"I remember the stream that lies just beyond that ridge. No water runs colder or sweeter. We are halfway there."

"Yes."

"My sister will know I want to lay alongside my mother."

"Yes."

"He loved me, always, and I loved him. Always." Serena's eyes seemed to be focused beyond Catherine, beyond the sky even, as if she both watched scenes unfolding from the past while looking toward a future Catherine could not see. Catherine knew that it was her father who was the "he" in Serena's heart.

"Yes, he did. Always."

Maisie pressed the olive leaves into Catherine's hand. She tried to curl Serena's fingers around them but they would not stay, and so she stroked them against Serena's fingertips. She could not tell if her friend felt anything any longer—she hoped not.

"You know the way to Lucia, Catherine."

"We visited your sister a dozen times."

"She is expecting me. Not so soon."

"No, it should not be so soon."

"You will explain."

"Yes."

"I am so tired."

Serena said nothing more. Catherine held her. She could tell the very moment she passed from unconsciousness to death, and she sobbed when it happened.

They gave her a moment, no more.

And then well before she was ready, firm but gentle hands pried hers away from Serena's body, and more firm but gentle hands pulled her to her feet and held her there when she would have flung herself down, weeping.

"Mr. Kenby says we have dallied too long," said the soldier holding her upright. "We must be on our way."

"Four times as many men." Vincent repeated, to be sure.

"Aye." The soldier giving him the news stood glum and dispirited. "Their horses weren't so bad off as ours, probably because they did not fight the weather. They were not at sea so long as we were."

Hedgeford's forces could well catch them in a day, Vincent calculated, if they guessed right about the route to follow. "Tell me, did you happen to cross paths with a small party of Burgundians on this road."

"Aye. Snooty lot."

"How so?"

"Tried to make us feel small for not joining the Crusade, and then tried to wheedle our horses away from us. And us carrying a hurt lady!" From the soldier's offended expression, Vincent judged he considered himself more knightly in regard to the lady than the knights themselves.

"Did they make mention of meeting our party?"

"No, Mr. Kenby."

The knights had at least kept that much of the bargain.

Apparently encouraged by Vincent's silence, the soldier continued. "I told them it weren't likely we'd give up our beasts, since there weren't no more to be had, even in Genoa."

With great effort Vincent stifled the groan that walled within him at the news.

He rubbed a hand over his eyes. A superior force on its way from Hedgeford. Horse-hungry mercenaries within striking distance. God alone knew what dangers lay ahead.

And within the group itself, a green-eyed temptress who haunted his thoughts both awake and asleep, so that there seemed no room in his brain for anything but thoughts of her.

Her pleading with him for understanding, that he of all men should know why she could not bear to be locked away in a convent . . .

Her hand, reaching but not touching . . .

His body, yearning for that touch . . .

Worst of all, his conscience had begun to plague him. For he did know what it was like in a religious house, and he did know that the vital spirit that shone within her like a lone torch illuminating a dark, dangerous passage would be deliberately smothered. He did know that her hand would always feel empty and unfulfilled.

All of this had been brought about by his own hand. He'd been the instigator. His conscience still rebuked him for not admitting to her the truth of his role when he'd been presented with at least two clear opportunities to do so. She continued to believe her father had developed the plan, when it was he. He owned an intimate knowledge of what was in store for her, and still he'd consigned her to this fate.

Responsibility for the dead woman lay on his soul, too. He'd suspected Hedgeford would attack the palazzo. He should have left a better-armed force to protect Serena, or urged her to take shelter elsewhere. He should, in truth, have brought her with them. His confidence, his certainty that he'd planned for every contingency, had made him dismiss that possibility. He had been so convinced that keeping Catherine isolated and frightened would serve his purposes better. Serena had paid for that decision with her life. So had he, for with no buffer between himself and Catherine, she had wound her temptress's fingers around his heart.

He need not bother assigning more hours of prayer to his penance. Hours would not suffice. He would need to spend years atoning for all the wrongs he'd committed within a hand's span of days.

He could not allow himself the luxury of regretting his sins. He could pay for those later. For now he had to clear his head and figure a way out of their present dangers.

"It will take at least three days to reach the village from here," Catherine said.

Vincent thought that she must have gone off her head, addled by grief. Their destination lay many days ahead—he would have gladly finished the journey in three if it were possible.

He ignored her and issued instructions to the sergeants. "Do not go too far into the woods to bury the corpse. Scatter leaves and brush around so the grave is not readily noticeable from the road. Then catch up to us."

They would need every man to guard their flanks. Hedgeford's men might have already left Genoa. This small group that had included one mortally wounded woman had caught up to them so quickly, he couldn't bear to think how fast his enemy would find them once they scented their trail.

"Do not touch her!" Catherine cried out, and wrenched herself free of the men who held her. She ran to Serena and crouched close to her. She batted away the hands that sought to lift the body. "She will not be buried here. You heard what she said. She wants to be buried alongside her mother."

"And I'd like to be buried alongside the king," Vincent said. "Unfortunately, neither of us are destined to get our wish."

Catherine stared at him in disbelief. "You heard me promise her. 'Twas a deathbed promise. It cannot be broken."

"You had no right to make promises you cannot keep, my lady."

Vincent turned and began to walk briskly away, when a clod of earth struck him in the middle of his back. He stopped. He turned back, slowly, and another clod caught him directly in the middle of his forehead. Small bits of it fell loose and trickled down his face and tunic; he could feel the main gob of it sticking to his skin. With a slow, deliberate movement, he wiped it away.

She stood straight and fine in her fury, dignified even though blood and mud mucked her gown, and more mud oozed between her fingers from the handful clutched in her fist. "You can pelt me with dirt all you like, but kindly do so while walking back to the cart," he said.

"I promised her." Catherine's voice was heavy with anguish.

"You had no right."

"She was right about you. You are a fool who cannot see beyond your own prejudices."

"I see more than you think I see."

"Let me tell you what I see—I see a man so intent upon getting his own way that he cannot see the advantage to be gained from what has happened here."

Although Vincent doubted there were any advantages to be gained, he never dismissed ideas proposed by another without first considering them. "Tell me."

"This party caught up to us with ease. Michael cannot be far behind."

"Aye." She had so eerily echoed his own unspoken fear that he wondered if she possessed a sorceress's skills to read his mind.

"You tried to dupe him once by foisting off another woman as me. You could do so again."

"How?"

"Let these men go ahead with Maisie pretending to be me. I will guide you to Serena's sister, deep in the mountains."

Vincent glanced toward the hills. "The cart could never travel those trails."

"I shall ride."

"You cannot ride."

"I never said I cannot ride. I only said I do not ride. You will recall how I arrived here with that soldier who fetched me."

That was true. "Do you ride well?"

"I can stay on a horse." She must have sensed that Vincent meant to say more skill would be required, for she did not let him make any comment. "Lucia's village is well fortified. We could ask sanctuary there until you feel it is safe to travel again."

The soldiers all nodded at the wisdom of her plan.

Only Maisie appeared against the idea, her face white with dread, and shaking from head to toe, and no doubt for good reason—the dead woman at their feet proved how little care Hedgeford's men showed toward females when they were in a mood to make war.

Vincent laughed, a little bitterly. "By your own admission, you are known to those villagers. You expect me to ride you straight into their arms, and gain sanctuary for yourself while I am packed off to explain my failure to your father."

"I would not. I give you my word."

He shook his head. "Attend to the burial." He turned to walk away, to find Rangold blocking his path.

Rangold cleared his throat. "Mr. Kenby, the lady's idea holds merit."

Vincent knew it did. He could not say why it went against every fiber of his being to split the party and improve his chances of completing his task, except that it would mean he would be thrown ever more closely into her company.

"My word has been given, Mr. Kenby." She called out like a knight casting a gauntlet.

He glanced over his shoulder at her. She had risen and stood straight, tall, determined.

"If you fail to accept it, you will have dealt me—and through me, my father—an insult of the deadliest nature."

Her assertion was ridiculous; nobody credited a woman's word with holding any weight, and certainly never accorded it the same importance as the declaration of an earl. But he could see the men appeared affected by her statement, and even Rangold was glowering at him with a judgmental scowl.

"You are right, Rangold," he said, though the words

threatened to choke him. "We shall split the party as soon as the burial is attended."

Her peremptory "No!" rang out in the air. "She comes with us."

"She is dead."

"I promised her. And I gave you my word only to ensure she would be returned to her home for burial."

Vincent refused to get caught up in what promised to be an endless round of bickering. He did not know why he was so set on thwarting her in this, except that an unfamiliar sort of fear within him demanded that he prove to himself, to everyone, that he was immune to her influence.

He was about to order one of the soldiers to tie her onto the back of a horse when she said, "If we do not take Serena's body to her sister, then I have no reason to go to the mountains. It would suit me well to let Michael's men find me."

"It might suit you the way it has done to her," Vincent said.

"Do you think I mind death any more than I mind what you intend to do with me?"

He'd carried his unreasonableness too far. Her eloquent cry, heavy with true anguish, had caused a subtle shift in the allegiance of his men; he could see it in the way they looked at her with such sympathy, at the way they looked at him with contempt. He had never considered himself to be stubborn to the point of stupidity, and yet he could not seem to stop acting stupid.

"You will show me the location of this well-fortified village whether this body comes with us or not."

"I think not," she said. "I think I shall assume the role of cloistered nun here and now, and practice the vow of silence. Nary another word shall cross my lips."

She made the motions of lacing her lips together.

He knew instantly what she meant—if she held her tongue, he would have no idea where this mysterious hidden mountain lair might be. One or two of the soldiers seemed to understand as quickly; he fancied he saw them hiding smiles behind their hands.

"Very well," he said, through lips so stiff they more rightly belonged on the corpse. "Wrap the body and tie it to a horse. We shall lead it, and pray God, lady, you do remember your oath and dare not steer me wrong."

Twelve

Vincent assessed the terrain. The road they traveled cut through a heavily wooded valley. The abundant sunshine, the temperate climate, encouraged an almost profligate growth of greenstuff. The soil under the trees would be rich and loamy with centuries of leaves and rotting wood enriching the earth, and although backbreaking work would be required to clear it, a man could wrest a bounteous holding from this land. . . .

He was thinking like a farmer instead of a tactician. This assignment, which ought to cement him more closely to his lord's side, and ensure his place for years to come, had instead reopened the paths to his past. It was almost as though something within him questioned whether what he'd striven toward so diligently was worth what he had left behind.

Since leaving Genoa, something had happened almost every day to insert a little invisible wedge into his contentment, to make him behave in ways contrary to his well-practiced methods. He had to put a stop to this insidious erosion, or else he might wake one morning to find his entire life had been washed away like the gilding from a base-metal statue to reveal that the Vincent Kenby beneath the false coating had not really changed at all.

He *had* changed, he told himself forcefully. He had struggled and sacrificed; he had overcome the limitations decreed by his birth and burst the bonds that held most men in place.

So why did Serena Monteverde's last words haunt him so? She had been speaking to Catherine, not to him, when she'd said, *Be proud of yourself. Never let him or anyone make you regret what you are.*

Vincent had been proud of what he'd accomplished, but never proud of himself. Every day of his life, he shuttered his heart and guarded his expression so nobody could see inside, for he did regret what he was. Nobody had ever really tried to look beyond the face he showed to the world, until this day when Catherine poked and prodded and somehow wormed her way past his defenses, and found something somewhat admirable in what he'd tried so hard to hide.

She had known the truth about him when she reached toward him, a woman to a man.

Because she was a temptress . . . a seductress . . .

He'd whispered the cautions to himself so often that they came into his mind now, but he had to reject them if he meant to be honest. He excelled as a lawyer because he had an uncanny knack for sensing the truth behind words and smiles. Catherine's interest in him had been genuine. She had made no effort whatsoever to use what she'd learned to her advantage.

She'd been interested in him. Nothing more. No harlot's tricks or courtesan's wiles, just a woman's interest in a man.

"Mr. Kenby, the lady says you're to head off toward the right," Rangold said.

Vincent welcomed the interruption. He scanned the roadside verge. "I reckon a small party could enter the woods through one of the narrow game trails," he said.

"Aye—a small party," agreed Rangold. "Taking too many with you would bust up those branches and gouge the trail so hard that you might as well post a marker showing which way you went."

A small party would do best, too, in passing through the thick growth they were sure to find off the road. He could afford to take no more than two men with him. Two men and a corpse would surely provide at least some sort of buffer between himself and Catherine. A dozen men, a hundred corpses, would not be sufficient.

"Truth to tell, Mr. Kenby, I worry more about yon mercenaries doubling back on us than I do the men who might come after the lady."

"So do I," Vincent acknowledged.

Rangold appeared to be surprised. "I thought you would take the part of the knights."

"I am not a woman besotted with the tales of love and honor that abound over such men," Vincent said. "My dealings with the knightly class have taught me much about the true natures their pretty manners and glib words can hide."

"Aye," said Rangold with approval.

"They did not say much, but they took note of everything. If they do come back they will be sure to notice that some of our party has gone missing, and they will wonder why. Solving the mystery may be of more amusement to them than stealing our horses."

"And a ripe plum would our lady be for them," Rangold said, muttering as if to himself. "They could hold her for ransom, pitting our lord and Hedgeford against one another. Better yet, one might just force himself upon her as husband and claim all our lady's dower . . . aye, I see why you're flummoxed, Mr. Kenby."

They stood in gloomy commiseration for a moment, and then Rangold brightened. "We have the new men. Put one of them into the place of every one who departs with you, just like putting in a new onion set soon's you pull out the old." Rangold seemed very pleased with his idea, and then frowned. "The clothes would give it away, though."

"The clothes?"

"Aye. You dress very fine, Mr. Kenby, and spoke out as our leader when they were here. Did yon mercenaries come after us, you would be their first target. So they'd be huntin' for the man wearin' that fine jerkin. They'd know straight off you was gone."

"That is easily remedied. I have a change of garments in my pack. I'll change into those, and give these—"

"Seems to me you'd fare better traveling as a commoner, Mr. Kenby."

Rangold wanted him to swap, it seemed. Aversion coursed through Vincent; not because he was too squeamish to wear another man's clothes, but because he wore his clothes as a uniform, much like knights flaunted their armor.

"All of you," urged Rangold. "The lady as well as yourself. You could run across all sorts out there, aside from those we already know about. Should anyone see a workingman and his woman in the wood, they'd think naught of it. 'Twould be a different matter, did someone spot a man and lady of quality."

Rangold's advice had been proven right time and again. Vincent had resolved to accept it, and he did so now without hesitation. He pointed to a sergeant that seemed closest to him in size. "You. Trade garments with me."

Rangold ordered the others to stand together to make a human screen so the ladies would not accidentally catch them shucking off their clothes.

The soldier made quick work of divesting himself of tunic, jerkin, hose. Vincent found it more difficult. He gave himself a mental scolding: did he fear that removing the thin layers of fine cloth would reveal him as an ordinary men, just like the others? But he could not think it through just then, or else he'd keep the other fellow standing naked as a peeled turnip.

He handed over his garments, and accepted the others, so quickly that he ought not to feel any self-consciousness over his nakedness. Oddly enough, even when the new tunic settled over his head, when he'd tugged the hose into place, he still felt unclothed.

The soldier did not seem to share his discomfiture. He marveled over his new garments, holding his arms aloft and swiveling his head between, gawping at the well-woven linen. "Would that my wife could see me now!" he crowed.

"Take care with yourself and those things and she can marvel over you when you return to England."

"Feel like a lord, I do," said the man, strutting like a cock preening for the hens, while the other men chuckled.

Vincent wasn't sure what he felt like, only that he felt different, as if in shucking off his counselor's garments he'd shed his old self at the same time.

It was an absurd fancy, and yet possibly not surprising considering the recent questions that had consumed him. Clothes had been important to him in his rise to power and influence. He had sworn, when he attained his position in the household, that he would never again wear rough homespun, never again own so few clothes that he possessed but one old outfit, and one even older.

Giving up his garments was just one more thing he'd had to let go of during this ill-fated task.

He'd forgotten that homespun conformed so well to the body that seams were not noticed, that the best of it helped a man stay cooler in the summer and warmer in the winter. This borrowed jerkin he wore had to stretch a bit to fit over his shoulders, but it did so without reminding him with every movement that he was wearing something a shade too small. A man could forget his clothes entirely when they settled upon him like a second skin; perhaps that was why the former owner had taken no care to keep food from spilling down his front. The odors, coupled with the stink of sweat, made him resolve to wash the garments at the first stream they happened upon.

But in the meantime, whether it was the coarse weave of the cloth, or the way it stretched over him, something about these new clothes made them less impervious to the elements. He felt the sun more keenly, felt the breeze tickle his skin to a greater degree than he'd noticed for many years.

"I feel like a different man," he heard the soldier say as he rejoined his fellows.

So do I, thought Vincent, *so do I.*

He noticed yet another difference when he gathered the men around him and dictated the strategy he wished them to follow. Two men to ride with him and Catherine, one right with them, and one far to the rear, to keep watch in the event the knights or Hedgeford's men discovered their departure and sought to follow them. Three of the newly arrived men to stay where they were and keep watch for a day and a night, and then move ahead, so that if the knights or Hedgeford's men approached the main party, two of them could do their best to delay the attackers while one rode ahead to warn the others.

In the event the main party was attacked, they were to simply disperse in different directions—with nothing to defend, there was no need to risk their lives, and spreading out would serve to confuse any pursuers.

"What about the girl, Maisie?" queried one.

"One of you must take charge of her. It should not be onerous tasking, judging by the way you relished her company throughout this journey."

To his surprise, they guffawed where before his comments about the woman had brought naught but carefully blank faces and stiff silence.

He noticed then that the soldiers had crowded around a little more closely as he talked, where before they had stood a respectful distance away. It seemed they nodded with greater approval, that the reserve they'd shown toward him had melted somewhat. Could such a change be attributed to the change of clothes—or had something within him changed as well, that made it evident he cared more about their safety than the successful completion of the task?

"'Tis a good strategy." Rangold set his seal of approval on the plan, and the men nodded, adding a few "ayes" to confirm.

"Go with God, Mr. Kenby," said one. Another clapped him one the shoulder—one quick touch, almost furtive, and then a second, strong and conveying solid goodwill.

None of the men had ever offered him personal good wishes before.

Vincent's throat tightened as he said, "And with all of you."

Maisie led Catherine back to the cart, and once sheltered within stripped the filthy, blood-soaked gown away and redressed Catherine in her own, marginally cleaner serving maid's garb. Catherine stood paralyzed by grief through it all. Maisie sorted through Catherine's belongings and chose a tunic to slip on. While dressing herself, Maisie muttered dire imprecations against every man who had ever taken up arms in battle.

"Treat us no better than a hen staked out to lure a hawk," she grumbled. "Well, I don't intend to sit here waiting for an arrow to pierce my heart. The minute you go off with Mr. Kenby, I'm making for the woods myself."

"I don't think he will allow you to come with us," Catherine said.

"Nor do I want to go with you," Maisie retorted, and then she grimaced. "What I mean is, I would go with you, my lady, but not to where you're bound. I'd sooner strike back toward that Genoa place. Mr. Kenby hustled us from port so fast we didn't get to see much, but it seemed a right nice town."

"Do you not wish to return to England?"

"Why would I want to go back there? Wretched weather, and bound to go hither and yon at the lord's whim. Naught but a lifetime of scrubbing and starving back in England. I shall take my chances here, my lady."

"I wish I could come with you," Catherine said.

"Why don't you?" Maisie plopped onto her knees and gathered Catherine's hands in her own. "We could sneak off right now while they're making their plans."

"I cannot. I promised Serena."

"Aye." Maisie's eyes filled. "Well, my lady, if you should decide to strike out on your own after you finish your task, then mayhap we shall find each other wandering in the woods."

The notion of a woman enjoying the freedom to go where she would, to wander if she willed, was enough to give Catherine new heart. She took greater notice of what Maisie was doing—she was busily folding Catherine's garments to fit as many as possible into the one wool sack Vincent said she could bring.

Maisie's hands, deft and determined, were smoothing the wrinkles from a bit of red silk. It was the nightdress she had secreted in her apron, the thing Vincent had declared too frivolous and unseemly.

"No—you keep that for yourself," Catherine said. "You might have need of it in Genoa."

"You might have greater need," said Maisie. She peered at Catherine with great earnestness. "He could be swayed, my lady. I don't think I'm mistaken—there is a feeling between you two."

"The only feeling between us is enmity."

"No, my lady—the way he looks at you is in the manner of a farmer's stallion coveting the lord's mare, but helpless to claim her on account of the high stout fence between them. An enemy's regard does not carry the same sort of heat." Maisie dangled the red silk. "You could make him change his mind."

Catherine's face burned. She could all too easily imagine herself garbed in that silken wisp, beckoning toward Vincent with an eagerness that would confirm the horrible opinion he had of her.

"Not that way," she said. "Never that way."

She wondered, once their small party entered the shelter of the woods, how long Maisie would wait before making her escape. She whispered a prayer for the girl's safe conduct, and then tried to marshal her wits, for she had a formidable task ahead of her.

The road they'd traveled snaked through the center of a valley, and on either side mountain peaks soared tall toward the sky. The lords of Italy built their mountain fortresses in the manner of barn swallows who hung their nests to the sheer side of a barn. If they had stayed on the road, the castle, walls, and fire smoke of Lucia's husband's demesne would have towered overhead, mocking anyone foolish enough to believe its defenses could be breached. Approaching from the woods, however, meant the castle lay out of sight, for which Catherine gave thanks—otherwise Vincent need only look to see where their destination lay, and she would have had no bargaining power with him at all.

They followed a path worn by deer, a trail so narrow that tall weeds brushed their legs as they rode. Eventually they broke through the trees to a wide meadow, affording a clear view of the mountains.

Catherine turned her head slowly from side to side lest she be caught staring directly toward where they were bound. Far, far ahead she could see the peak that marked the remote village. Years ago Serena had pointed out how one side-jutting protuberance appeared to be the thumbs, and the balance of the mountain the hands of hands joined in prayer. Lucia's village nestled at the joint, sheltered from the worst of the wind, protected from invasion by the mountain.

Catherine would have joined her hands in just that way now, except she didn't dare remove her hands from the reins and saddle. She had not lied to Vincent; she had, as a child, enjoyed rides on a sedate, well-controlled pony. Until she'd ridden pillion with the sergeant, she had never mounted a horse. Never been solely responsible for keeping it under control. This animal seemed huge and loud, often snorting and shaking its head for no reason, so she was somewhat afraid of it.

She was even more afraid of losing her grip and tumbling to the ground. She clung tight with hands and legs and felt the tremors in her legs announcing that she'd overstrained her muscles and would pay the price later. The horse, moving not with calm grace but odd stoppings and startings, seemed confused by the conflicting signs her stance was sending to it. While she preferred this open meadow to the narrow woodland path, she couldn't help worrying that the horse might take it into its head to dash through the tall waving grass—or more dangerously, heave itself over and roll around the way horses sometimes did.

She would not allow herself to think about how this was the easiest part of the journey they faced. She would only think about the promise she had made to Serena. If she could manage the horse through this low-lying terrain, perhaps by the time they reached the mountainous areas Vincent would be so committed to the project that he would not declare an end to it and consign Serena's body to an unhallowed grave.

"How long until we reach the village?" Vincent asked.

He rode behind her, and behind him trailed the horse carrying Serena's body. Catherine was glad she had to look at neither of them.

"It is difficult to say," she said. "Every other time we came, we followed the roads."

"If you would point out our destination, I could perhaps map out a quicker route."

Yes, he would like that—if she pointed toward the mountain and said, "There it is." He had at first demanded to know where they were bound, and in the face of her silence had repeatedly tried various disarming comments, all to no avail. She knew that telling him would allow him to dispose of the body. She deigned not to answer.

She had little energy to dispense upon conversation, anyway. Riding a horse took more strength than she'd imagined, and beyond that, her spirit sagged, wounded beyond measure by Serena's death, compounded by the numbing agony of knowing that her parents' love counted for so little that they would be willing to never see her again. And yet she would not fall to despair. Deep, so deep within that it was threatened with suffocation, was a small flame of hope that by fulfilling her promise to Serena she might find some opportunity to escape her fate. Perhaps Michael's men would find her. Perhaps she could run away while Vincent was not so vigilant.

Just now, her promise to Serena must be fulfilled, so she dare not allow herself to fan that hope lest she be tempted to forget her promise when an opportunity arose. But once Serena was delivered into the hands of her family and consigned to the earth, then, then . . .

She did not know how long they rode, for her aching muscles had gone so numb that she no longer felt pain, or the passage of time. When the meadow ended they traveled through thick-grown woods again, and then through another small meadow, and again into woods. She had no idea how much time had passed when at long last Vincent called out for her to stop, and though she was not conscious of doing anything different the horse came to a standstill. She swayed in the saddle.

"Shall I help you dismount?" Vincent stood at the horse's side. He had not reached for her, but stood there obviously expecting her to appeal for his assistance.

She wanted to dismount on her own. But she found she could not unclench her fingers from the reins, and when she tried to swing her leg up and over the broad back of the horse, it simply hung there, unresponsive.

"It appears I am in need of your help after all," she said.

He grabbed hold of her then, and some of her numbness gave way to a sizzling little thrill. He seemed unaware of the change jolting through her. He tugged at her waist. She remained clamped to the saddle as if she'd been glued in place.

The horse disliked what they did, and attempted to sidle away from Vincent.

"If you would just leave go of the reins, my lady," he suggested.

"I cannot."

"Ah."

With more gentleness than she would have credited him for possessing, he unclamped her fingers one by one. And it could not have been easy for him to do what he did next. Somehow he supported her at the small of her back, and pulled her down off the horse and stood her on the ground the way a child might try to stand a rag doll, holding her carefully lest she topple over. She would have moved away at once, if she could, but her legs were no more responsive to her wishes here on the ground than they'd been on the horse.

"I can stand on my own," she said.

"I doubt it."

Though she heartily wished she could dispute him in this manner, her legs chose that moment to fail her. Her knees gave way; both limbs trembled and then sharp stabbing pains commenced at her feet and spiked their way upward, causing her to cry out involuntarily at the sudden pain.

"Walking will help."

She did not know how he had come to be so knowledgeable about what was ailing her, but she was grateful for it, even though each step he helped her take seemed at first to increase the agony. Back and forth he led her along the narrow trail, a puppeteer guiding his marionette, until gradually she was aware less of the pins-and-needles in her legs and more of the strong arm wrapped around her shoulders at the back, at the other arm curled tightly around her waist from the front.

It could not have been easy for him to walk with her plastered against him. He held her so snug that when he moved his leg, hers moved with it, letting her limbs regain some feeling before taking her full weight. His head bent so close over hers that she could feel his breath stirring her hair.

Another slight trembling shook her, but it was different.

As if he sensed the difference, he stopped, and set her just slightly away from him. He held her at arm's length until reassured she would not pitch headfirst onto the ground. "Do you think you can stand alone now?"

"Yes."

"Walk?"

She thought he meant her to begin walking toward the mountain, now that he'd realized how poorly she rode. "I had hoped we might rest for a moment."

"Of course. I meant are you able to walk into the brush without my help?"

She felt embarrassment creep up from her neck to color her face. She nodded. He nodded, too, and then left her to manage on her own.

Vincent eyed the swift little stream with longing, but reluctantly decided he would have to wait to launder his borrowed garments. He was anxious to make as much progress as possible before night fell. He knew Catherine would not ask for respite.

Vincent did not want to be, but he found himself growing increasingly admiring of her courage.

He had employed every trick of intimidation that he knew upon her. Most people were ridiculously easy to cow, and those who were not usually boasted the blood or the money to defy attempts to control them.

She possessed the blood, but it coursed through a woman's body, which should have rendered her meek and weak. She owned nothing, save for the small sack of clothing and essentials he had tied to the packhorse carrying the courtesan's corpse. He carried a fortune—ostensibly her dowry—but she had no right to claim a single coin for herself. And yet she had levered the one thing she possessed, the knowledge of the location of a mountain stronghold, into a bargain that essentially put him into her hands while she led him God knew where.

He could credit part of her determination to a desire to prolong as long as possible the moment when she was handed over to the cloister. But in his heart he knew that her grief over Serena's death was genuine, that her determination to carry out her deathbed promise was sincere, and that, too, invoked admiration.

She staggered back out onto the trail, moving with obvious difficulty but asking for no assistance and making no attempt to call attention to her plight. She was a mess; she had smoothed her hair back behind her ears but it was in need of brushing. Smudges of fatigue and simple grime darkened her skin. Frays and snags showed where her borrowed gown had battled branches and twigs.

Yet she held herself with pride, and when her glance flicked toward the horse burdened with the body of her friend, her eyes grew moist but no tears fell. She did not, he realized, burst into tears continually as most women he'd known were wont to do, and when she had cried, the tears were shed for Serena, and not for herself.

Another reason to admire her.

The Earl of Ardleswyck, who had only daughters, would have been proud of a son who possessed her qualities. Michael of Hedgeford would have treasured these qualities in a wife. Any man would.

"A little food and water," he said, offering her some things. "And we should not tarry."

"Yes, I know—we must hurry," she said, somewhat

resignedly. She took what he offered and began consuming with neat, delicate motions.

His reason for haste was different from what it had been up until now, he realized. For most of the journey he'd been worried about the maneuvering for favor that was undoubtedly going on behind his back, worried about reclaiming his position. That concern had given way to the immediate threat posed by Hedgeford's forces, and was compounded by the possibility that the knights might double back and attack.

Now, he knew they could not tarry, for doing so would cause her more discomfort.

"When your muscles cool, you will find it less comfortable to ride," he said.

She blanched at that, but finished her water and bread with alacrity. "I am ready," she said.

He could feel her stiffness when he helped her mount. He saw the slight hesitation in her hands before she took the reins and knew when her fingers spasmed that her hands had cramped in protest, but never did she cry out, and never did she beg or plead for more rest or anything to ease her discomforts.

For himself, he resumed the journey with a little less resentment. The woman whose body they transported was no doubt responsible for much of Catherine's strength and integrity, despite the other less admirable qualities she had instilled in her. She deserved the honor of a Christian burial near to her family.

Thirteen

Catherine managed until the foothills.

From afar, the mountains appeared to be tall, forbidding peaks rising straight from the valley. Up close, though, the foothills the Italians called the Apennines, Little Alps, hugged the bases of the taller peaks. These giants were themselves dwarfed farther north by the cloud-piercing peaks of the true Alps.

Tough, twisted trees dotted the foothills, with only scattered clumps of grass and brush managing to poke through the rock-strewn soil. The horse's gait shifted from a relatively smooth walk to a bone-shaking scramble, as it clambered and hitched its hindquarters to maintain footing on the rocky ground. The reins were useless to her; she fell forward against the horse's neck and clung with all her strength, and still almost toppled off.

"Catherine—stop!"

Vincent had never before called her by her name; always, it was the proper "my lady" this, "my lady" that, even when he'd spoken in anger or contempt. Did he think she attempted to escape him at this late moment, or did he call her name out of concern, somehow realizing she no longer controlled her mount?

"I cannot!"

She did not think he could hear her over the clatter of hooves against rock and the horse's loud chuffing. The horse made one more clumsy leap, and she started to slide sideways, and knew she would never manage to stop her fall. But suddenly he was there. He'd spurred his horse alongside hers, so close that she fell against him instead of to the ground. He grabbed the reins to bring them both to a halt, and then steadied her back into her saddle.

"Get down before you break your neck."

No polite "my lady," no worried "Catherine." Just a curt order issued by a man whose whole demeanor conveyed annoyance. She slumped over the horse's neck, while a terrible trembling shook her. She supposed it was a reaction to her near-brush with death, and she was not altogether certain that he'd done her a favor by stopping her fall.

"I don't care about my neck."

"And I don't care about delivering your friend's body to where you promised to take her. We can abandon this witless task. Just say the word. I'll bury the body here and now."

He studied her with cool dispassion, daring her, she realized, to admit she could not do what she had promised to do.

There were advantages to admitting defeat. If they buried Serena here, and she kept to herself the location of the mountain village, he would have no choice but to take them back to the road to resume their journey. Michael's men might still find her.

But she could not follow the course most advantageous to her without turning her back on the promise she had made. Serena had lost so much in her own life, the love of the one man she had truly loved, the chance for children of her own body . . . She had asked nothing of the child of the man she loved except for this one thing, and Catherine had looked into her dying eyes and promised "yes, yes." She could not abandon that promise now, within sight of the place she'd promised to reach, even if carrying on reduced her chances of rescue.

Forcing herself to sit upright once more, she shook off her malaise and nudged the horse's side with her heels. But Vincent did not release his grip on the reins. The horse, no doubt as tired as she, whinnied a protest as it danced sideways, unable to go ahead as she wished, unable to escape Vincent's hold.

She almost fell again.

He came off his horse so quickly that she knew his legs had not gone numb, that his hands had not cramped into claws. He quieted her fidgeting horse with soothing murmurs, and then before she realized what he was up to, he pulled her down off the animal's back.

He tried to help her stand as he had done earlier, but this time too much strength had seeped from her, and to her horrified embarrassment she knew she would collapse into a heap right there on the rocks.

He shifted her, and then lifted her, so that he carried her across his arms the way she'd been told amorous knights carried off their ladies.

But he did so muttering curses and imprecations, and after scowling first at the setting sun and then at their comfortless surroundings, he lowered her to the ground and propped her against a tree trunk.

"I am not fit to kiss her hem," said Catherine, distressed beyond belief to find herself virtually unable to move.

Vincent cast her the indulgent, fearful look one usually directed toward idiots. He probably thought she'd gone off her head.

"People often chastise themselves when bereaved by a sudden death."

"She is not dead!" Catherine said scornfully.

"Then whose hem are you not fit to kiss?"

"The old queen's. Eleanor's." He still did not seem to understand why she was so disappointed in herself. "Eleanor has traveled the world on horseback—though once, she was forced to ride in a litter. At this very moment she is said to traverse Italy on the back of a mule. And I . . . I cannot manage one day without almost breaking my neck."

"You admire Eleanor? I've heard her to be difficult, obstinate, and opinionated."

"A man would think so. I admire her more than I can say."

"Well, even Queen Eleanor would have had to stop sooner or later. Stay there," he commanded, and if she had any strength she would have laughed at the lunacy of his believing she could force her numb legs to totter even one single step.

"Is aught amiss, Mr. Kenby?" The soldiers who guarded their flank caught up to them.

"We shall stop here for the night." He made a motion with his hands. "You, go back and keep watch. And you, help me with the horses."

The soldier who remained helped Vincent unsaddle the horses. Working together, they unlashed Serena's body and maneuvered it—respectfully, Catherine was relieved to see—over to a large boulder where they laid it gently.

Vincent came to her, and handed her a bit of bread

he'd pulled from one of the packs. "The horses need water, and I must confer with both of these men about our plans for the night. We will return soon."

She wasn't hungry, but she tore off a bite-sized chunk of the tough bread and made herself chew. She'd learned her lesson about losing her strength, losing her will, by not eating.

Bread or no bread, he had no need to worry she would try to escape—even if she could run, she could not leave Serena's body lying there for the wolves, and she certainly could not manage a horse well enough to carry both her and Serena.

If she ever had a daughter, she would teach her to ride and use a sword. She would entrust her with an allowance and teach her the value of money. Men did themselves no favors by keeping women weak and helpless. Women never suspected the depths of their ignorance until they were faced with situations they could not conquer, all because they had been denied the chance to learn.

If she ever had a daughter . . . but she never would.

Vincent's heart still hammered, his whole being still shook, from the fright that had gripped him when she'd started to fall from her horse.

He'd been harsh and curt with her to cover how profoundly affected he'd been. His was not the panic of a man who feared he would fail in his assignment. His heart-stopping terror sprang solely from believing he had lost her.

Lost her, when she was not his, and never could be. And words came hard when a man waged an internal battle pitting what he must do against what he wanted to do.

He heard a stream splashing just out of sight. Dousing himself in cold mountain water might clear his head. Better yet, if the stream was deep enough, he could strip naked and immerse himself, and hope that he would turn numb. He could do that, and tend to the cleaning of his filthy borrowed clothes at the same time.

First, he must make arrangements for the night.

A quick look at his fellow travelers told him they were unfit for guard duty. He felt a pang of conscience, remembering how he'd goaded and pushed all of his men. The idea he'd had of letting them sleep in shifts had not progressed beyond the first pair of men before all his plans had gone awry with the arrival of Serena.

He would have to insist they rest in shifts now, too, though they both looked near to collapsing. They'd started a small campfire, and both hunkered down around it staring glumly at the dancing flames.

"You can decide between yourselves who will take first watch with me," Vincent said.

Their glumness deepened into scowl. They glanced at each other, but neither of them offered to stand guard with Vincent.

"Why two guards, Mr. Kenby?" ventured one after a long pause.

He reminded himself that he'd regretted his earlier heedlessness of their rest and well-being, and so rather than issuing an order to do as he said, he explained himself. "One of us must keep watch on the trail, and one must guard the lady, lest she try to escape."

"Where would she go?"

"Aye. Even if she tried to run, we could catch up to her soon enough."

"Not if she stumbled straight into the arms of one of our pursuers." He did not delve more deeply into an explanation—they knew he had been charged to deliver her to Saint Justinius, and it was enough for them to believe that if she were abducted he would fail in his mission.

They did not have to know that the thought of her falling into another man's hands roused a jealousy within him so severe that he'd never suspected he was capable of it.

"We could make do with one man, if she promised to stay put," grumbled the man. "Seems to me she's a lady of her word, Mr. Kenby."

He glanced toward where he'd left Catherine. She sat as she'd been placed, with her back braced against a tree. Her hair was a lank, snarled mass of gold, her dress nearly in tatters, her eyes red-rimmed but no tears spilled. She paid no attention to them; her regard was fixed upon Serena's remains, and her lips moved—he could not hear her, but could recognize that she formed the words of the Hail Mary. Her hands lay still in her lap, open, as if she lacked the strength to fold them together in an attitude of prayer.

He could understand why the soldiers thought she lacked the spirit to escape. But he knew how quickly a little rest could fortify a body, knew how bright was the spirit that burned within her.

So, too, would a few hours of sleep let his men recuperate. He need only ask for her word, and believe she would honor it.

It came hard to him, accepting a person's word. Much of the work he did for his lord was occasioned when someone failed to honor a promise, or broke a bargain sealed with a handshake. He'd learned while growing up that adults seldom meant what they said, and nothing he'd experienced afterward had altered that impression.

He had not been exactly circumspect about keeping his own word. In his position of service to the earl, he thought nothing of promising one thing yet doing another if it better suited his lord's purposes.

And yet . . . his instincts told him the soldier was right. Catherine would honor her word, if given. He wondered if she would trust him to honor his.

It had never mattered to him before, that someone would trust him in a matter not bound by law.

"I will ask her," he said to the men.

He dallied, first stopping to rummage through a pack and withdraw her cloak, so she might either lie upon it or use it as a cover if the night turned chill. He found other items within that she might have need of—a comb, some lengths of ribbon. He took the things to her, and dropped them onto her lap. Then he, who prided himself on arranging words and covering contingencies, managed only to blurt out the proposal in the roughest fashion.

She listened without comment until he'd finished, and then cocked her head. "You mean, you want me to swear I will not try to run away from you, and in return you will promise to stop threatening to abandon Serena?"

He felt the sting of shame to be reminded of how he had attempted to bully her.

"Aye."

She did not hesitate for a moment. "I promise."

"Do you want to take a moment to think it through,

my lady? I know you are tired, and sometimes exhaustion leads us to make mistakes."

"There is nothing to think about, Mr. Kenby. I gave my word to Serena, and I will do whatever it takes to keep that promise. You may rest assured I have given my word to you with equal intent."

He had to restrain himself from pressing and probing, and when trying to determine why he was so dissatisfied with her easy capitulation, it came to him: he had wanted to hear, from her own lips, the words *I trust you, Vincent.*

He left her before he embarrassed himself by asking.

He told himself, as he walked back to the campfire, that only a fool would weaken himself in the eyes of another by asking to hear such words. But a part of him mocked this sensible withdrawal, and taunted that the real reason he did not ask her was because he feared she would laugh, would say that of all the people on this earth, she trusted him least of all.

As she had every reason to do.

"'Tis set," he told the soldiers. "I will stand first watch myself."

The sergeants didn't even bother with food. They stretched out near to the fire and in no time their snores punctuated the campfire's crackling.

Catherine had curled away from the tree and wadded the cloak under her head as a pillow. She was turned away from him, so he could not see if she slept or continued to pray for Serena.

He left the camp and took up a watchful position overlooking the valley they had so recently traveled.

The moon cast a silver glow over the verdant growth, bright enough that he could see the tree branches waving in the breeze, the meadow grasses bending in the wind. Providing no clouds came to cover the moon, he would have a clear view of anyone who sought to follow them.

An hour passed. Two. The soldiers would not complain if he woke one of them now and asked for relief. He let them sleep, for despite his exhaustion he knew he could never escape his thoughts long enough to find oblivion.

He had become a mass of contradiction. His life seemed all of a piece up until the moment he'd disembarked from the ship in Genoa. He'd been Vincent Kenby, upstart farmer's son, secure in his beliefs, strong in his commitment, certain of the way he must act and think to hold everyone at bay lest they probe— and find—any weaknesses.

The port had been ringed with the remnants of an ancient Roman aqueduct, and to reach Serena's palazzo they'd had to pass right beneath one of the massive stone arches. The Vincent Kenby who'd walked into the port side of that archway seemed to be a different man entirely from the man who had passed through the far side.

He wasn't fanciful enough, or fool enough, to believe walking through an archway would change him so profoundly.

He was surrounded by the same men who had started this journey with him. Set upon the same task that had sent him here. The only thing that was different was the presence of Catherine of Ardleswyck. She with her glorious eyes, her unshakable pride, her gentle smiles.

Temptress. Seductress . . .

The words no longer carried any weight.

Something had dulled those warnings, rendering them toothless. Here, with the clear eye of the moon shedding its light upon the world, he had to admit Catherine had said nothing, done nothing, that would tempt men into foolery. He alone had been ravaged by need, by lust, virtually from the moment of meeting her, but nobody else appeared to be similarly afflicted.

He was no nearer to figuring out the mystery when one of the sergeants stumbled to his post.

"You did not call us to take our turn," he said, yawning and stretching. " 'Twas kind of you, Mr. Kenby. Grab yourself a bit of sleep now."

Vincent nodded, oddly touched that the man had called him kind. He found himself a grassy spot midway between the embers of the campfire and where Catherine rested. Sleep eluded him, for every time he closed his eyes he was plagued with the image of her, of knowing that she slept near to hand, with her head pillowed on her hands, breathing softly in the moonlight. He understood, then, the curiosity she'd shown in studying him while he'd slept in the cart, for he wanted nothing more than to sit next to her and watch her sleep.

He remembered the stream, then.

He followed the rushing and splashing sounds and heaved a sigh of relief when he found more than a stream—the sounds he'd heard marked a small waterfall cascading into a wide pool that promised to be deep. He decided a thorough dousing was in order.

Her knees ached. She stooped to peer through the narrow viewing window. "Catherine of Ardleswyck! I come for Catherine of Ardleswyck!

And for the first time ever, the rectangle expanded, telling her that she had always taken too narrow a view of her life. She saw the whole of the chapel on the other side. Striding across the marble floor, calling her name, came the man she loved, soaked through from traveling through the rain to find her. She reached toward him. He caught her hand and bent low to kiss her hand. Water dripped from his hair to cool her skin as he pressed firm, commanding lips into her palm. As if he branded her as his, this man she loved.

Vincent.

Catherine sat bolt upright, yanked from her dream by . . . she did not know.

She winced a little, since the sudden movement had taxed limbs grown stiff and cold. Her heart raced, but not from discomfort. She felt a sweet, mellow joy, a sense of rightness that told her she had admitted in dreams that which she would not allow herself to even think while awake.

She loved Vincent.

Impossible.

She had fallen prey to the very danger Serena, wise Serena, had warned her against. Catherine clutched her head between her hands, wishing she could squeeze out the memory of that dream. She could not love Vincent Kenby. There was nothing about him to love.

Her head told her so. Her body, it seemed, had other ideas. He could set her aflame with a single glance, could rob her of sense with a hot look or his rare smile. He talked to her, with words she knew he'd never revealed to another, and he honored her promises with vows of his own.

Her head throbbed with confusion. She worked her fingers through her hair, grimacing at the knots, the tangles. Perhaps dreaming of Vincent, of his wet hair, had reminded her of the sorry state of her own. She had never been a vain woman, but did take care of her appearance. She glanced toward the heavens; she did not know how to judge the hours by the moon's position, but there was no lightening of the sky to hint dawn approached.

Once they resumed traveling the next day, she would have no time for grooming. Perhaps she could go now to the stream she heard rushing beyond the trees, and at the very least wash her hair.

The moon lit her way through the trees, around the rocks, toward the splashing water.

She thought at first that she must still be dreaming, for much of the splashing came from the man who stood waist-deep in the middle of a woodland pool, facing a small waterfall. He plunged his head into the rushing fall and held it there for a long moment before pulling back and shaking the water away. His hair, just as she remembered, just as she had dreamed, fell slick and dark against his head. The water dripped down his neck, down his back, trails and droplets of water against his bare skin. Bare, for he wore no clothes.

His tunic and chausses hung from a branch, and they shed droplets that glistened like crystals in the moonlight. His boots lay off to the side, one standing upright, the other toppled against it.

Surprise and fascination held her motionless as a statue; she did not even remember to breathe. He shoveled another double handful of water from the stream, and tilted his head back to let it cascade over his face when he, too, seemed to freeze in position. The water glittered like ice as it splashed over him, and he moved as if intending to do it again, when somehow he sensed her presence. He turned to see her standing there, watching him.

Neither spoke for a very long moment.

"My lady," he said eventually. "You have caught me in an uncomfortable position."

Not nearly so uncomfortable as she found herself, Catherine thought. She felt helpless to look away. She'd never seen a man without his shirt. She'd never realized how sculpted, how ridged a man was shaped. She'd never realized that the chest hairs Serena had told her about would grow in the shape of a vee, copying the shape of his torso.

"'Tis your good fortune I am not one of the pursuers you are always guarding against," she said, striving for levity amid the awkwardness.

She succeeded. He smiled, and she wished she had simply turned and run away from him rather than let that bright happy flash from him shaft straight into her heart.

"I believe we both had the same idea," she said.

She raised her comb, and went to work on one of the knots in her hair, giving the task far more attention than it required.

"If you would hand me my chausses and turn away while I don them, I would be grateful."

"Oh! Of course."

The garments were cold, but no colder, she supposed, than the water in which he was immersed. She tossed the wet chausses and turned away as soon as he caught them.

She concentrated furiously upon her knots, welcoming each painful tug as a slap reminding her to stay facing away. She wanted to turn and look at all of him as he forded his way out of the pool.

It seemed to take him an inordinately long time to dress, for she had finished with her hair when he said, a little breathlessly, "May I help you with something, my lady?"

"I intend to wash my hair. Nothing more."

"Are you able to manage?"

"I have been washing my hair all my life, Mr. Kenby."

That wasn't exactly the full truth, for she had always had a maid to help her.

"I forgot to provide you with soap."

"I did not think to pack any."

He rummaged through some things that lay on the bank and handed her a small clay bowl. "I have a little left. Not sweet-scented, but it will do the job."

She dipped a finger into the soft soap pooled at the base of the bowl. She sniffed; it was clean, plain, and yet evocative of him.

"Take care, for the eddies swirl strong and the pool is deep."

"I do not intend to go into the water. Just kneel at the edge."

"Banks are notoriously treacherous."

"I am surefooted."

By then she stood at the bank. She intended to drop quickly to her knees and make quick work of her hair. She found to her dismay that her stiffened limbs would not obey her orders.

For once, his stubbornness worked to her advantage, for he had obviously ignored her assurances that she required no assistance. He stood at her side. He cupped her elbow.

"Please indulge me. I promise not to hover over you," he said.

With his support, she was able to kneel. He stepped away, leaving her to do what she would. She set the soap within easy reach. But when she tried bending forward she could not prevent crying out. Her hips, her waist, overly strained from riding, protested the movement. Surprised by the pain, she lurched clumsily. Her knees dug into the muddy bank, and her hands landed in the shallows. Her head was mere inches above the water, but she knew she would never be able to bend her neck at the required angle without the rest of her body screaming in protest.

She had never cried in front of him, had taken pride in hiding her inner wounds. But now . . . with her heart all aflutter from realizing she loved this man, with her body pulsing with appreciation for the sight he'd made, naked in the stream . . . with so much of her in turmoil—the futility of finding herself on all fours like a dog, and not being able to wash her hair, broke her control.

She made no sound, and she splashed a little water on her face to cover the tears, but somehow he knew.

He knelt beside her, heedless that his newly washed chausses would be ground into the mud. He pressed one hand against her back, hard, which somehow eased the pain, and lay his other between her shoulders. With that hand he made small circular motions which loosened her stiff muscles. Heavenly. Perversely, her tears increased.

"Those who ride every day soon forget how hard the body complains when learning the skill," he said.

"I just wanted to wash my hair." She hoped he didn't realize she was blubbering like a babe. "I must needs bend forward just a little more."

His hand stilled. "Very well."

He shifted, and gripped her hard around both shoulders.

The thought flitted through her mind that he could so easily pitch her forward and hold her under. Be rid of his promise to bury Serena, be rid of her and the whole unpleasant business. And yet that doubt was gone as quickly as it had come, as if her mind had felt obliged to consider the other side before wholeheartedly placing complete trust in him.

She dipped the forward portion of her head into the water, and then one side, then the other. His hold altered; he curved one arm under her, above the waist, just below her breasts, and then she felt his other hand gentle at her neck. He lifted the mass of her hair to the side so that when next she bent toward the water, most of her hair got wet. His fingers stroked her skin as he captured trailing strays. She shivered.

"The water is cold," he said.

"Yes."

She tried to curve her arms so she could massage the water into her scalp, but again the stiffness defeated her.

He sighed. And then he changed position again without letting go his hold, until he sat on the bank next to her, his bare feet planted in the water. She was draped inelegantly over his thigh, which felt hard as a tree trunk and yet at the same time the most wonderfully comfortable place she'd ever rested. He kept one hand on her back, as if to hold her still, and she did not know what he meant to do with the other until she felt the cool glop of soap on her crown.

"Hang on," he said, giving her permission to grip onto his leg as he let loose of her. His strong fingers began working the soap through her hair, into her scalp.

She thought she might faint from the sensation.

And she was glad that the frigid water provided such an excellent excuse for the tremors that shook through her as his thigh bunched beneath her breast, as his hands cupped her head and trailed the length of her hair.

It ended too soon. Ended with a thorough dousing of her head with cold water.

He helped her to stand. He helped her find her comb, and from his own things drew a length of sacking for her to use as a towel.

"Can you find your way back to the campsite?" he asked, not quite looking at her, but off to the side, as if marking the path she was to follow.

"Will you not return with me?"

"Not just yet. I need . . . these chausses could use another scrubbing."

She nodded, and left him, though with each step she ached to turn around and ask him to touch her all over the way he'd done with the washing of her hair.

But she heard a loud splashing and knew he'd gone back into the water.

Vincent had managed an hour or so of sleep, enough to take the sharpest edge off his exhaustion. He'd paid dearly for the relief, though, for his dreams had been haunted by the memory of Catherine held so tight within his grip, of his hands moving over her with a freedom that should only be claimed by a husband.

So little . . . he'd but washed her hair. And yet even in his sleep he felt its heavy silk slip through his fingers, felt the tender skin of her neck . . . He woke in a cold sweat, his body aroused, demanding he find her and claim more from her than he had any right to take.

He put those thoughts out of his mind and studied the rock-studded hillside they would have to climb.

The soldiers, rested but just as glum as before, frowned at the terrain.

"We're doomed," said one.

"Aye. She cannot ride well enough, and no woman could scale this path on foot, even were she not half lame."

They turned as one when Catherine came toward them. She moved with care, obviously still stiff and sore from the previous day in the saddle. Vincent knew that the soldiers had spoken the truth: Catherine's horsemanship was nonexistent, and in her current condition she could no more climb these slopes on foot than he could leap from a tree and fly.

What to do? She could not ride. She could not walk. They could not remain there and let her recuperate without risking discovery. On a more delicate note, they could not tarry long without consigning the body of Serena Monteverde to the ground.

What to do? He could think of only one option, and after the way his senses had flown from being with her the night before, the thought filled him with dread.

"Mr. Kenby?" asked a soldier.

"Make ready to leave."

She seemed unaware that they studied her so closely and remarked her painful progress. She tottered to her horse and placed her hand upon the saddle as if she meant to mount the animal on her own.

"Not that one," Vincent said. "The other."

She glanced back at him quizzically, and even that

small movement roused a little line of pain on her forehead. A slight shudder passed through her, and then she took a few slow steps from her horse to the packhorse.

"Not that one," he repeated. "The other."

"Your horse?"

"He's young and strong, and best suited of them all to carry two."

"Carry two?"

She seemed determined not to understand what he meant. "You will ride with me."

"Pillion."

"No. That requires more skill than you have shown, and requires more strength than you can spare just now. You will sit in front of me," he said.

"No."

He had promised not to threaten her with the abandonment of Serena's body, but what he had to say was only the truth and not a threat. "She must be put in the ground within a day, at the most two. We must move quickly, and that means you cannot ride alone."

Catherine's lips tightened. She did not have to answer. She took the stiff, jerky steps toward the side of his horse. He had won this battle.

But never had victory felt more like defeat. The moment he levered himself into the saddle behind her, he knew he was in trouble.

She felt so small, so fragile.

She tried, for the first quarter hour, to hold herself away from him. If she thought this would reduce their contact she was mistaken, for the way proved treacherous footing for a horse, and Vincent continually had to hold her close to prevent her from falling. Eventually she gave up her stiff-backed seat and rested against him, lightly.

Better for her; worse for him.

His arms encircled her. His legs enclosed her from hips to thigh. His senses swam, filled with her, her warmth, her suppleness. The smell of his own soap came from her hair. Although she did not obviously employ her seductress's skills, his body responded to hers as a man's body will.

"How much farther?" he asked, his voice strained.

She hesitated.

"My lady, I would remind you that I gave my word we would see Serena to her sister. There is no reason for you to withhold the direction from me now."

And still she hesitated. In the past, he would have flared with anger over her refusal, but now it simply hurt to think she did not, after all, trust him.

But then she lifted her arm and pointed toward the right, toward where a large peak and its stony offshoot formed a shape somewhat like hands joined in prayer.

"There," she said. "Right where the thumb joins the hand. And now"—she paused and made a little hic-cupping sound—"now everything is yours. I have nothing else you want."

He held her tight, his senses swimming, and dared not tell her how very wrong she was.

Fourteen

They started off on the same course Catherine would have chosen, but after long hours of travel, Vincent struck off in a direction that seemed to head away from Lucia's village, rather than toward it.

"Are you trying to prolong our journey, Mr. Kenby?" she asked.

"No."

The rumble from his chest when he spoke felt delightful against her ear. She wondered if he noticed anything when she talked, or if his body, which seemed so much harder than her own, was impervious to sound and vibration.

"We were almost there before you turned away." She could not stay silent on the matter; something within demanded to know if he deliberately sought a way to grant them a little more time together.

"We're closer now," he said, dashing that hope.

Sure enough, they skirted a wide boulder and the new vista presented showed the twisting trail that led up to the stronghold.

She had to bite her tongue to keep from crying "No."

No, she did not want this journey to end.

But end it would. In less than an hour they would dismount in the courtyard and she might never again

feel Vincent Kenby's arms around her. She nestled
more fully against him, something she had resisted at
first and he had seemed to repel, but as the miles had
passed beneath their horse's hooves they had both
made accommodations.

She regretted now every moment she had held herself away from him. Her stiffness had eased as his
warmth seeped into her. She was glad she had washed
her hair, for sometimes his face brushed against her
head and she preferred he find her soft and clean, although he could not have faulted her if she had been
otherwise. She loved the way she felt surrounded by
him, and yet not restrained.

She rested her head against his breast, and relished
the way the sun struck her exposed cheek. Her other
cheek lay cushioned by the springy hair lying beneath
his homespun tunic, but even so she could feel how
hard, how firm was his chest. And despite so many layers of clothes and man, she could hear the strong,
steady thud of his heart against her ear.

Sometimes, when she moved her bottom to relieve
a posture held too long, his heartbeat quickened. Hers,
as well, and not from her slight exertion.

Their hearts beat in accord, and even the near silence in which they traveled came about naturally, not
from either of them forbidding the other to speak.
Much as she enjoyed hearing his voice, conversation
held the virtue of passing away the time, and she desired nothing more than to savor every minute she had
with him. What an improbable change of heart!

Could it mean, possibly, that he might have experienced an equally confusing change of heart regarding
her?

Serena had told her that most of the problems between men and women came about when one or the other—and sometimes both—held to their pride rather than bare their heart. Catherine had never truly understood, but she did now. It seemed such a simple thing, to ask a man if he would like to keep her with him, and yet doing so meant revealing a love so new and impossible that she scarcely dared believe in it herself. If he laughed, if he repudiated her . . .

That was her pride speaking, just as Serena had claimed it would do.

"What if we just kept riding?" Catherine asked, barely above a whisper. "What if we rode on and on?"

She almost hoped he had not heard, and yet she waited breathlessly for how he might answer her. She waited so long that she thought perhaps he had not heard her bare her hopes after all.

"You must know that is impossible," he said at last. His voice, too, held little more than a hint of its usual strength. If not for the vibration against her ear, if not for the coldness that pierced her heart, she could have pretended he hadn't spoken.

She had offered herself. He had rejected. There was nothing more to say between them.

Serena had been wrong about this.

She gathered in the shattered remnants of the pride she had abandoned. She straightened her spine, ashamed of the abandon she'd shown in cuddling against him. He was not the betrothed to whom she owed her heart, but rather her father's lackey sent to lock her away. What a fool she had been, mooning about heartbeats, bemoaning the closeness of their destination.

This journey could not end soon enough.

They gained the trail, and though each twist and

turn was familiar to her, she was so blinded by unshed tears that she saw nothing.

He tensed, his arms tightening around her, his legs clamping more closely around her hips, and despite knowing the movements meant nothing to him, her woman's body welcomed the slight possession.

"Someone approaches."

She had to blink wetness from her eyes to see, but before she made out what had set him on alert, he relaxed. "'Tis only a villein, gathering wood."

Catherine leaned forward to see around the horse's neck, and then she laughed. "Look again, Mr. Kenby. He is a sentry. We are very near the village."

The peasant held a mattock, the usual blunt tool designed for lopping dead branches from trees. He also carried a long knife thrust through his rope belt, commonly carried by anyone who intended to hack through tough bark. Its dull finish did not even reflect the sun, in the way of metalware long past the ability to hold a sharp edge. A net lay stretched out on the road. A few lengths of wood lay within it, with plenty of room for more that would be foraged by the peasant.

Catherine recognized the man, though. She knew he possessed fighting skills any knight would envy. The tools, cleverly smoothed in secret ways the Italians had learned from the Saracens, could slice through a man's throat without pause, could sever a man's hand from his wrist as easily as cleaving an apple in two. That net could be pulled out from under the few chunks of wood with one swift tug, swung around the peasant's head, and flung over an intruder so quickly that he would be immobilized before he realized what had happened.

He approached them with the fawning shuffle adopted by any villein in the presence of his betters, so convincingly that she wondered if Vincent noted the sharp intelligence gleaming in his eyes, if he realized the hands twisting his cap near his waist meant he could grasp his knife in an instant.

She knew him. He knew her. If she called out for help, he would send that deadly blade straight toward Vincent Kenby's heart, and she need only duck to the side to avoid the killing blow.

But she had promised . . . and even more than the loathing she would feel at herself for breaking her word, something within her rebelled at the notion of Vincent Kenby falling dead at her feet.

"Roldano!" she called out a greeting to the man.

The villein went still. He squinted suspiciously, and then a huge smile of recognition brightened his sun-darkened face.

"Signorina!"

The hail, the acknowledgment; she need only ask Roldano in his own tongue to help her and he would.

Vincent dismounted. He stretched. He yawned. She knew he feigned ease by the tight grip he used on the bridle and the stiffness of his shoulders. She remembered those strong fingers soothing her, rubbing her back, cupping her head; she remembered those shoulders bared to the moonlight. She could never speak the words that would end his life. She said nothing as Roldano approached.

He spouted forth a torrent of words, waving his hands from her to Vincent to the body tied to the pack-horse, and gesticulated even more wildly when the soldiers who accompanied them drew close.

He cried unashamedly when she told him that they had brought Serena home for eternal rest.

Vincent stood silent through it all. Roldano wiped the tears from his eyes and busied himself with releasing the packhorse from their little caravan so he might lead the animal himself. Only then did Vincent glance up at her.

"I thought I might understand more of what he said. He does not speak the same as those in Genoa."

"Each village develops its own twists on the language. It is not unusual that a Roman cannot understand a Sicilian, and many Italians from the large cities cannot understand the people from these small villages at all."

"It is the same in England. Some of the country speaking Anglish, some Norman French, some a godawful mixture of both."

They discussed this topic, which was of no interest to Catherine, as neutrally as a teacher and student might do when discussing the vagaries of language.

The strain in Vincent's expression did not ease.

"Does it embarrass you, to be unable to understand a language you have never heard?"

She caught the tiniest flicker of acknowledgment in his eyes, but he did not admit to embarrassment. "They could say anything to you, and I would not know."

It was bad enough that this conclusion to their closeness affected him not at all; it was worse that he would choose this moment to reveal he truly did not trust her to keep her word.

"I promised that I would not thwart you."

"I am not worried on that account." He said it with utmost sincerity, and something warm and fine bloomed in her heart. "I would like to object if they hold you to blame for Serena's death."

Her treacherous heart softened toward him once more.

He made a clucking sound to gain the horse's attention and tightened his grip on the bridle. She thought—she hoped!—he would jump back into the saddle, but he did not. She rode alone as he set off on foot, leading the horse, following Roldano.

Vincent deliberately allowed the peasant to put a great deal of distance between them. He told himself that the slow pace was to accommodate Catherine's lack of riding skill. Or to spare Catherine the ordeal of breaking the news of Serena's death herself.

A little voice inside him whispered, *These may be the last moments you will ever spend alone with her.* Already his arms missed her shape, his chest missed her weight, and if he meant to retain some peace of mind, he could not acknowledge at all what his lower reaches missed.

The villein who led the packhorse would deliver Serena to her family. Catherine could rest assured that her promise had been kept. His must now take precedence.

His lawyer's mind probed the agreement they had made. She had given her word to not try to escape or ask sanctuary, but within a short while she would be surrounded by people who knew her, who perhaps loved her, who would be sympathetic to what she had to tell them. He could not explain why he believed so implicitly that she would not break her word to him. But these villagers were not bound by her oath.

Once they knew the whole story, they would blame him as the instigator of the circumstances that had led to Serena's death. It would not matter that he had been carrying out his lord's orders. Nor would the lord's orders hold any sway in this remote place—the Earl of Ardleswyck exerted no more influence here than would Vincent himself.

Here, he thought, Catherine's station meant nothing—she carried no noble Italian blood in her veins. In a way, he and Catherine were equals here.

By great force of will, he drove the notion from his mind to concentrate on his duty.

He ought to turn them about at this very moment and race away from the village as quickly as her lack of riding skills would allow. His brain ordered *Do it!* and yet he kept placing one foot in front on the other, moving up the mountain.

Here, they were equals.

Again, he shook the thought away. He had a very good reason for not turning back. Hedgeford's men might have sniffed out their route, and could at this very minute be patrolling the road they'd left behind. And those mercenaries, he must never make light of the threat they posed . . .

He knew in his heart that neither of those reasons kept him heading toward the village that might take Catherine away from him.

The trail curved, showing him the junction between the two sections of mountain that formed the praying hand. A fine stone arch bridged the gap. A sentry stood atop the arch, and he called out something and was answered by another whom Vincent could not see.

"You were right," he said to Catherine in the flat,

almost formal way they'd adopted. "This place possesses formidable defenses."

"Difficult to breach," Catherine agreed.

But not impossible. Someone who knew that the villein gathering wood was a sentry, someone who knew how many men guarded this arch, might succeed in piercing through. Catherine held such knowledge. Hedgeford's forces did not. He seized on that notion; it provided a solid reason for not turning back.

The trail did not widen for a long time. They walked between sheer walls of stone for a good quarter hour before the path widened suddenly to reveal the center of the village.

A courtyard paved with stone boasted a water well, not a dug well but a stone-lined pool. It brimmed with fresh sparkling water fed by a stream that tumbled down the mountainside and was coaxed by troughs into the pool. Across the courtyard from the pool a tight cluster of buildings clung somehow to the side of the mountain, piled one against another, in the way Vincent noticed Italians favored their homes. At the farthest curve of the courtyard, a narrow path snaked upward to a stone castle that seemed to grow straight out of the mountain.

Wherever earth erupted through gaps in the stone, someone had planted small clumps of wheat, vegetable vines, fruit trees, olive trees, up the mountain and in all directions, as far off as he could see.

Vincent had not heard anyone call out their arrival, and yet in no time a somber crowd gathered and formed a semicircle around the packhorse holding Serena's corpse. Loud sobs and wailing, punctuated by words he could understand—ancient prayers—echoed against the natural enclosure.

Some of the cries and sobs were directed toward Catherine. *Carina,* they called to her, *carina,* reaching toward her, but they did not break rank to approach her.

The castle gate creaked open. Roldano came through, his head bowed, his hands twisting his cap. Next, a woman, supported on either side by a man gripping her arm, lurched through the opening. They made a slow, somehow dignified procession down the twisted path. The woman certainly would have fallen without their support. Tears streamed so heavily that she could not possibly see. Vincent had never witnessed such an open display of grief.

Catherine cried out when she saw the woman, and before he could help her she scrambled off the horse. He started to follow, certain that her own physical woes would cause her to stumble, and she did—but straight into the woman's arms.

They clung together, crying, stroking each other's hair. The sight and sound seemed to serve as permission for the others to intensify their own weeping and wailing until the whole mountain reverberated with this manifestation of sorrow.

Vincent did not know how long ago Serena had left this village, and still they mourned her passing as if she had lived there every day of her life, and died as one of them.

If he should die on this task, he could not think of one person who would remark in even the slightest way on his passing.

Vincent had retreated once more behind his invisible shield. She could see him as clearly as ever, but it was as though a vast distance separated them, as though they had never touched, never talked, never laughed together.

He stood apart from the sorrowing villagers, and she recalled how often she had seen him standing just so, an observer at the edge of life.

"How did it happen?" Lucia asked, drawing Catherine's attention away from him.

"She died because of me." Choking on her tears, stumbling over the words as she sought to explain, Catherine began to tell Lucia what had transpired in Genoa. But mindful of Vincent's uncertain grasp of the language, she switched midway through to English, which she knew Lucia understood.

Lucia listened without comment.

"Vincent—the man who brought me here—is not to blame," Catherine ended.

Lucia gave her a very strange look, and when she did speak did so in her own tongue, deliberately ignoring Catherine's lead. "You would defend a man who means to do you so ill?"

"At the instigation of my father," Catherine reminded her.

"The hand that fits the last nail finishes the door," Lucia said somewhat enigmatically. And then her expression hardened with determination, and when she spoke again, she did so in English. "You are not responsible for my sister's death. Nor is this *man,*" she spat the word contemptuously, "who seeks to make something of you that you are not. The one who attacked a defenseless house is the one who killed my sister."

"The forces attacking the palazzo came for me,"

Catherine said. "They serve my betrothed. Even now they scour the countryside, searching for me."

Lucia's eyes narrowed.

"You and this Vincent shall stay here while our men make a search of the road. If we find those responsible, they will pay."

"We cannot stay," said Vincent. "The lady and I must continue our journey. Her father, my liege, has ordered it so."

Lucia gave him a humorless smile. "Sirrah, you are now in my domain and subject to *my* orders. Your English lord's whims mean nothing to me."

Vincent would object. He would lash out with a quick order and remind Catherine of her oath. She just knew he would.

But he said nothing, and stood unperturbed, as if he had expected Lucia to say what she'd said.

His silence touched something inside her, reminding her that he had promised to believe she would honor her word. She had to prove to him that she meant to do it. "I vowed to go with him," Catherine said.

"My sister acted as a mother to you, and in her absence I will do the same. Daughters are always making rash promises that should not be kept."

"I had good reason, the best reason, for making this promise."

Lucia dismissed her protest with a shake of her head. "I must think through this situation, my dear, and cannot do so while grief over my sister's death overwhelms me. In a few days I shall decide whether your father's wishes must be honored."

A few days? Catherine's heart leaped to think that she would be granted more time with Vincent, and yet her spirits plunged, for she knew she would only fall more in love with him the longer she spent with him. "It can be very difficult to wait, Lucia," she said.

"You will be too busy to fret. Every one of us must work here, for your English king's Crusade has lured many of our men away. We all do our part to raise food. You shall not sit idle while you wait."

Serena would be consigned at once to the grave, but neither Catherine nor Lucia could bear the thought of her going to the earth without tending her as carefully as they would if she still lived. The old woman who did the laying out for all of the villagers shooed them from the chamber when the men first carried Serena's body inside, but eventually she called to tell them Serena was ready.

To Catherine's surprise, Vincent came with them to the barn.

"I did my best." The old woman wrung her hands, agonizing. "She has been waiting too long for her rest."

The crone's ancient eyes brimmed with tears of grief and frustration. Lucia lay a gentle hand against her cheek. "You have done well. Her soul carried her beauty straight to God."

They prayed over the body that had once been Serena, but was no more. Catherine closed her eyes as she prayed, so she might see Serena as she had been, beautiful and vital, laughing and loving. The corpse lying on the bed took its proper role as vessel of the soul and spirit, the temporary host of the true nature of the woman.

"Her life was like a circle," said Lucia. "Beginning with one Crusade, and ending with another. If you would not mind, *carina,* I would like to be alone with her."

Vincent took Catherine's elbow and led her out into the sunshine.

"What did she mean about beginning with one Crusade and ending with another?" Vincent asked.

"My father took the cross during the last Crusade, some fifty years ago." Catherine had seen the stained remnant of the white cross that had adorned her father's armor. He kept it near his bed, and one morning she'd burst into his room to greet him good morning, to find him standing over the cross, with his hand resting lightly and yet familiarly on it, as if touching it was part of his morning ritual.

"He followed a route that took him along the very road we just recently traveled—it has ever been a main route through Italy to the southern sea. One of his men took ill, and soon they all suffered from the malady. Lucia's husband found them and brought them here. Serena cared for my father."

"They fell in love."

"Aye." They walked to the well, and she rested on the ledge, letting her hand dip into the water. "He left to fight the infidels when he regained his strength. He should have gone straight back to England when the Crusade failed. Instead, he came back here. I think he would have stayed, would have abandoned everything for her, but she would not let him."

"She sent him away?"

Catherine nodded. She'd known this story of her father's and Serena's doomed love for many years. She'd called them sinners at first, in those days before she'd learned to love Serena herself.

Afterward, she'd secretly admitted that the story was

wildly romantic, if immoral, and dreamed she might find a similar kind of love with God's blessing, with Michael. It wasn't until now, when she'd tasted the merest hint of forbidden love herself, that she realized how truly heartbreaking the story was.

"They both pined near to death, and so my father sent for her, and she went to him. She knew they could never wed. She knew she would be treated as an outcast, and despised, and still she came when he asked. She told me that once an Italian woman gives her heart, she can never accept another man."

"And yet he sent her away, in his turn. He never explained why, though anyone who knew him recognized he was not the same man after she left."

Catherine felt a sudden kinship toward her father. She knew she would never be the same woman now that she'd fallen in love with Vincent. "My mother brought it about—she appealed to the pope himself. There is a slight family connection. The pope said he would excommunicate everyone in this village if Serena did not leave my father. You cannot imagine how terrible of a threat this was."

"Ah," said Vincent. "Remember—I know something about the inner workings of the Church. Serena's sacrifice proved how much she loved this village. Her dying wish was to return here, so why did she live in Genoa?"

"She felt her example was not good for the young girls who lived here. And Genoa is right on the sea, so if things ever changed and she could return to England without risking the immortal souls of the family she loved . . . But circumstances never changed."

* * *

They buried Serena at dawn, as the sun shed pale golden rays upon the mountain and birds sang her soul to heaven.

The villagers gathered for a second leave-taking before the sun reached its midday peak.

Lucia's husband Massimo, lord of them all, stood fully armed and surrounded by a dozen of his finest fighting men. "We shall find those responsible," he said.

"Let me go with you." Vincent stepped forward.

Massimo shook his head. "This is our fight. I believe you have your own battles to wage."

Fifteen

Catherine twirled, and laughed with delight at the way the full skirt belled around her. She'd never worn a garment like this one given to her by Lucia. It fit more closely above the waist than her usual tunics and gowns, but then flared out with carefully crafted tucks that would allow her legs more freedom of movement than she'd ever enjoyed.

"Let us now do something with your hair, *carina,*" said Lucia.

Lucia tended Catherine herself. With deft hands, she parted Catherine's hair at the middle and then braided each half into long, thick plaits, which she wound around Catherine's head. "There. You look a proper garden wench now."

"As do you." Catherine smiled at Lucia, who wore her hair in the same fashion.

"The others await—let us go." They each caught up a basket by the handle and left the castle. A group of women clustered near the well, gossiping, casting indulgent eyes at the children who tumbled and played at their feet.

Catherine knew these children would accompany their mothers. While the women worked, the children would remain free to explore, free to play. She could not help contrasting these happy, laughing children with the little ones on her father's English estate, who were put to work picking stones from the fields or chasing off crows, as soon as they were steady on their feet.

The women greeted their lady with warm smiles, and included Catherine in their welcome. How different from her own home, she remembered, where her mother's presence brought about nervous bows and averted gazes, where competent serving women grew clumsy in their efforts to please someone who refused to be pleased.

Catherine had learned from Serena that it was not necessary to terrorize servants. But she knew Michael must manage his lands and people in much the same way as her father had done, as noblemen had always done. If she married Michael, she would sit down at table every day to eat food that had been sweated over by men who had no hope of improving their lot, and by children who had never enjoyed the luxury of play.

"If I must leave Italy, I would almost rather go to the convent than return home," she said to Lucia.

"We will not speak of such things now."

"I cannot stop. I . . . I almost think I would not marry Michael now if I could."

"Shhh. Not just now. Not just now."

Across the courtyard, men gathered, too. They made a far more boisterous crowd than the women. They joked and taunted, poked one another with their elbows. Some carried spades slung carelessly over their shoulders. Others leaned against rakes or hoes. One of the men caught Catherine looking their way, and he blew her a flirtatious kiss. Startled and yet pleased, she smiled, which seemed to encourage him, for he sent her a broad wink. Still smiling, she shook her head and turned away, when from the corner of her eye she spotted Vincent at the fringe of the group.

She wondered if he had ever blown kisses to a girl. Wondered, for the first time, if he loved someone back in England so much that it accounted for the restraint everyone attributed to monkishness.

Some of her delight in the day dimmed.

As always, he stood apart from everyone. It was not so much a matter of distance, for he was at most an arm's length from the core of the group. Rather, no hint of camaraderie relaxed his stance, no easy smile lifted in appreciation of the jibes and jokes. He was the only one who carried no tool, the only one with arms crossed over his chest, with his gaze fixed steadily upon something that seemed of interest only to him.

He couldn't understand them, Catherine thought suddenly. He truly was alone among those men.

"I should help Vincent," she said to Lucia. "He will not know what they want him to do."

Lucia didn't even spare him a look. "Leave him be. There are things he must learn on his own before he can make use of anything you can teach him." She handed Catherine a square of cloth to tie around her head, and the women set off, the children scampering with them.

The men climbed, with a man veering off here, another there, a pair there, until only Vincent and one older but exceptionally spry fellow continued up the mountain.

As the trail steepened, Vincent's companion never paused for breath, never slowed the torrent of words that poured from him. He didn't seem to care whether or not Vincent understood, he just seemed happy for the company.

Vincent concentrated on the babble and tried to sort out the words as best he could while picking his way up the steep slope. He realized Catherine had been right about the language; if he listened carefully, he could identify the Latin roots in some of the words.

They climbed several hundred feet beyond the castle, to where a long narrow patch of earth had been planted with exquisite precision. Vincent did not recognize the vegetable that grew there. Each plant occupied just as much ground as it needed, no more, so that an amazing abundance grew from a plot that would've gone to weed in most English farms.

The language of the land was universal. The Italian squatted alongside the plants. He pointed toward slender vines that twisted along the ground, and showed how the weed sent shoots to encircle the base of the desirable plant. *"Cattiva,"* he spat, dislodging the weed with care, to demonstrate the task Vincent was being set.

Weeding. They'd taken his measure, and without him saying anything, they'd known at once what he was suited for. He crouched down next to the Italian, and with a few deft motions yanked the offending weeds from the soil without disturbing the vegetable plant's roots.

"Bene!" The Italian clapped him on the shoulder. *"Bene, Vincenzo!"*

It was the second time in as many days that a man far below him in prestige and power had shown him approval. The second time in as many days that he'd enjoyed a quiet satisfaction from the gesture that put to shame all the moments of pride he'd indulged while in service to his lord.

The Italian stood and moved away, just a little, to keep watch as Vincent worked—no doubt to make sure his weeding skill wasn't just a fluke. Without thinking why he did it, Vincent plunged his hand as deep as it would go into the well-worked soil and caught some of the fine loam and crushed it, then let it dribble through his fingers. He had not done such a thing for more years than he could remember. But the blood of farmers ran through his veins and rejoiced at the friable, moist, rich dirt.

"Bene," he echoed the Italian's earlier remark. "Good."

His borrowed homespun tunic and chausses stretched and shifted to accommodate his movements as he worked his way through the patch. The sun beat down, warming his back; the breeze felt cool and clean against the good honest sweat that dotted his forehead and streaked down his back. After a while loud birdsong surprised him; he realized then that the Italian had left him on his own, apparently satisfied with the quality of his work, and he'd been too engrossed in the task to notice. Not like himself at all, to have grown so unwary when his back lay exposed.

In fact, none of this was like him: the meek acceptance—enjoyment, in truth—of the menial task, the complete faith in Catherine, that she would honor her word . . . and most of all, the satisfaction he found in doing this thankless job, the type of job he had scorned as a youth and thought never to tackle again.

When he finished weeding the patch, he noticed a small peach tree nestled in yet another pocket of earth. Creeper vines wound around the base of the trunk. He could see his father's face, hear his father's voice echo in his head: *Peaches dass not like being squeezed about the roots.* Vincent's throat tightened; the ghostly image of his father's face had not visited him in many years. He thought he had forgotten his father's face.

It was the work of a few moments to remove the vine's strangling presence. He leaned back on his heels and wondered if it was his suddenly overactive imagination, or whether the little tree did look a bit perkier, its leaves a little less droopy. Years from now, someone might be working this same patch of land, and pluck a fruit from this very tree to be refreshed by the juice, to savor the taste. They might spare a thought to thank the fellow who had helped this tree to thrive.

Years from now, would anyone reap the fruit of the work he'd done for his lord? This job he ought to be doing right now, delivering Catherine into a convent—years from now, would he be able to look back on it and congratulate himself for a job well done?

No.

A small word, much like a near-invisible seed that a man might plant. The word took root in his head. A few days earlier it would have fallen on fallow ground. But something within him had changed.

Change seldom came easily. He thought to himself, *No, I cannot take her there,* and knew he would have to think it through in his usual, logical manner, and knew he would have to wrestle with it during sleepless nights.

He glanced toward the sun. At least an hour remained before most good farmers would consider even thinking about supper. That suited him; now that he'd begun the task, it felt good to get his hands into the dirt, good to fight the endless battle against weeds. The sun struck hot and pure against his skin, and everywhere he looked offered a feast for the eyes.

But nothing about the Italian landscape compared to the beauty of Catherine. She had outshone every woman in the courtyard this morning, although they'd all been garbed alike, and all wore their hair in thick coils around their heads. She alone stood regal as a queen, her braids shimmering like a crown of gold. Her hair—he had thought to put her in a place where they would cut away all her glorious hair . . .

No.

The word echoed within him again, a little louder this time.

Hedgeford wanted her. He would take her to wife, make her his lady, give her his children.

No.

The most resolute denial of all, even though he lacked a moral reason for handing her over to the man she thought she loved.

Did she love Hedgeford? She had said she did. But how could a woman love a man and say to another, as she had said to him, *What if we just kept riding? What if we rode on and on . . .*

She did not love Hedgeford. She could not.

So, he could not put her in the convent. He could not give her to Hedgeford. Her father did not want her in England.

But she could stay here.

Any woman could do worse than live out her days in a place like this, where status mattered so little that the lord and lady worked alongside their villeins in the dirt.

So could any man.

* * *

The women harvested garlic. One of the women explained to Catherine how they had planted individual cloves the prior autumn. The sturdy plants developed below the ground through the winter and spring. The heads were fully formed by early summer, heralding the beginning of the summer growing season.

Lucia showed Catherine how to identify the browned, drooping spikes that marked each head, how to gently loosen the earth around the hidden bulb and pull it free.

"We shall let them dry, and then braid the stems together and hang them all about the hall," said Lucia. "The ancient ones taught us that the scent wards off evil humors, and my cooks make good use of the spice in our food."

They worked for several hours, and though Catherine had thought the job absurdly easy at first, she was glad when Lucia announced a break for the bread and cheese they had carried with them.

Catherine stood, grimacing a little when her back protested its unfamiliarity with bending for so long. She pressed a fist into the small of her back, remembering how Vincent had eased the ache that night alongside the stream, when he'd helped her wash her hair. Her hands felt strange, as if the mud drying upon them pulled all the moisture from her skin. Her knees, too, reminded her that their most onerous duties to date had been kneeling for hours at the *prei deiu,* while she watched Mass. The *prei deiu,* where she'd first seen Vincent.

Some of the women noticed her discomfort and nudged one another, laughing, but not mockingly.

"You will get used to it," one called encouragingly.

"I have never worked," Catherine marveled to Lucia. "Sometimes, to relieve tedium, I mended or embroidered and *thought* I was working—I was wrong."

Lucia laughed. "This is one of our easiest tasks. Digging is much more difficult. And do not forget that at the end of the day these women still have homes and children and husbands to attend."

They had everything she had ever wanted, Catherine thought. Her hopes and dreams had ever centered around a husband, children. She'd endured tedium, certain that one day her life would be full and happy. What did a nun do to pass the day? She knew all too well that her faith was not deep enough to allow her to lose herself in prayer.

She must have betrayed something of her feelings, for Lucia caught her by the hand and drew her away from the other women. "We will walk, and we will talk a little, just the two of us," she said.

She aimed them toward a tree-shaded rock, and they settled on the rock's generous contours. Catherine lifted her face toward the sky. The leaves dappled her skin, and she enjoyed the coolness mingled with warmth.

"Do they allow nuns to sit outside and enjoy the day?" she asked, somewhat bitterly.

Lucia caught her hand. "You must know I will not let that man take you away from here. Unless you want to go. And I can think of one reason why you might want to leave with him."

"I cannot. I have never felt the slightest urge to take up a religious life."

"I know that, *carina*. I meant, I can understand if you want to leave, to be with him."

Catherine thought she had kept her love for Vincent well hidden. "I suppose it is easy for one woman who is in love to recognize when another woman is in love."

"Oh, I am not in love, *carina*."

"But you and Massimo—"

"We like each other very well," said Lucia. "We suit each other in ways that our parents were able to recognize when they made the match. But I have never felt for Massimo the sort of love I see shining in your eyes when you look upon your Vincent."

Your Vincent.

"He despises me," said Catherine.

"His eyes burn with the same fire when he looks at you."

"Because . . . because of what he thinks I am." Haltingly, she explained to Lucia what Vincent believed of her. "And so he looks at me the way a man will look at a whore—I know, for I have seen this myself when a soldier cast covetous eyes upon my maid."

"You are too innocent to recognize the difference between lust and love."

"Oh, Lucia, I thought I loved Michael, the man I was to wed. I don't know what I feel anymore. I had a thought, earlier today, that I did not even want to marry him now if I could."

Lucia squeezed her hand, and they sat in silence for a little while.

"You may change your mind about that. You can take all the time you wish to decide. I think that if you marry your Michael, you might well end up as Massimo and I have done. It is not a bad life, *carina*. The children make it worthwhile. Besides, Massimo can make me laugh, sometimes, and he can be a generous and considerate lover, sometimes."

"That is more than Serena and my father ever had," said Catherine.

"Oh, no—you are very wrong. One great love in a lifetime is enough to sustain a person all her days, even if the lovers are together for only a brief time."

"How can you be so certain?"

Lucia grew very still, but rapture seemed to light her from within. "Because I had my moment."

"You—and another man?"

Lucia nodded.

"Then why did you marry Massimo if you loved another man?"

"I could say, because it was expected of me. Massimo and I were betrothed, as was my true beloved. But I would have gladly caused the scandal, and risked exile, to have stayed with him all my days. Alas, I was so young, and I made mistakes."

"What sort of mistakes?"

"I did not let him know how I felt. I never asked him to run away with me."

"I have done that." Catherine blushed, remembering how she'd cuddled against Vincent and asked him to ride on and on with her. Remembered how he'd refused. "He said it was impossible."

"Ah—but did you declare your love to him before making such a request?"

"No. I thought he might be able to tell."

"Men lack the ability we women possess, to look beyond the surface and find the truth. You say he believes you to be something you are not. Until he changes his mind about that, he will not believe anything you tell him for fear you might be trying to trick him."

"Then he won't believe me if I tell him I love him. I do not believe my pride would permit me to go through that again."

"A woman's pride is more resilient and far deeper than a man's." Lucia squeezed Catherine's hand. "Men like to think themselves bold, and daring, and uncaring of what others think of them. And yet a man bases his pride on his status, his accomplishments, his assurance of his place in the world—all things that can be taken away.

"I do not know your Vincent, but in him I sense a man engaged in constant struggle with himself. His pride is all he has, and he may fear that if he lets loose of it to bare his heart to you, he will have nothing. This man you love carries with him a terrible burden. He will never willingly reveal his feelings unless he is certain they will be reciprocated."

"So I must show him that I love him."

Lucia nodded.

"How? I have told you what he believes about me. He will suspect anything I do, anything I say, of having ulterior motives."

"You must first tell him that he no longer holds power over you, that we will keep you here with us regardless of what he wants to do. And so he cannot suspect you if . . . well, if things happen between you after he knows, he cannot even think you deliberately sought to sway him."

"I must find the right moment, when we are alone."

Alone, in this small village, where the age-old castle boasted such few comforts that the lord and lady shared an alcove, and nobody had a chamber to them-selves.

Lucia sat silent for a long moment, and then smiled. "I think that tomorrow will be the perfect day to gather the first strawberries. They grow in a sheltered place far from the castle. 'Tis a job for two, and I know exactly who I shall set to the task."

The fine evening lured the entire village to the courtyard. Vincent knew that as summer deepened, and the food production demanded more effort, these people would be glad to take to their beds directly after supper. Or would they? Nothing in this place was the same as what he'd known in England.

"Vincenzo!" One of the men wagged a jug of wine toward him.

Vincent could understand so little of what these men said, and yet he felt more welcome, more part of the group, than he'd ever felt in his life. He held out his mug, and when it brimmed with the rich red wine they produced on this very mountain, he propped himself against the low wall, right next to the fellow who'd poured for him.

Right next to him.

He sipped, and he saw Catherine over the top of his mug.

There was a sweet wistfulness about her. She mourned Serena, he knew, and yet she was obviously enjoying this humble evening pleasure. How much of her melancholy stemmed from believing that soon she would be taken away from it and never know it again?

No.

His last doubt melted beneath that sad, sweet smile.

He could not take her to the convent. There would be repercussions, as he'd said to her father on that day that seemed a lifetime ago. But this time the repercussions affected him personally, and on a level he'd thought he'd obliterated long ago.

As he'd done that day with her father, he set his mind free to work through the problems that would present themselves. This time they were not laws written down in books, or customs so old that they'd gained the weight of written laws.

This time, he was himself the root of all the problems. He had to cast aside all the projections and defenses he'd built so carefully, so that she might see the real Vincent Kenby and not the false one. This time, there were no tricky maneuvers, no subtle phrasings that could substitute for the truth.

He would have to admit to Catherine how he felt, how he had come to love the woman she had proven herself to be. He would have to tell her how loving her had changed him so profoundly that he questioned the way he'd built his life. He would have to ask her to forgive the wrongs he had done her.

He would have to admit that what he intended to do—or not to do, really—meant he had no status, no job, no real purpose in life . . . except for loving her.

It was not the sort of declaration a man could shout across a crowded courtyard.

She might not believe him, even if he did. Words, he knew, were cheap things, capable of being ignored and retracted. She knew this, too. He would have to show her how he felt.

The solution formed in his mind, so full-blown that he knew it must have been lurking there all the way, waiting for the right moment to spring forth. He would simply offer Catherine something she had always been denied. The best gift he could offer Catherine, the gift that would prove to her that he loved her, was to offer her the right to make her own choice.

Which meant she could go to Hedgeford, if she wished, reasoned the part of him that ever probed a course of action for weaknesses.

His hand shook, and he lowered his mug before he spilled it.

He would prove nothing to her if he offered freedom but anchored it with conditions. That would be no gift, to say, "Very well, I have changed my mind about doing this, providing you do that."

He would have to find some time alone with her, and somehow convey all of this in a manner she would believe. He could not afford to make a mistake. Which meant he had to fall back on the skills that had served him so well up until now. One last time; he must once more call upon his old manner of doing things to make sure he got this right, and then, then . . .

Then he could banish the old Vincent Kenby.

Sixteen

The mornings started off cold so high above the valley. Catherine wore her cloak fastened tightly at her neck. Vincent wore his usual jerkin and tunic, and knew that soon enough the sun would warm the air and he could shuck off the topmost layer.

He wished he could be equally certain about the more important outcome he hoped the day would bring. Lucia's assignment meant he had the time alone with Catherine that he wanted, but it happened too soon. He'd meant to argue his case more fervently than he'd ever presented at court, but now he would have to just . . . talk. He'd resolved to bare his heart to her, to drop his defenses. He'd just expected a little more time to prepare. Once again Serena's predictions haunted him. He'd planned to do this, and yet his throat seized, his mind went blank, whenever he tried to summon the words.

"Lucia assured me that we would find the best pickings right around this boulder," Catherine said.

Every word she'd said to him so far was spoken with the same stilted formality that she'd adopted since he'd dismissed her appeal to ride on and on together.

He knew some of his difficulty stemmed from Catherine's demeanor. Her polite conversation. Her impeccably correct posture. Her neutral expression, which revealed none of the warmth and passion he knew she held within.

Trying to say anything meaningful to this cool stranger was so difficult. As difficult as she must have found it to talk to him, he realized.

He noticed that her hand moved a little toward him, and he was familiar enough with watching her to know that any other person who walked with her would have received a gentle touch when she talked. But she did not touch him, and she soon switched her wooden pail to that hand. So she wouldn't inadvertently touch him, he knew.

As they rounded the boulder, they startled birds already gorging amid the lush growth. The birds launched themselves into the air with loud squawks of protest. Their thrumming wings stirred the air and fanned the perfume of ripe strawberries over them.

"Now I know why bees act wine-flown when the berries are ready for picking," Vincent said. He inhaled the heady scent with pleasure even as he decried his own adherence to their formality.

"I can't even see the berries, yet they announce their presence," said Catherine, cool, remote.

The strawberries grew like true wild things, with profuse bunches of the distinctive leaves sprouting from crevices so narrow no man could plant in them. Here and there trailing runners tumbled over the top of rocks and boulders, seeking footholds against the rock, clinging like ivy. White blossoms dotted the foliage. Here and there one could see the pale-green nubs of newly formed berries, and the mottled pink-and-green of berries only half ripe. The ruby-red ripe berries, no bigger than a thumbnail, lay beneath the shelter of the leaves and had to be hunted like the tiny hidden treasures they were.

Catherine knelt next to a likely looking patch, and her cloak fell around her so that only the soles of her shoes poked out of the folds. He remembered the time she'd challenged him in the hall of the Genoa palazzo, wearing that very cloak, claiming that she could sleep naked beneath it. It was easy to imagine that she knelt there with nothing but the thick soft fur covering her . . .

The day had not appreciably warmed, but sweat sprang to his brow.

He found his own patch to forage, one not as lush as the one she'd chosen, but with the advantage of facing away from her. He needed more time to think, and this mindless chore promised to give it.

He easily remembered the picking technique he'd learned so many years ago, freeing a likely berry from its fragile stem and tucking it toward his palm until he had a handful. He dropped all but one into the bucket. That one he ate himself, a farmer's reward, his father had always called it. He quickly developed a rhythm; so many in the fist, *plop,* into the bucket, and then one for him.

They picked in silence. Eventually the birds lost their fright and took up perches in the closest trees. Occasionally one would dart from branch to ground just long enough to snatch a crimson treat, and when it returned with its prize in its beak, its fellows seemed to both cheer and scold it. One appeared to take offense and opened its beak to chatter back, whereupon it dropped its treasure—which was snatched from the air by another.

Catherine's delighted laughter mingled with Vincent's, and he turned to find that she'd taken off her cloak. Perhaps learning that they'd both enjoyed the sight would ease some of the strangeness between them . . . but his laughter died in his throat while he found himself captivated by the bright sparkle of her eyes, the lovely curve of her lips . . . lips a deeper red, more lushly moist, than those that haunted his dreams. He watched, spellbound, while she licked a bead of juice with the tip of her tongue.

"You caught me!" She looked contrite, but that did not stop her from popping another ripe berry into her mouth. "My bucket is almost full," she added.

"Mine as well."

"We should go back."

The sun still shone as brightly, the birdsong sounded even more joyously than before, but somehow the day's brightness dimmed. He had to keep her there until he found the right way, the perfect way, to present his case.

"Lucia will know what you've been doing. You wear the mark of the strawberry upon yourself like a thief branded on the forehead."

"Truly?" Her eyes widened in consternation, and she rubbed the back of her hand vigorously over her mouth. "Better?"

Not better. More seductive. The rough action had only heightened the color in her lips, and made them look even fuller and riper.

She misunderstood his paralyzed silence.

"No good, hmmm? Well, since you have obviously enjoyed your treats as well, we shall both be punished!"

"Me?" He repeated what she'd done, and gave his mouth a good rub.

She shook her head.

Intolerable, to think they would leave this mountain without his having said what needed to be said. "If we walk back to the village as we look now, with our mouths all smeared, they'll think us no better than two children who could not keep their hands off the treats. There's bound to be a stream close by. We'll wash away the signs."

She folded her cloak into a bundle and tucked it under her arm, and carried the bucket in her other hand.

They found a stream just past the first growth of trees. He crouched next to it and was assailed with the memory of that night when he'd held her, when he'd helped her wash her hair.

"We always end up at the water's edge, you and I," she said, somewhat shakily.

In that moment she sounded like the Catherine who had leaned close against him, the Catherine who had asked him to ride on and on.

"Do you remember what we said to each other?" he asked. The question sounded harsh and rough, betraying how difficult it had been to choke out.

"Aye. You told me to mind my step, for stream banks are known to be treacherous."

He did not know if she'd misunderstood his question, or if she'd deliberately deflected it.

He caught up a handful of the clear frigid water, cupped it over his mouth, and rubbed.

"Better?" He turned and found her so close that his shoulder brushed against her skirts.

She shook her head. "No. Let me try."

She withdrew a length of cloth from her sleeve and bent toward the stream.

"Mind the bank."

"Yes, I know." She dipped the edge of the cloth into the water. "You see—I can keep my feet dry!"

Just then, the loose soil shifted and she almost lost her balance, would have fallen right into the water, except his arm shot out instinctively to pull her back to safety.

Safety? He didn't feel the least bit safe with his arm wrapped so tightly around her, with her soft breast pressed hard into his chest. He shifted so that one knee dropped to the ground while the other supported most of her weight, somewhat awkwardly, so that he continued to hold on to her for fear she might go sliding into the stream. Her breathing seemed a little labored, and he wondered if perhaps he held her too tightly, making it difficult for her to breathe, but she made no effort to escape his hold.

Nor did he let loose of her.

With her eyes fixed upon his, she raised the wet cloth. "I shall tend to you." The words seemed little more than a whisper, and he spared yet another worry that he might be holding her too close, but both of them seemed welded in place. "Then you shall tend to me."

"Aye."

She touched the cloth to his lips, and not even the icy chill of mountain springwater could cool the fire that leaped within him at her touch.

Her eyelids fluttered. Her lips parted. The fingers pressing the cloth to his mouth trembled. Tremors shook him, as well, from the effort of denying himself. He wanted nothing more than to tear the cloth from her, to draw her head toward his and claim those strawberry-stained lips with his own.

And so it seemed at first that it was a dream, when

the cloth landed on his knee and her fingertips, smooth and chilled from the water, traced his lips with a gentle curiosity that threatened to drive him insane.

"Your lips are soft," she marveled. "They can look so harsh." She leaned closer; he felt her breath against his skin, and then with a movement that might have been an attempt to turn her head away, or might have been an attempt to steal a kiss without his knowing, she brushed her lips over his in a featherlight caress.

The knee he'd so firmly planted into the ground wobbled, and he toppled over, with her landing right on top of him.

He remembered how he'd wakened in the cart to find her over him much like this. How he had yearned with every inch of his being that she would truly press herself against him! Now, she was there, her every curve molded to him the way those trailing strawberry runners followed the contours of the rock. The water he'd splashed on his face earlier had soaked down the front of his shirt, and the wetness made it seem as if he wore nothing where her breasts rested against him.

He cupped the back of her head with one hand and drew her face toward his, and did as she had done, brushing against her lips so gently, somehow holding back so that the kiss he gave her was almost elusive as one given in a dream.

That would be all he ever had of her, he told himself, unless he managed to say the things he'd planned so inadequately.

And then . . . and then . . .

Her mouth found his. At first, the touch was as light, as tentative, as if a ghost kiss had brushed across his lips. But then she melded her mouth to his, parted her lips so that his followed, and he tasted strawberries.

The restraint, the control he'd maintained for so many long years dissipated like snowflakes falling into a campfire. So did the words he needed to say fly straight out of his head. Urgent, undeniable need claimed him entirely, consuming him so thoroughly that he could not even think.

He groped blindly for her cloak and pulled it toward them. He heard the clatter of wood against rock, and the scent of strawberries told him he must have knocked over a bucket of what they'd gathered. No matter. Hunger surged through him, a hunger that could not be slaked by food, a hunger that strengthened him rather than weakened.

He swiveled, tumbling her onto her back with the cloak beneath her, with himself lying hard atop her. She sighed, a sound of invitation that heightened his appetite. He kissed. He devoured. With soft sounds and eager movements she stayed with him, her lips parting to the command of his, her tongue touching as his demanded, she rising slightly, infinitesimally, to follow when he drew away in the rhythm of kissing, to return to the right place once more.

Her hands were upon him, stroking, pressing, pulling. He kissed her forehead, her eyes, ran his tongue along the ledge of her jaw and found the exquisite pulse in the hollow of her throat. He tasted the flesh there, let his lips quest lower, let his hands play at the ribbons holding her peasant's blouse gathered above her breasts. He tugged the ribbon free and the folds of cloth parted to reveal her to him. He caught his breath at the beauty, the perfection of her breasts, and he claimed them as his, first taking them into his hands, then tasting them with a slowness that maddened them both. He brushed his lips against the sides, lightly, and when she would surge upward, crying out wordlessly but somehow telling him that she wanted him to take the hard, throbbing peaks into his mouth, he held her hips hard against the ground. He tasted his way completely around each breast, and then giving in to his hunger, he swirled his tongue around each tip and drew them into his mouth, sucking, savoring, aching for more.

He would have it. He would have *her.*

He twisted and drew her partly atop him, bearing her weight with his hip against the hard ground while he pulled away the clothes that covered that which he desired.

She helped. She lifted her hips, she raised her arms, she parted her legs, and when she did, he did not allow her to close them again, but kept his hand there, caressing, stroking, thrilling inside to every sound she made, every squirming, straining motion that told him she ached for him as much as he yearned for her.

He would have her. He would have all of her.

He rolled her onto her back again, and the rich ripe scent of crushed strawberries sweetened every breath they took.

While his hand teased and tormented her, his mouth found her breasts again, and then began working its way lower. Across the taut ridge of her ribs, into the concave valley of her belly, up the mound that opened into the heat of her sex. She cried out when his tongue found the places his fingers had brought to life. She shuddered, her whole being vibrating with the wonder of discovery. He had to draw away lest the storm raging through him explode. He watched ecstasy bloom upon her face, and wondered if he would have the strength of mind to watch again when he brought her to a true woman's joy.

He rose up, and drew her legs even farther apart, molded her thighs to press against his middle. He throbbed against her, felt her hot and wet against the hottest, hardest part of himself, and remembered why she was so wet and hoped that she had moistened on her own as well as from his tongue.

She opened her eyes then and saw him watching, and he thought that if she pulled away just then, if she said him nay, he might, *might,* manage to draw away and douse himself straight into the stream. But her lips parted, her eyes darkened with passion.

"Vincent," she said. Just his name.

The tip of his shaft found her cleft, found it wet and slick and welcoming, and he had to pause again. She clutched at his back while he buried his face against her breasts and drew a harsh breath. She made a tentative motion with one leg, drawing it slowly over his hip, and then joined it with her other so that she was completely open to him, so that he need not even move for his shaft to slip toward the very brink of where he ached to go. Any movement at all . . .

With a little cry, she lifted her hips, and he was inside her.

He maintained enough presence of mind to try to spare her his weight. He gritted his teeth and held himself in check as he penetrated her by the smallest degree when he wanted to thrust, and then again, the tight silky wetness of her turning his blood to molten iron. A little more, his whole body quivering from the strain of holding himself back when he wanted to devour, wanted to stake every inch of her inside and out

as being his. A little more, and he was brought up
against the internal barrier that told him he was indeed
the first, the only, the one whose handling of her now
would determine how she felt about love for all her
days.

He had never deflowered a virgin.

He was beyond being gentle.

And she, eager, gasping, moving beneath him, asked
for no quarter.

Wondrous sounds came from her. Wondrous sensations spasmed from inside her. He sheathed himself
deeply, and then more deeply, into her body, his senses
flown by the friction, the heat, by the startling wetness
that eased his passage and told him that all this wet
was not from his tongue, but from her, from what he
had done with her. What they had done together.

He was lost.

He knew, on some level, that the deep male cry that
echoed from the mountains came from his own throat.
He drove into her, again, again, and she met every
thrust, every shudder, with one of her own, until a long
while later they lay limp and unmoving save for the
quivering that announced each muscle's relaxation
from the thundering climax they had shared.

She was his.

He had been the first, he would be the only, and she
had let him be the one before he had told her he could
not lock her away.

His pride wanted to crow his triumph to the heavens.

And then that part of him that ever analyzed, ever
probed, brought to the forefront of his thoughts a
repercussion so devastating he went rigid with paraly-
sis.

If he told her now that he meant to set her free, she

would think she had bought her freedom by letting him use her body.

Maybe that's exactly what she meant to do, the voice within him taunted.

No. He had lain with enough women to know the difference between those who brought affection to the act, and those who sought to earn something for their trouble.

With his endless fretting over choosing the right words, the perfect words, he had missed his chance.

A pain not unlike a well-thrown spear shafted straight into his heart.

Catherine lay dazed, happy, her body replete in a way it never had been, breathing the scent of strawberries mingled with the even headier scent of man.

Vincent had one arm curled around her, and her face was buried against his shoulder, and so she could not see his face. Did she dare ask him if he had enjoyed what they'd done?

He held her as if he cared. He held her as if he'd changed his mind about her being a dangerous temptress.

She had completely forgotten everything Serena had told her about coupling with a man. She had moved by instinct, responded to what he had done to her; she had kissed and licked and touched where her body had commanded her, without ever once worrying if she was doing it properly.

Serena had promised her that a woman could find no greater joy than coupling with the man she loved. She loved him, this quiet, complicated man who thought he hid himself so well from the world. She would tell him.

She turned a little, stretched like a contented cat, and Vincent went rigid against her.

Not in the same way as he'd been before, hard and honed with the movements of love, but stiff and restrained, the Vincent of old, as if he'd suddenly come to his senses and despised himself for lying there with her.

She tensed, too, with her declaration of love frozen on her lips, understanding in that moment why he never allowed himself to be the first to betray a weakness.

"Catherine," his voice was a hoarse sliver of itself as, God curse him, he turned and put her below him and looked down into her eyes with his own filled with stark pain, and something like fear. She looked away. Her woman's instincts told her that look boded ill. He ran a shaking hand along her face, cupped her chin and tilted it up, forcing her to look at him.

"Everything has gone wrong," he said. "I did not mean for things to happen this way."

"How exactly did you mean for . . . things . . . to happen?"

"Not this way."

The last shreds of her ecstasy vanished. She had done it again! Offered herself, when she'd sworn she would never do so again. This time he had taken everything she had, used it, and now cast it away.

She had never been ill-tempered, and yet a fine fury rose within her, so fully fledged that it might have been waiting within for all her life for this very moment to explode. She was more angry at herself than at him, but it served to strengthen her either way.

She struggled free of his hold, and some part of her noticed that he made no great effort to keep her near, which only fired her anger more.

"I should have listened to Serena. She warned me. She worried I would be too susceptible, too eager to believe myself in love. Why did I not heed her?"

"You . . . you believe yourself in love? With me?"

He looked as stunned as a bull that had been poleaxed, stunned and disbelieving. Something died inside her, something that would have stayed alive if only he had said, "I am happy to hear that," something that would have flourished if only he had said, "I believe I might love you too."

She'd abandoned her pride to wallow in the woods with him, but she gathered it back to herself now. Somehow, she had to pretend that what had happened meant as little to her as it did to him.

"I love Michael," she bit out. The three-word refrain had been a part of her daily litany for so many years that she could say them with as little true feeling as a person might acknowledge a sneeze with a "God bless you."

She did not know who she strove harder to convince—Vincent, or herself. "I have always loved him, and always will. I will nevermore forget the lessons taught to me by Serena. She promised that when I coupled with the man I truly loved it would be an ecstasy unequaled by anything here on earth. This . . . thing . . . was pleasant enough, but it did naught but whet my appetite for my betrothed. I give you fair warning, here and now, that I will no longer honor the promise I made to you."

She wriggled free, while he seemed immobilized by the torrent of words she'd flung at him. It was the work of a moment to slide her shift over her head. Her hair was beyond help, and she thought of using her cloak pulled well up as a sort of hood to hide it when she scurried back to her chamber in the castle, but one look at it threatened to break her heart. It lay beneath Vincent, wrinkled and stained, her virgin's blood mingled with the stains of crushed strawberries, thoroughly ruined as she was.

He sat up, reached for his clothes. It would take him a little time to don his tunic and chausses . . .

She bolted.

"Catherine!"

She glanced over her shoulder to find him hopping on one leg as he tugged on his chausses, and despite her anger at him she was about to call a warning, yell out that he ought to heed his own advice, for he teetered too close to the treacherous wet earth at the edge of the stream.

Just as he succeeded in pulling the garment to his waist, his leg shifted awkwardly beneath him and he toppled over into the stream.

There was a loud splash, and then the stream babbled as prettily as ever, as if the water had not been disturbed at all.

"Vincent?"

He groaned, but did not answer her.

"Vincent?" She ran back to the stream.

He groaned when he saw her, and then closed his eyes as if embarrassed. He made some ineffectual movements with his hands, splashing water over her, over himself. She didn't think he realized what he did. He'd landed with his torso in the icy stream, with his legs splayed out on the bank so that he was tilted with his head down. It was an awkward position for someone fit, an impossible position for one whose left leg twisted at the knee in a way she was certain no leg was meant to twist.

He dug his elbows down below the surface and lifted his head and shoulders above the water. Already the bare skin of his chest, visible below the surface, had gone white with cold. His lips, too, were compressed into a thin line, white with pain.

"Your leg!" she cried, pressing her hand to her mouth. His ankle seemed to swell before her eyes.

"Will you help me?" he gasped.

How could he even think that he had to ask? She added his lack of faith in common courtesy to her list of things to hate about him. She did not deign to answer but studied his position. There was something wrong with his left leg, so she could not pull him out that way, especially with his torso going downhill as it did. Once she started pulling, his head might go under the water. She would have to haul him to the other side.

Catherine sloshed into the stream. She caught him under the arms and tugged him toward the opposite bank, but it was like trying to move a fallen bull. Her feet, up to mid-calf, went numb almost at once from the frigid water and she dared not think what it must be doing to his vitals. "You will have to help," she managed.

And he did manage to get his good leg levered against the ground so that he pushed as she pulled. She could tell he bit his tongue to avoid crying out; she could feel the agony grip him every time he moved, but he never made a sound beyond a stifled moan. After an endless time she had him out of the water, on the bank, where he shivered despite the sweat profusely beading his forehead.

She crossed the stream and returned with her ruined cloak, which she spread over him.

He would never be able to negotiate the mountain trail on his own, not even with a stout stick to bear his weight, not with the break so fresh and new.

"You saved my life," he said, and she acknowledged it with a nod. He would have perished, certainly, either from the chill water stealing his blood's warmth, or when his strength failed and he would no longer be able to hold his head above the water.

She stood, looked down at him for a long moment. "Now I must save mine," she said.

Seventeen

Inch by excruciating inch, Vincent dragged himself toward a tree whose forked trunk promised a hand-hold. He knew he'd lost consciousness at least once, for he'd come to spluttering and spitting mud from his mouth.

Gritting his teeth, he forged on, moving by digging his elbows in and hauling his lower half forward. All the work was being done by his arms and yet his leg all but shrieked with agony with every lurching inch he gained.

But that torture was nothing compared to the sear-ing pain that caused him to retch and sway as he pulled himself up, hand over hand, when he reached the tree. Somehow he managed to hoist himself and wedge his torso into the split trunk, where unconsciousness claimed him once more.

And so he wasn't sure, at first, when he opened his eyes and saw Catherine's beloved face in front of him, heard her beautiful voice urgently calling his name, felt her slender hands grip his shoulders and shake.

"Vincent!"

"You are here," he said witlessly.

"Did you think I pulled you from the stream just so you could die in a tree?"

She seemed so angry. His head swam as he tried to remember what he'd done. No, it was not something he had done, but something he had *failed* to do . . . talk. That was it. He'd missed his chance to talk to her. He'd been so concerned about choosing the right words that he hadn't said anything of importance at all. So talk he would, blurting out every word that was in his head until he got it right.

"I thought you had run," he said. "I thought . . ." Even half out of his head, it wasn't so easy to say what he wanted to say. He didn't know if he could impress upon her that he'd thought he would die when she'd turned away from him, for his heart had splintered into shards with every step he thought she'd taken away from him, a pain that hurt worse than his leg.

"You look beautiful," he said.

Her hair hung loose and still held bits of woodland chaff. Her skin still carried the flush of loving, her lips still red and slightly swollen from his kisses. Anybody who saw her so would know she had lain with a man. He could not bear to think somebody might make mock of her, or hold her in low opinion for loving a man to whom she was not wed.

"But do not let anyone see you like this." He croaked like a frog, he thought, as he raised one shaking hand to pull a bit of leaf from her hair. "You must not let anyone know what happened between us."

She jerked away from his touch, and he saw that his blathering had not helped his case at all. Before he could marshal a new line of reasoning, she turned away from him. Other faces crowded close, took her place. Familiar faces crowned with dark hair, their dark eyes full of concern. Reassuring smiles, and hearty words he could not understand—men from the village.

"Catherine—come back!"

The men nudged one another and joked, beaming with masculine approval at Vincent.

One of them crouched down and caught Vincent's foot between both of his hands. He rotated Vincent's foot, and though his touch was gentle, the turning of his knee nearly sent him swooning again. The man *tsked* and shook his head. Vincent gritted his teeth and gripped the tree trunk so hard that the sharp bark bit into his palm with enough pain to divert him from the ankle.

He had been wrong about her not leaving him. She had gone and found help, and come back for him, and in the process let the whole village know what had happened between them. Curse his stupid tongue, for she could not help but misunderstand what he had been trying to tell her.

"Catherine!" He had to explain. He pushed himself away from the tree and without regard for his injured leg took the first step toward following her, and promptly pitched headfirst when his knee gave way beneath him.

The men surrounded him, and ignoring his struggles to bat them away, they heaved him onto a litter, where more torturous prodding and poking went on. Endlessly, when he had to hurry. When it all ended, what seemed like hours later, his leg had been immobilized between two strong sticks and a cloth binding wound around and around.

"Broken?" he asked.

They did not understand and so he made the motions of breaking a twig over his good knee.

"Ah!" Understanding dawned. "No, *Vincenzo.*"

A sprain. He let his head fall back. Laid low by a sprain on the most important day of his life.

Cursing his luck gave him something to occupy his mind while they hoisted the litter. The bandaging helped; he felt discomfort but no more of the excruciating agony, even though he was jarred and jolted as they made their way down the mountain.

He stared past the shoulders of the man who bore his litter, straight up to the sky, and thought.

Catherine's father and Serena Monteverde had fallen in love in the very place he was being carried, when the earl had been sick and Serena given the task of caring for him.

Now, he was wounded, and Catherine would care for him. Perhaps his accident had been no accident at all, but fate's not-so-subtle push to teach him a lesson. No more planning, no more analysis for him! He would tell Catherine everything, expose his heart, keep nothing secret. He needed only a moment alone with her.

Catherine found her way back to the village by instinct, the way a horse finds its stable in the dark. She chose to enter the castle by a small rear door for she could hear a commotion in the courtyard, and could not bear facing all the villagers.

She found Lucia standing near a window, looking out at the courtyard.

"I am the world's worst fool," Catherine sobbed. "I thought my heart hardened toward him, but I see now that I still held hope he might care for me. Instead I learned the truth—he is ashamed of what we did."

Lucia turned so slowly that it seemed she had aged

and stiffened by a dozen years in the last hour. Tears streamed from her eyes. Her shoulders heaved with silent sobs. This display of grief had begun long before Catherine blurted out her anguish. Lucia must have suspected how Vincent truly felt.

And then Catherine heard, from the courtyard, someone calling her name.

"Catherine of Ardleswyck! We demand Catherine of Ardleswyck!"

As if in a dream, Catherine walked toward the window.

The commotion she'd heard in the courtyard, the commotion she'd sought to avoid, was not a happy gathering like that of the night before. Instead, several dozen fully armored English knights stood with their weapons trained on the warriors of the village, including Massimo, who had ridden off so boldly to avenge Serena's death.

Their numbers had been decimated, Catherine noted with despair. By her count, only half of the men who'd ridden out now stood shackled, with their hands bound, before their captors.

"Catherine of Ardleswyck! We demand Catherine of Ardleswyck!"

She opened her mouth to announce her presence. Lucia stilled her. "No, *carina.* We promised you sanctuary. We knew what doing so could mean."

"Lucia, no—"

Before Catherine could complete her objection, a new uproar marked the arrival of the men bearing Vincent upon a litter. A few of the knights left off guarding the warriors and trained their swords and spears on the newcomers.

There was no hope of resistance. The fighting men

had been conquered, and those who carried Vincent had gone after him unarmed, and returned to the village joking and laughing, having no reason to expect their defenses had been so terribly breached.

"Catherine of Ardleswyck! Mark me well!"

Catherine knew that very few of the villagers could understand the knight's demands, for he spoke in her native tongue. But nobody could fail to understand his actions. He used his feet and the flat edge of his sword in the way a man might cull a sheep from its herd, to separate Massimo from the huddle of defeated warriors.

Lucia ground her fist against her mouth to stifle a cry.

Catherine remembered what Lucia had told her about a man's pride when she saw Massimo forced to his knees. The knight grabbed Massimo by the hair and pulled back his head to expose his neck.

"I will call my lady's name once more." The knight's voice rang from the stone walls. "If Catherine of Ardleswyck does not answer, I will slit this man's throat. And I will do the same for one man each time I call and the lady does not come forth."

"Do not hurt him! I am right here!"

Catherine leaned out the window as far as she could, waving wildly to draw the knight's attention.

"Catherine of Ardleswyck?"

"Aye."

"I bring to you the fond greetings and felicitations of my lord, the Earl of Hedgeford."

Incongruously, he bowed toward her without letting loose of Massimo's hair.

"Did my lord Hedgeford order you to treat my hosts with such disrespect?"

"My lord ordered us to do whatever it took to bring you to his side, my lady."

So far, Michael's orders had taken Serena's life, and the lives of half the village's fighting force. The extent of the devastation wracked her to her soul. But she strove to sound confident, demanding, when she shouted back to the knight.

"Here is what it will take; you will order your men to lower their weapons and step away from your hostages. I also demand your oath as knights that you will harm none of these people."

"Agreed, my lady."

He let loose of Massimo, bowed again, and issued a quick order that led all of the knights to lower their weapons to resting position.

"We await you, my lady," the knight called.

"A few minutes—I must needs gather my belongings."

Catherine stepped away from the window. Tremors shook her, and she thought, a little wildly, that the human mind and body were amazingly resilient, to be able to survive the onslaught of emotions that had assailed her throughout the past hour. Love. Life. Death. Sacrifice.

"Oh, Catherine." Lucia sobbed freely. "I am so sorry, but so grateful."

"There have been too many deaths already. I could not bear another on my account."

It was true, she could bear no more death—but she had learned in these past moments that she could survive almost anything.

It seemed a lifetime ago that she had knelt in the palazzo's prayer room, begging God for exactly what waited for her now. Then, she had been so naive, hopeful, yearning to become Michael's wife.

Perhaps she could regain that innocent anticipation. Perhaps she could forget those moments amid the strawberries when she'd discovered what she truly wanted in her life, only to lose it.

Perhaps she could find contentment, as Lucia had done, as Serena had done.

Except . . . they had their perfect moments to look back upon, to savor all their days. Her moment would not glow so brightly in her heart and mind, for it would forever be tainted by the memory of Vincent telling her that nobody must ever know what they had done.

He'd touched her hair when he said that, and she did so now, finding what he'd discovered—tangles, bits of woodland chaff. *Do not let anyone see you like this.*

"I must comb out my hair," she said to Lucia. "Clean myself, and change into a different gown."

Lucia nodded, her eyes dark with the knowledge of what Catherine sought to obliterate.

They worked quickly, and soon Catherine looked the same on the outside as she had on that day that seemed a lifetime ago.

Inside, both physically and emotionally, she had been irrevocably changed.

No one must ever know.

She gave Lucia a lingering hug, but dared not tarry too long lest the knights grow impatient.

She held her head high as she left the castle and crossed the courtyard. She tried to emulate, as she walked, how Eleanor of Aquitaine would have acquitted herself when moving under her own volition toward the party of soldiers who would escort her back into the dreary imprisonment she'd endured at Winchester. By all accounts, the queen had walked with so much dignity and pride, that she might have been on her way to a new coronation.

"Carina!"

"Vada di Deo!"

The people called out to her. Dear heart. Go with God. An outpouring of love and caring for her, whose presence had cost them so much. This would be her moment to treasure for the rest of her days.

She prayed Vincent would hold his tongue as she walked past the litter. She doubted he would survive if the knights knew he had been the one to take her from Genoa, the one who sought to keep her away from her betrothed. She knew he would not survive if he betrayed what had happened between them on the mountainside.

She could see from the corner of her eye that he propped himself up on his elbows as she passed. She dared not look more closely at him. Everything within her yearned to run to him, to ask him if she had understood him aright—but she dared not.

She went to the leader of the knights, extended her hand, accepted his obeisance with as much calm as she could muster, as if she abandoned her dreams every day of her life.

She thought that now, if she chanced to meet Queen Eleanor on the road, the old queen would be proud of her.

Vincent watched Catherine turn regal before his very eyes.

She refused to play the meek and conquered maid. She demanded her things be fetched, some special foods prepared, a litter readied to carry her. She caused these mighty knights far more trouble than she had ever caused him.

But at length there were no more delaying tactics at her command, and she was borne out of the village on the shoulders of squires, with an escort of three dozen mounted knights.

The entire village seemed to be spellbound, held by a tense silence that held until the clopping of hoofbeats faded. And then, in a frenzied burst, women and men ran to each other to cling and babble aloud their fears, their relief. Some women were left to cry, for their men had not returned. They all grew silent again when a deep-voiced bellow of pure agony echoed from the stone walls.

His cry.

Lucia, clinging to Massimo, approached Vincent where he lay helpless as a legless beggar. She could understand him, he remembered, and he had to pour out the anguish in his heart. How much he had changed in just a few days—but one minute too late. One minute, one fateful hesitation, and he'd lost her forever.

"You did not say good-bye to her, or even wish her well." Lucia looked at him with contempt.

"She is impulsive, and far too loving. She would have betrayed—"

"She would never have betrayed us."

"She would have betrayed herself." Vincent drew a shuddering breath. "Those knights will honor her as their lord's betrothed, providing they do not suspect what happened between us. If I had called to her, if she had come to me . . . Her eyes reveal her heart, my lady. The knights might decide she has been sullied. They might consider her an unfit bride for their lord, and as such she would be prey to their lusts."

Lucia nodded with some reluctance. "Aye. I can see why you let her go away without a word. You saved her honor, but you broke her heart."

Massimo burst into a rage, pounding one fist into the other, tears falling openly from his eyes.

"We are ashamed," Lucia whispered. "We let her sacrifice herself to save us. We must mount a rescue party."

Vincent shook his head. "They are a superior force. She will have gone with them for nothing, if more of you were to die after what she has done."

"Then *you* must do something," Lucia challenged.

Vincent nodded. "I will leave at once."

"First let me look at your leg. And truly it would not do to follow too closely at first. Wait until morning."

They carried him into the castle and laid down his litter near the fire pit—even though it was early summer, the nights turned cold here in the mountain. He scarcely noticed the temperature, and welcomed the dull throbbing in his leg, for it kept him focused when he wanted to let his mind wander back to the glorious moments when he'd held Catherine in his arms, when he had claimed her as his own.

His own, now in the hands of others.

He probed the problem from every angle, but in the end had to admit that his legal knowledge hurt more than it helped, for everything he knew told him Hedgeford had the right to do exactly what he had done. She was in his possession, and there was no legal manner to pry her free.

No legal manner.

He sat up, and noticed distractedly that the pain had abated somewhat in his leg.

No legal manner. Which meant taking her by force—except using force put her at risk, as Serena's death had shown. And he had no superior force to marshal against a cadre that had proven itself capable of conquering the best this village had to offer.

But the roads of Italy teemed with more of the best—mercenaries seeking God, glory, and riches.

He listed his assets: his desperate determination, and Catherine's dowry, which he'd been entrusted to hand over to the cloister. Putting that fortune to another use was as good as stealing it from his lord.

"I need one man to show me an alternate route to Genoa," he told Lucia and Massimo the next morning. "They will be forced to travel slowly—I have some experience with that."

"You and one man alone could never—"

"It is best you know nothing of what I plan to do."

"But can you ride with your leg injured so sore?"

"I can stay on a horse."

Eighteen

The villager who had led Vincent from the mountains to Genoa had refused to leave him when they reached the city. Pointing to the crutch Vincent needed to use in order to hobble around, pointing to his mouth and making exaggerated babbling sounds, he'd made it clear he considered Vincent unfit to arrange Catherine's rescue without his help, that perhaps Vincent could not survive at all without him.

And for the better part of two days, it appeared he was right.

When they'd arrived in the city, Vincent had been heartened to find Hedgeford's ship anchored out in the water. They had managed after all to get there ahead of Catherine and her kidnappers, and he did not regret a single minute of the excruciating agony caused by riding the surefooted little mountain horses at such a fast pace along the secret byways his companion had known.

Finding a champion and fighting force to beat Hedgeford's should have been easy in this city teeming with mercenaries. But none of the men he approached suited Vincent. Some spent their days sleeping off drunken orgies, others lacked experience and hoped to gain it on Crusade, while still others had experience aplenty, but all on the losing end of a battle lance.

Quite a few more than he expected claimed a true religious fervor, a driving need to fight the infidels, which meant they dare not risk their life on a pursuit so trivial as wresting a woman away from her betrothed, just so she might be given a choice.

Vincent had to take care, as well, to minimize Catherine's value. He could not defend her, curse his twisted knee, should the mercenary he hired decide his reward would be greater by stealing Catherine away than freeing her from Hedgeford.

He had never before understood why women feared being forced to marry against their will. Now he did. He'd been beyond arrogant in believing that a roof over one's head, a meal in one's belly sufficed in exchange for personal choice. Catherine might find a bit of irony in knowing that in this, her situation tied her closer to the woman she admired so much, the old queen Eleanor. Eleanor, he recalled, had had to fight off more than one kidnapping attempt herself when she was between husbands.

Vincent knew exactly what he needed—a champion so renowned, so feared, that nobody dared stand up against him. A champion so honorable, so just, that he would decry what was being done to Catherine. A champion so forward-thinking that he would believe Catherine should be allowed to choose her own destiny.

As the day progressed, as the sun moved through the sky and marked the passing of the hours, he grew ever more frantic to find his perfect champion, and ever more despairing that he would succeed.

The villager proved himself invaluable, running about and producing likely candidates for Vincent to interview, or sometimes just disappearing and reappearing with something cool to drink, something warm to eat.

He tried to coax Vincent into eating a grotesque, many-legged sea creature and some flat yellowish cakes that he seemed to be saying were made of beans. Vincent pushed the food away, and turned his head to avoid even looking at it, and thus found the answer to his prayers.

Superb animals, fearsome weapons glinting in the setting sun, banners and pennants so rich with gold and velvets that just one could be sold for enough to feed a family for a year. All this, backed up by a force of dozens to outnumber Hedgeford's eight to one—a champion the likes of which he had not even dared to imagine.

"No, *Vincenzo,*" the villager implored when he saw where Vincent's attention had settled. Vincent supposed he could not blame the man for doubting the champion would help him—so obviously wealthy, so obviously powerful, there would be no need of the fortune he'd hoped to dangle as an incentive.

But he wouldn't know unless he asked. He'd learned that much, at least.

They let him hobble fairly close before ordering him to stop.

"I have a business proposition," he called out.

"I will listen."

"To whom will you turn if I say no?"

Vincent had never endured such a stringent grilling, and it grew more difficult, rather than easier, as it progressed.

"I do not know," he admitted. He watched for a flicker of an eye, a quickly hidden smile, to see whether he'd betrayed too much desperation. "I will find someone."

"Will you? I wonder."

They sat apart from the others, so nobody could overhear, but even so Vincent felt the heat of embarrassment from being taunted.

"I offer enough money to buy the right man."

"But you do not guarantee the money even for a successful campaign—that is the rub. 'Defeat those men and set her free,' you say, and then, 'But ask her if she wants to go with them, and if she says yes she must be free to do so, along with her dowry.' Does this sound like the sort of challenge a sane person would embrace?"

Vincent rubbed his hands over his eyes. "When put that way, no."

"You love this woman."

It was not a question, not said in a joking manner—simply a statement of fact.

"Yes, I love her." It was the first time Vincent had said the words aloud.

"You are hoping she chooses you, rather than this Hedgeford?"

"Yes."

"What of the dowry then?"

"It is yours, if she agrees. I have no interest in it."

"You have considered her father's reaction if she chooses to stay with you."

"Aye."

"And the reaction of the man she will spurn if she chooses you."

"Aye."

"And you have deliberately sought the services of a stranger to this land to avoid repercussions falling on the Italian villagers she loves."

"Aye."

Vincent squirmed beneath the barrage of questions, which were but repeats of a select few of the hundreds that had gone before.

He felt once more like the scribe who'd dared to aspire to become a counselor, back in the old days. Then, he'd spent days, weeks, closeted with the best of the earl's lawyers, while they taught him to exercise his mind and consider all the options.

This keen mind testing him now dwarfed any he had studied under, bested his own. At any other time, he would enjoy the mental challenge of matching wits with such a quick thinker. But now, his own wits were so mired in worry, his own interests fixed upon the fate of one glorious golden girl, that he was beyond intricacies. Save her. Save her. That was all he could think.

This could go on all day, he realized. He'd learned too late that a man sometimes had to put aside planning in favor of acting.

"Have done with this!" He slapped his hand down on the table. "Will you help me, or will you not?"

The sigh prompted by his table-bashing conveyed a world of experience with similar fits of temper. "The only thing more pathetic than a man in love is a woman in love. Very well. I dislike involving myself in affairs of the heart, but I have need of the money."

Vincent recalled the splendid condition of the horses, the quality of the weapons, even the clothes and armor worn by the fighting men. "I did not realize."

"Nobody does. I have the devil of a time keeping them fed and healthy so they can be in fine shape to get themselves killed. If it were possible for me to marry the wench, I'd steal her myself for the dowry."

Vincent was not sure if the statement had been meant as a joke, but he did not laugh, and so nobody did.

"Here is the way I have planned it—" he began.

"You came to me because you believe—rightly, I assure you—that no man's forces dare test my own. I have experience in thwarting the plans of others. I will handle the rescue in my own way."

"Please use the utmost caution. A stray arrow, a carelessly flung lance—"

"Leave it all to me. You will not be disappointed."

Catherine's escort made a large procession through the rough cobbled streets of Genoa, but the city bustled with so many people, so many horses, so many carts, that their passage added nothing perceptible to the din. The clattering of hooves, the thumping of wheels, the trudging of boots, swirled like a trapped wind and circled endlessly through the narrow passages.

The sun beat down, adding its brightness and heat to air already close from the sheer numbers of people swarming about. The litter bearers made no complaint, but Catherine could see how their hair lay pasted against their necks, and dark vees of sweat darkened the backs of their tunics. She was glad, for once, to be reclining in the enclosed litter. The roof shielded her from the worst of the sun, and the openings on the sides allowed in a rare breeze. Now and then, she fancied she caught the scent of the sea.

They traveled the main road, a road so old that one

had to have a care for the ruts worn into the stone by Roman chariots. They passed an alley she recognized. Narrow corridors and twisting alleys crisscrossed Genoa like a maze, but she had learned the routes well in the years before the crusaders had begun arriving and she'd been confined to the palazzo for her own safety. If they would but turn left, and then right, and then left and right again, they would pass Serena's palazzo.

If only I could go back, Catherine thought. Not merely to the palazzo, but back to the time when she'd chafed at the long, leisurely days spent within the palazzo's cool walls, laughing and talking with Serena.

She'd yearned for excitement, yearned for the start of her real life. She had been given just a few days of that life. Now, she was done. Her heart had broken when Vincent urged her to hide the evidence that they had loved. Lucia had promised her that one moment was enough to sustain a woman for the rest of her life. Catherine's moment with Vincent had ended hers.

She would breathe and walk, eat and talk, but she would never again be alive the way she had been during those timeless moments held tight in Vincent's arms.

She longed for nothing more than peace and quiet. She hoped Michael would not be overly disappointed in her.

A bell tolled, rich and deep, the ancient solemn tones palpable, announcing that they were very close to the Cathedral of San Lorenzo. Some of the surrounding uproar dimmed as men paused to listen. The bell tolled again, and some men dropped to their knees. They bent their heads in prayer, and those who had failed to slow or kneel were forced to dodge and skip their way around them. The bell tolled again, and in an amazing transformation, the teeming masses came to a standstill; even the men bearing her litter stopped to gape at the sudden freezing in place of what had been a mad commotion.

The bell rang out a fourth time, and here and there, wherever a man wore the crusader's cross upon his chest, he stood tall and raised his right hand into the air. Once more the bell sounded, and it seemed they had been waiting for this fifth ringing, for as one the crusaders lifted their voices in something like a prayer.

"Help, help for the Holy Sepulchre," they intoned—English, French, Italian, each in their own tongue but united in meaning and purpose. Their vows echoed with the bell's reverberations.

Their fervor moved her. She understood why Queen Eleanor had joined in with the Crusade all those years ago, and why even now she traveled through this very land to do all she could to assist her son Richard mount another attack against the infidels.

The solemn moment passed, and Catherine's litter bearers took up the pace once more.

Vincent stood in the shadows, beneath the arches of the ancient aqueduct ringing the port. He studied the portside continuously, looking for any sign that would betray the presence of his champion. Even though the execution of the plan had been taken out of his hands, he knew surprise was the most valuable weapon—the only weapon—that might allow Catherine to be freed without dangerous conflict exploding around her.

He saw nothing unusual. Sailors and dockworkers tended to finish their work early in the day. Fishermen and their wives hawked what was left of the day's catch from a line of crude stalls near the water. There were only a few buyers lingering over the wares, since those who could afford to eat would've done their shopping hours before to have their meals ready by now.

A small group of drabs hid near Vincent, watching hungrily, hoping to swoop in and gather up anything the fishermen would discard, or sell cheaply. But no fisherman would beckon them forth until he'd made every possible sale to the few who shopped so late, or to the group of brightly clad foreign ladies who laughed and squealed with mock fright at the unusual creatures held up for their inspection.

And then Catherine was there.

Hedgeford's knights flanked her litter front and back. Their armor lay dull beneath the grime of road dust, the parts of their faces revealed by upraised helms were lined with exhaustion. But these were good soldiers; they looked about, sharp and wary, even though their ship lay anchored in sight and their journey was near done.

Vincent gripped onto the stone support. He wanted to see her, had to see her. Where was his champion? He searched the portside again, looking for the first flash of sun against sword, but nothing, nothing. Now was the time to strike, before those on board ship were aware the knights had arrived. There might be reinforcements on the ship, and Catherine could be caught in the middle . . .

They bore Catherine's litter to the edge of the water,

close to where a small boat had been pulled up onto the shore. One of the knights dismounted, and from somewhere on his person withdrew a small square of metal, which he aimed toward the sun and flashed a signal to the ship. An answering signal flared.

To the great annoyance of the fishermen, the knights' arrival distracted the laughing ladies. They lost interest in the market stalls. Giggling, chattering, they flocked toward the knights. Vincent cursed them, urging them silently to get out of the way of danger, but he knew it a useless effort. All women were drawn to knights, like butterflies to roses.

All of the knights dismounted. One of them helped Catherine out of the litter, very properly, but stood there offering his arm as support and she clung to it while she established her legs beneath her.

Vincent wanted to kill him. Wanted to kill them all and sweep Catherine away, deep into the mountains, deep within his arms.

Where was his champion?

"We shall row you out to the ship, my lady," said the knight.

Catherine walked slowly toward the little boat. These would be the last steps she took in Italy.

She heard laughing and chattering, and she had become so accustomed to hearing the knights speaking to one another that she didn't think much of it that the women coming her way were calling to one another in Norman French and not Italian.

She'd known several Italian women who spoke her tongue, but never so many in one group. She glanced up at them. It was a shame, in a way, that the last words she heard in this land were not spoken in Italian.

One of the women smiled at her. She held up something at arm's length and made a mock horrified face. "Lady—do you know what to call this thing?"

Catherine could not help laughing; she had had the same reaction to her first introduction to the little creature. "'Tis called an octopus. Surprisingly tasty, if one can get beyond its appearance."

"You are one of us, my lady?"

"I am English."

"English!"

Delighted, they caught up their skirts and hurried to her, save for one older woman who maintained a more dignified pace. The faster ones clustered around Catherine as they reached her, touching her hair, asking her name, chattering and laughing.

"See here, my lady," said one of the knights. He'd backed away beneath the onslaught of femininity, and had to rise onto his toes to look over their veiled heads to find Catherine. "We must be on our way. Ladies, kindly step aside."

The women paid him no mind and encircled her so thoroughly that the knights would've had to toss them aside to reach her. The knights backed away from the knot of femininity, looking befuddled and somewhat frightened, and then the older woman joined her ladies.

"I saw you climb out of that litter," she said to Catherine. "Did you enjoy riding in it?"

"I did not."

"I did not think so. I was once forced to endure a quite lengthy journey inside one, which caused me to develop a severe aversion. I have sworn to never ride in another for as long as I live." A delicate shudder passed through her.

Catherine felt a sudden surge of kinship. The woman was not one that a stranger could easily touch and say, *Oh, yes I do understand,* or easily confide in. But there was something . . .

She studied the woman. Very old, and yet she was as straight and easy in her movements as a young woman. The woman in turn studied Catherine. Her eyes, deep and piercing, held a wealth of knowledge. Her eyes reminded Catherine in some ways of Vincent's, as if one could see right through them into the intricate workings of the mind.

She was most likely somebody's grandmother—great grandmother perhaps—but there was nothing soft and indulgent about her. This was a woman to command respect, a woman to honor and admire . . .

A woman once forced to travel in a litter, a woman of obvious wealth and dignity, so old she ought to be home near a fire with her grandchildren at her knee and yet here, on the shores of the sea in a country not her own . . .

"M-Majesty?" Catherine whispered, hoping she did not sound too ridiculous.

"You recognize me." Eleanor smiled and looked pleased.

Eleanor of Aquitaine is smiling at me, echoed through Catherine's head while she stood there witlessly staring.

"Do you want to board that ship and marry Michael of Hedgeford?" asked Eleanor.

"No, Your Majesty."

"Very well. Come with me."

She pulled Catherine's hand into the crook of her

elbow, and began a slow, dignified walk away from the sea.

They had put maybe fifty feet between themselves and the knights before the men noticed.

"Hold on there!"

Eleanor continued walking.

"I order you to stop!"

Eleanor stopped. She looked over her shoulder. "What did you say to me?"

"I said—"

One of the ladies who barred their way tapped the knight playfully on his shoulder. "Make certain to add 'Your Majesty' when you give orders to the Queen Mother. If you do, the Lionheart may show mercy and order a quick slash when he cuts off your balls."

The knight paled.

Eleanor made a movement with her free hand, and at the signal mounted men spurred their horses from beneath the arches of the aqueduct. They took up position between the knights and their lady.

Eleanor resumed their walk as if they'd never been interrupted, as if they did but stroll near the sea on a pleasant afternoon.

"Now," said Eleanor, "I have a short list of questions to ask you yea or nay, and then we can all be back to our usual business. Mr. Kenby!"

Vincent came out from the shadows.

Vincent. Catherine had to grip tight to the queen's arm to keep from racing to him. She had not gone dead at all. She came to life only in this man's presence. She wanted to touch him, smooth his hair back from his face, examine the injury to his leg that forced him to hobble with a crutch fixed under his arm.

She wanted to ask him how he had gotten here. Wanted to ask him why he had come.

Eleanor pressed her arm against Catherine's, as if to remind her to breathe.

"As you can see, Mr. Kenby, I prevailed without a single blow being struck. I am delighted you did not rush out and ruin everything."

"I came close to it, Your Majesty, until I realized what you were doing."

"Rare good sense in a man," Eleanor said approvingly. She turned to Catherine. "Do you want to become a nun, Catherine of Ardleswyck?"

"No, Your Majesty."

"Do you want to return to England—I can order it so, even if your father does not wish it."

"No, Your Majesty."

"Do you want to throw your lot in with this man, who can offer you no wealth, no title, but does have an interesting mind—albeit somewhat hampered by a tendency to talk too much?"

Vincent—talk too much? Catherine found she could not talk at all, so confused, so overwhelmed did she feel. She'd managed to blurt out only the most cursory yeses and nos when she'd longed to say so much more. Could this be the way Vincent had sometimes felt, settling for the barest expression when unable to reveal all that was in his heart?

"This is a fairly recent development, Your Majesty," said Vincent. "I have learned my lesson about holding my words too dear."

"Prove it," Eleanor challenged.

"Very well."

And then, to Catherine's amazement, he tossed aside

his crutch, spread his arms wide, and bellowed, "I love you, Catherine!"

What with battle-ready knights staring daggers at one another near the shore, nobody in the area had any attention to spare upon the three of them. Catherine doubted anyone but she and Eleanor had heard, but she required no witnesses.

Eleanor nudged her. "He's quite lame without the crutch. Do not lose your dreams for the want of a few steps separating you, child."

She raced toward him. She stopped just before reaching him, for she was afraid to touch him—for fear of disturbing his balance, for fear of finding he was only a dream and not really here at all.

"Do you love me?" he asked.

"Yes."

He smiled, a smile so huge and so sweet that she thought she might melt right there on the paving bricks.

"I take it you want to stay with him," said Eleanor.

"More than anything in this world, Your Majesty."

Improbably, Eleanor's eyes sprang with tears. "Now you see why I dislike involving myself in affairs of the heart. They remind me I am but an old woman with a romantic nature."

Vincent laughed and drew Catherine into his arms, pressed her close against him so that she felt the vibrations clear through her skin.

"Pray do not forget the matter of the dowry in your fit of romantic weakness," he joked with the queen.

Eleanor chuckled. "Catherine of Ardleswyck, you should know that your Mr. Kenby bargained with me over your dowry. He promised it to me on two conditions—that I rescue you unharmed from Hedgeford's men, and that you agree to give it to me."

"Of course I will give it to you," said Catherine. "It has been nothing but trouble for me."

"Well, my son will make short work of it, so it won't be around to trouble anyone for much longer."

Vincent let loose of Catherine only long enough to remove a pack he wore slung over his shoulder. He handed it over to Eleanor who hefted it, and nodded. "A good day's work. Richard will be pleased."

"Pleased enough to claim Catherine as his ward?" asked Vincent.

"I have a father," said Catherine, though she held little regard for him at the moment.

Eleanor laughed aloud.

"Excellent idea, Mr. Kenby! My son cannot abide squabbling between his nobles. As his representative, I declare it necessary to declare forfeit to the Crown the source of the fighting, which happens to be you, my dear Catherine. You are now my son's ward."

"What does this mean?" asked Catherine.

Vincent answered. "It means your fortune, and your very person, belong to King Richard."

"No—I want you!"

"And you shall have him," said Eleanor. "My son will of course keep the dowry, but he will soon be saddled with more women than he will know what to do with. I am taking his bride to him, you know." She smiled indulgently. "So, he has no use for spare women hanging about. To save him the trouble, I shall place you right now in Mr. Kenby's keeping."

"Thank you, Your Majesty." Vincent bowed at the waist.

"You can thank me by remembering how you feel

about each other at this moment. Later in life, it is all too easy to forget, unless you take care to treasure the memory."

"We will remember, Your Majesty," Catherine promised.

"I quite like the two of you." Eleanor beamed her approval at them. "It occurs to me, Mr. Kenby, that you will have nowhere to live with your new bride, and no trade to fall back upon. And I have often found myself in need of sound legal advice. It seems that I now have a business proposition for you."

Catherine fidgeted. She'd always held Eleanor in such high esteem, and had dreamed that she might one day know the supreme honor of meeting the woman—but now she wished Eleanor would take herself away so she could be alone with Vincent.

She supposed it was important to arrange their future, but her heart cried out the need for just one moment, one moment with her love.

Vincent tightened his arms around her. She rested her cheek against his chest, and thrilled to the strong steady beat of his heart.

"Majesty—I shall attend to your proposition in a moment," said Vincent.

And then he tipped Catherine's chin up. He left a queen waiting while he claimed Catherine with a kiss that told her one moment would not be nearly enough time for all they had to say, all they had to do with each other.